THE DEATH OF THE PARTY

The screaming had stopped for a moment, which I took as a positive sign, but now it started again. As I moved closer to the trouble, I heard the violence in the sounds of the retching and coughing that were punctuating the screams of pain.

I heard the man in front of me whisper to his date, ''Don't look!''

Of course I had to.

It was Lily who was standing over Bruno and shrieking. It was Bruno who was laying on the dance floor, writhing and convulsing.

And then he just stopped. Brown eyes open, distorted mouth gaping, long body rigid in a contortion one moment and frozen deathly still the next.

SYMPATHY FOR THE DEVIL

A MADELINE BEAN MYSTERY

JERRILYN FARMER

AVON BOOKS
An Imprint of HarperCollinsPublishers

AVON BOOKS
An Imprint of HarperCollins*Publishers*
10 East 53rd Street
New York, New York 10022-5299

Copyright © 1998 by Jerrilyn Farmer
Library of Congress Catalog Card Number: 97-94413
ISBN: 0-380-79596-5
www.avonbooks.com

First Avon Books printing: May 1998

Avon Trademark Reg. U.S. Pat. Off. and in Other Countries, Marca Registrada, Hecho en U.S.A.
HarperCollins® is a trademark of HarperCollins Publishers Inc.

Printed in the U.S.A.

10 9 8 7 6 5

For my mother,
Molly Sarnoff Klein,
who sat pretzel-style on
the kitchen linoleum
and taught me to play jacks

ACKNOWLEDGMENTS

The author wishes to offer her sincerest thanks to the following individuals—those talented writers who gather regularly at Dietra's house on Tuesday nights: Howard Gantman, Bruce Kelton, Erica Bailey Rudnick, Jean Shriver, and Dietra Simon; Leonne Schillo for her inspired guidance; Ken Adashek, M.D., Jay Orringer, M.D., Jim Waisman, M.D., and Ondine for their expertise; Chef Alex Lombardo of Cucino Paradiso and Chef Octavio Becerra for their culinary advice; Robert and DeLores Klein, Heather Haldeman, Omara and Lauren Insalaco, Joan Farmer, Sheryl Lombardo, Martha Brown, and the gourmet chefs in the Crestview family for their enormous support; Richard Klein, Brandon Hoskins, Steve Wilson, Melody Johnson Howe, and UCLA Extension for their many talents; Evan Marshall, my warm and wise agent; Lyssa Keusch, my excellent editor and new best friend in New York; Sam and Nicholas, my darlings, and their incredible father, Chris Farmer, for all their love.

Chapter 1

"**A**ny last words?"

A puff of dense steam clouded the hot kitchen as the young man pulled the lid off an enormous stainless-steel stockpot. His remark had been addressed to a tank filled with ten dozen live Maine lobsters.

In the warm air, the pungent smell of garlic and hot frying butter mixed with countless other delectable aromas, blanketing the crowded room with the fine perfume of many cooks' efforts. I stepped into the din and swirl and heat, instantly embraced by the heady atmosphere.

"Madeline!"

Wesley, half a head taller than any of the assistant chefs in the room, saw me at once and met me at the door.

"The truffles never arrived. Fifteen pounds for the love of France!" Wesley checked his watch, the kind with a digital readout and timers and buzzers. "It's seven. The schedule's shot. There goes the artichoke and Swiss cheese tortellini topped with fresh truffle shaved to order."

I met the eyes of Wesley Westcott, my dearest friend and business partner. Wes was usually granite right before guests arrive, when it's one hour to dinner and counting, but this was the first time we'd spent fourteen thousand dollars on one fragile ingredient.

"Wes . . ."

"Coming through!" Our assistant backed her way into the huge kitchen, leading three young men. Each pushed

1

handcarts stacked with crates marked PERISHABLE and AIR FREIGHT.

"Who's got the crowbar?" Holly's strong voice rose above the commotion of thirty cooks and helpers hard at work.

I said to Wes, "The truffles have arrived fashionably late."

"Ah. Good." He rechecked his digital. "Fine."

Someone moved aside, and I felt a blast of smoky air from the fireplace where several legs of lamb were roasting on a spit. I was getting high breathing in the succulent aroma of rosemary-scented lamb. I love this. The fun, the noise, the smells, the elevated temperature, the sensuous pleasures of cooking.

I smiled at Wes and he seemed to relax a notch. After all, the truffles had arrived.

Our track record for keeping some of Hollywood's biggest stars happy at their own parties, perhaps even more than the excellence of our cuisine, was adding to the growing word-of-mouth popularity of our company, Madeline Bean Catering.

And this is a great town for caterers. Here, clients desire parties that are extraordinary and are prepared to pay the extraordinary costs. It's this outlandish disregard for thrift that the small-business person such as myself can come to appreciate in their clientele. And such parties!

Wes and I once set up a bar mitzvah for the son of a talent agent in a mock rainforest. It included a parrot that recited the first line of the bar mitzvah boy's Hav Torah. In Hebrew. And the *L.A. Times* wrote up our "wrap" party for Mel Gibson's last action movie. We blew up the catering truck right after dinner.

Tonight we were standing in the kitchen of TV producer Bruno Huntley's grand estate, on the evening of October thirty-first, preparing dinner for six hundred guests. And as for our reputed ability to soothe cranky hosts, this evening could be the acid test. If we could keep a famous asshole like Bruno Huntley happy at tonight's Halloween party, we would soon achieve a new "personal best."

"Hey, Madeline!"

Manny Martinez, working on the other side of the kitchen, was waving his wooden spoon at me. He didn't appear happy.

Holly flattened herself against the crates she was working on as Wes and I squeezed by.

Close up Manny looked more worried. "Taste it."

I picked up a fork and dipped it into the souffle he proffered. It flaked. It crumbled. It pulled away from the sides of its dish pathetically. Too dry. Too brown.

"Overcooked."

Wes grabbed the fork. "Is this the arugula and chevre souffle?"

It was something less than the golden, well-puffed mixture of garden greens and goat cheese that was our hostess's favorite dish.

"It was fine when it came out of the oven," Manny said. "But now . . ."

I pointed at the pretty round baking ramekin decorated with hand-painted black cats. "It's the dish."

Wes considered. "It's the right shape," he said. Its sides were straight and tall and in the correct proportion to send the fluffy mixture towering skyward as the beaten egg whites expanded in the heat of the oven.

I clinked the side of the dish with my fingernail. I loved the fine art of detective work and I loved being right. "It's stoneware."

Wes began to nod. Stoneware retains more heat than porcelain. "It's still cooking after it's out of the oven."

"Manny," I advised, "your eggs are getting scorched by the dish."

"I knew I didn't overcook nothing," Manny pointed out. We cooks have egos more delicate than, well, a souffle.

"So we adjust the recipe for stoneware. Make a note." Wes turned and gave me a fond smile. "Oh, you're good."

And then the screaming began.

"Oh no! Oh my god!"

First a woman's guttural shriek. Then men shouting.

"Get them off me! Get them off! Jeez!"

I turned quickly and spied Holly, usually calm as toast, now swatting at her legs in a panic, swearing like a teen-ager.

She had pried open one of the crates marked PERISH-ABLE. Instead of containing outrageously expensive deli-cacies air-shipped from the Perigord region in France, the crate had instead disgorged thousands of wriggling earth-worms.

Freed from their wooden prison, they had oozed out onto the floor, squirming in their peaty-smelling packing earth, and over the shoes of Holly and several of her mates.

Wes was all business. "Okay. Get them the hell out of here. Then I want the floor bleached and sanitized. Got it? Oh, and all those of you who have been . . ." He smiled graciously. ". . . wormed, please change out of those clothes and shoes as soon as the creatures have been re-moved."

A few nods as those on the front lines now stood their ground, six Levi-covered legs holding back the tide of earthworms until they could be contained and removed.

I was already on the phone calling to the airport. Ah. A mixup at LAX. Our two hundred and forty ounces of ir-replaceable gourmet fungi were, at this moment, being trucked to a bait shop near Long Beach.

I signaled to the guys, who had renailed the crate shut. "Holly, drive the worms back to the airport. They'll radio the truck that took our truffles to meet you there."

"Right." Holly pulled off her apron and ran for the van.

I started to laugh. "We're always looking for new and exotic ingredients." Wes and I liked to provoke each other.

Wesley was now back in his element and he grinned at me while he stirred a pot of pasta. There he stood, tall and thin as a strand of spaghettini. Wes is really very nice look-ing. He has good hair, straight and brown and immaculately cut, and even better clothes. This evening it was khaki slacks and a starched white shirt with the sleeves rolled up. A short, black, mannish apron was his sole protection from flying tortelloni and splattering pumpkin seed oil as he worked the room.

The kitchen in the Huntley house was wonderfully equipped with two of everything: two dishwashers, two double sinks, two ovens, two icemakers in two separate sub-zero freezers. It had been remodeled in recent years, after Bruno wed Wife Number Three.

Since he had moved all his wives into the same historic mansion, it had become something of a tradition in Bruno's world to allow each new wife the pleasure of spending unquestioned amounts of money to redo the kitchen. And so, just days after returning from her honeymoon in Greece, his newest young wife and her decorator got to work. They turned the twenty-by-forty-foot space into an English fantasy, complete with two-hundred-year-old wooden beams shipped from Gloucester, and about a hundred thousand dollars worth of honey-colored pine cabinets made in London by Smallbone.

As I surveyed all the activity in this dream kitchen, I heard a distant wail. The door flew open, and a small, red-faced boy darted into the crowded room. He was running hard, heading straight at me. Then, to my astonishment, he ducked between my legs, jumped into the bottom cabinet, and pulled the door shut behind him.

Now, technically, on party day, the kitchen is mine and the kitchen's actual owner and family are encouraged to stay out. On party day, perfectly nice families can turn testy. I didn't even want to think about what it could do to a family like the Huntleys.

Just then, a petite woman rushed into the kitchen. Wile E. Coyote, I guessed, in the chase scene in progress. Her entrance had silenced the throng of hurried, concentrating chefs. The noise of knives hitting chopping blocks halted as everyone waited for the requisite cartoon anvil to drop.

"Babalu?" she called, her voice heavily accented with Spanish inflection.

Wesley and I shared a look of appreciation. It's not every day that one is treated to a tribute to Desi Arnaz.

"I'm Madeline Bean. Can I help you in any way?"

She turned to me like to a life preserver. Sounds of chopping resumed as my staff remembered their deadlines.

"I'm sorry Missus Madeline. It's my Babalu. Little Lewis. He is running away from me," she explained. "It is the Gummi Worms. I say, 'No, no, Babalu! You have too many.' But he don't like me to say this."

A dispute over candy worms. A particularly unsavory mental picture in light of our recent visitors.

And in an evening of dramatic entrances, the swing-door banged open on its antique hinges yet again.

"Where in the goddamned hell is he?"

In strode Bruno Huntley, producer of soap operas and T.V. movies. He liked to claim that *his* version of the Joey Buttafuoco story pulled damned decent ratings, despite having been the fifth one to air. It was his lavish dinner party we were all working on tonight, so I guess he figured he could yell if he wanted to.

"The kid is four goddamned years old!" he bellowed. "Find him and I'll thrash his butt til it bleeds, dammit! I'm ready!"

And, I swear, the man unbuckled his belt, shouting obscenities and threats, and ripped it from his jeans. The room went stark quiet as Bruno Huntley, apparently gone berserk, began swinging the lizard belt in frantic arcs over his head.

The heavy brass belt buckle swung low and knocked a glass crashing from the counter. And as it whipped by again, it just missed the nanny's face by inches.

Chapter 2

*B*runo Huntley was a tall man, about six foot two or three, lean and paunchless even in his late sixties. He wore tight, faded, hundred-dollar jeans. With his flinty blue eyes, thinning gray hair, and overtanned face, he liked to comment on his perceived resemblance to whatever elderly movie star he admired at the moment. Imagine Clint Eastwood in some kind of red-faced, spitting rage, recklessly swinging a snakeskin lariat in an overcrowded room.

With a flourish, he released the belt, letting it fly. It struck my shoe as it whipped across the floor, its lethal buckle etching skid marks into the terracotta tiles.

"You!" he said, pointing at the woman whom he had very nearly whipped. Then he changed his mind once again and decided to share his ire with the rest of us.

"Rosalinda here lost the boy again," Bruno complained. "She can't keep up with a toddler, for Christ's sake!" Most of my staff were studiously avoiding the shocking scene.

"I'm so sorry, Mr. Bruno," Rosalinda began. "Please . . ."

"Ah, cut the crap! *I-want-the-boy-found-now*! *Comprendes*?"

"*Si, señor*," she whispered. She knew where to look.

"No! No! *No*!" The boy was yelling and hitting at his captor. "No Rosa, let me go!"

Lewis must have bit Rosalinda, because she let go fast and cried out in pain. Bruno moved closer to the action.

"H-e-e-ey, buddy?" In a dizzying instant, Bruno's tone of voice changed dramatically; his deep voice now hearty after all that out-of-control wrath.

Meanwhile, I helped Rosalinda wash her injured hand in cold water. Wes took injustice very seriously. He told the young woman she should leave, but she protested. Then he gave her our business card. "Call Madeline," he urged her. "She can be a good friend."

Rosalinda stared at me.

Bruno ignored our scene at the sink and moved to the cabinet.

"Hey little man! Come on out of there!" Bruno overpowered the boy and dragged his uncooperative body from its hiding spot.

Lewis was a beautiful child with long blond bangs. He wore a pale flannel shirt, tucked into crisp white overalls. The tiny clothing was stamped with the words "baby armani," like some upscale gang had tagged him with their Beverly Hills graffiti.

"It's Halloween, pal! Time to get into your costume."

"No!" Lewis squirmed in the old man's tight grasp. Then he stared defiantly at his father, puckered his beautiful mouth, and spat.

Saliva dripped down Bruno's cheek.

It was bad enough having to silently witness Bruno's horrible temper as he abused his staff, but I honestly didn't know how I'd react if he hit his son. I'd never walked out on a client before. My hands clenched. That's how tense it was in that kitchen.

But Bruno Huntley, erratic as ever, simply laughed. "Hey, you want to dress up as a sprinkler?"

Lewis jumped up into his dad's arms. I heard Wes take a deep breath, watched Rosalinda stop shaking, and realized that we had all been poised on the sharp edge of that ugly, dangerous moment.

And if my "no family in the kitchen" rule hadn't already been shot to hell, into this overcrowded set walked the newest Mrs. Bruno Huntley. Her name was Lily.

Lily Pamela Goldman had become a Huntley almost six years ago, but due to her youth in contrast to her husband's advanced age, it was still hard for the casual observer to distinguish her from one of Bruno's grown children. He had two sons, now in their thirties, from his first marriage. At family outings, I imagined Lily looked a little younger than their wives.

Lily was dressed in a white cashmere "sweatsuit," although I could never actually picture Lily working up a sweat, and certainly not on the cashmere. It was the sort of outfit I imagined Nancy Reagan wore when she was at home. It seemed an odd choice for such a young girl, but I had heard people describe Lily as twenty-five going on fifty.

Her pale, waist-length hair had expensive streaks of blonde, but now it was twisted in a knot at the back of her neck. She looked apologetic. She knew my rule about family in the kitchen.

"Hi, Madeline. Did you find everything you need?"

"Of course she has!" Bruno answered her, gruffly. "But what's your problem, huh? Why haven't you gotten your son dressed? And look at you! You look like hell. Where are the costumes? For nine grand I want to see them on you!"

"We're getting there, dearest," she answered in a little-girl voice, smiling sweetly at him.

Bruno unloaded the child into his mother's arms. "And as for you, little buckeroo . . ." Bruno smiled and winked at Lewis. He seemed calm now after the violent storm.

"Yes, Daddy?"

The father drew back and spat hard into the boy's face. "Funny, huh kid?"

I heard a gasp and a cry coming from my startled crew. Lewis began to wail. And Lily, followed by the nanny, left the room quickly, cooing loving words into her son's ear.

During the fracas, Wesley had moved out into the butler's pantry, a small service room connecting the kitchen to the formal dining room beyond. I joined him.

"That man." Wesley was truly angry. It's less than ideal working conditions when one of the caterers hates the client. If Wes didn't walk out, it was only to make me happy. "So, you going to defend him? Again?"

It was complicated. At his worst, Bruno could be a monster. Every nasty thing people said about him was probably true. But he and I had our own odd history, which had to be factored in.

"I owe him," I remarked. "He gave us our first important job."

"Yeah. Right. You're probably the finest chef who's willing to do crew lunches. And for the first few years, what Huntley paid us was a joke. I think, my dear, what you 'owe him' is a bill."

The door to the butler's pantry was on a swing-hinge, and our privacy was interrupted by three young women balancing trays with dozens of tiny, lit candles destined for outdoors. The candles would illuminate hundreds of miniature pumpkins along the walkways.

Right behind them came Bruno.

"There you are! You guys need anything? Hey, Wesley, how's it going, guy? Madeline!" His voice, booming in its loud hearty way, was much too big for the small room. "It looks great outside. I love it." Our efforts had transformed the expansive grounds of his estate into an eerie, haunted landscape.

"You need anything, just let me know, huh?" He grinned at the kids holding their trays of candles. "Hey, did you gals know I discovered Madeline slaving away at a stove at some hole-in-the-wall bistro seven years ago and made her a star?"

He stood there, master of the tiny room, beaming. He clearly thought he was charming.

Bruno turned to me. "Say, what's up with that fellow of yours—he gonna marry you, or what? You've got to nail that son-of-a-bitch down and set the date! You hear? I want to buy you a big, fat wedding present!"

Bruno grinned at my workers. "Hey! Am I right?"

They giggled.

"Thanks for the romantic advice, Bruno."

The thing is, my relationship with Arlo Zar is on the complicated side. Arlo is a writer for that popular sitcom, "Woman's Work," the one about a feisty lady lawyer. Writing for prime time means he works sixteen-hour days. What with my nights and weekends schedule, finding time together is a challenge.

Bruno was having a great old time, probing for a possible sore spot. "Listen to me, girl! You've got to hog-tie that runaway dogie and bring him back to the fold. Beautiful girl like you, no husband, that's alarming! Am I right, Wes?"

I held my breath at how Wesley might react. Would he kid around with the now playful Bruno? The pause was long.

"I'm alarmed," Wes said, with no inflection at all.

We had gotten past a bad spot. I sent Wes a grateful look as I endured more of Bruno's legendary "wit."

"What are you now? Thirty-three?"

He was doing this on purpose, deliberately adding a few years.

"Not yet."

"See there? She can't even admit her age in public!" Bruno chuckled and gave me a fond look. This is the way he treats the people he likes. "So what can I do for you? Any problems?"

"We're fine, Bruno, thanks," I said.

"What about Holly leaving? Wasn't she going to be the soothsayer tonight?" asked a cobweb girl. Bruno had wanted a fortune teller at the party and Holly volunteered for the part. Now that she was returning worms, we were short one soothsayer.

"We'll be fine," I said quickly. Too late.

"Leave it to me." Bruno loved to take charge. "There's a gal I know who is a terrific little actress. She'll fill in for us."

Bruno pushed on the swinging door into the kitchen and

held it open. There, making a grand show of his largesse to all the kitchen staff, he yelled back, "I'll take care of everything."

I was all set to turn him down when Wes said, "Thanks."

"That's what I'm here for, pal," Bruno said, beaming, "to help my friends!"

The fact that not one person laughed at the insanity of that statement was proof of just how adept in the ways of Hollywood my young staff had quickly become.

Chapter 3

*Y*ou haven't seen upscale real estate until you've gazed at the enormous hacienda-style mansion at 32 Winding Oaks Drive. The house, perched on forty expensive acres, is located in Los Feliz, an old L.A. neighborhood rich in filmland history. Movie idols and studio moguls from the golden age of the silver screen built their posh mansions here. The charming twisted streets of Los Feliz are studded with these residential jewels, the brick and stone rewards to Hollywood's first superstars for inventing themselves.

The magnificent Los Feliz estates, as befitted the giant egos that had them built, seem more the product of set designers than architects. As the building boom spread from the 1920s into the 1930s, impossible Tudor castles elbowed aside giant Mediterranean villas until they ran out of space on the Hollywood Hills.

Los Feliz (which the natives pronounce "Fee-liss," blissfully bludgeoning its proper Spanish pronunciation) is one of my favorite areas of the city. I cater a lot of parties here, since new Hollywood has moved in where old Hollywood moved out, and, as befitting their own egos, remodeled big time.

I stood at the top of the driveway, in front of the ten-foot-tall arched mahogany door that was set into the main entrance of Bruno Huntley's estate. The cars for tonight's party would never be brought up here. The driveway was built in 1928, like the rest of the house, and it was too steep

to provide safe passage for all the modern exotic cars that
were expected. From where I was standing, I could look
down the pitched hillside to the narrow street below where
the valet action was taking place in the winding streets of
Los Feliz. In the still night, a wind gusted against my white
dress, and although it wasn't cold, I shivered.

It was 8:35, and guests were arriving in serious numbers.
It's a perverse law in Hollywood: No matter how unlikeable
an important host might be, it never seems to affect his
popularity. Men like Bruno can be so dangerously important to one's prospects, so routinely ruthless, that it seems
wisest not to cross them. They are the ones, after all, who
get their pictures made and their series renewed. And everyone in this town needs work.

So everyone comes to Bruno's parties, to drink his champagne, to eat his food, to admire his latest Rookwood vase
or latest wife, and maybe even do a deal with the bastard
himself.

New Ferraris and lovingly detailed Mercedes were pulling up at the foot of the drive down on the street. I watched
as the owner of a mint-green BMW850csi disembarked
from his hundred thousand dollars worth of imported metal
and shrunk back against his car as a valet parking attendant
moved towards him. With Bruno's sense of twisted humor,
he'd thought it would be tremendous fun to costume the
valets as the "homeless." They were dressed in dirty rags
and carried signs that read, "Will Park for Food." The
concept was having its effect.

"Homeless" Jason left his "prop" shopping cart and
opened the door for Mr. 850's leggy date and then moved
around to the driver's side and Jason tried to slide behind
the wheel. Mr. 850 looked horrified. Only when he caught
the startled looks on the faces of Mr. Testarossa and Mr.
600slc as their "homeless" valets took off did he get the
joke. Yeah, Bruno could be funny. At someone else's expense.

After leaving their cars, the guests ascended the wide
stone steps that staggered up the short hill to the front of

the house. They followed a trail of hundreds of tiny jack-o-lantern faces that flickered their loony smiles and daggerlike frowns all the way up from the street to where I was standing. The effect in the dark night was mesmerizing, like each pumpkin face was in on some evil secret.

Mr. 850csi was dressed as Captain Hook, with a terrific black satin cape, a patch over one eye, and an expensive-looking long curled wig. I noticed that he couldn't stop fiddling with his hook. His companion was dressed as Peter Pan, all in green. And the tights revealed very shapely legs.

"John Parmentor and Drew Barrymore," said Mr. 850. The guard at the security table took the proffered invitation and checked off their names on his master list.

"You may pass," Rudy told them and he handed them each an appointment card printed with the time they'd be expected at the soothsayer's cottage for a personal reading. Then Rudy pushed a hidden button that lifted an artfully creaky iron gate, and they were able to cross a humped bridge and move on back to where the party was taking place behind the main house.

Rudy was dressed as a giant, menacingly ugly troll. He stood at his post shirtless, so that his overdeveloped pecs and delts, smeared with black soot, were clearly visible under the gray cape flung back over his shoulders. He wore black tights and knee-high boots and his face was disguised by a wart-covered rubber mask.

A large sign was posted at the medieval table at the entrance that read: "No invitation or no costume and absolutely no admittance!" These had been Bruno's orders.

It was pretty difficult to throw guests out at the door when they were actually holding an invitation to the party. Not to mention impolitic when the guy you're tossing owns a movie studio. Virtually all of my bouncers, including Rudy, were "the next Stallone," and they worked my parties to make a little money while they were waiting for their *Rocky*. At my parties, they might even be discovered. However, it doesn't take someone with the genius of a Schwartzenegger to realize it's more difficult to make that important contact when you're humiliating the very man you need to make you a star.

It had been decided that the only way our bouncers could turn away important guests would be to do it incognito—hence the warty masks. It was still early yet, but so far no one had arrived without proper paper and cloth and things had been going smoothly.

"Halt! Who goes there?!" Those were Rudy's lines and he spoke them as if he were at an audition.

After a small exchange, Regis and Joy Philbin were admitted, looking like a rather compact Batman and Catwoman.

"Nice work," I whispered to Rudy. "Keep it up." Then I turned after the Philbins and followed them back toward the party.

I met Wes on the pathway next to a lush hillside covered with ivy. We eyed each other's costumes and chose not to comment. The Wizard of Oz and Glinda the Good Witch. Bruno had taken his own pleasure in selecting what the staff was to wear.

"Your hair is perfect," he said. Good old Wes, straining to find something nice to say.

I dragged my fingers through the nest of light reddish-goldish hair that I almost always wear pulled back, just to keep the weight of it off my face. Tonight, the mass of heavy curls had been left down, sprayed with silver glitter.

I made a face and Wesley laughed.

The party had started and, as usual, I was beginning to enjoy myself. Just then, I felt something lightly touch my ankle and I absentmindedly rubbed my other shoe against the spot out of reflex. Looking down, I watched a rat with a foot-long tail streak across the garden path and out of sight in the darkness.

"Ugh! Oh my God! Where'd it come from?"

"Don't you know what lives in the ivy on these hills?"

"Rats?"

"Rats, snakes, lizards, spiders . . ."

The hillside was blanketed with fluttering, dark green,

heart-shaped leaves. I controlled a shudder. ''But ivy is so pretty.''

''Looks nice, sure. But underneath? You don't want to know!''

Wesley turned to go check on the cooking and I quickly made for the patio in order to survey the party scene.

The staff was in motion—trays of hors d'oeuvres swirling through the clusters of arriving guests. And I was jolted from any inward ratty concerns by the startling sight of the waiters. The sixty men and women were dressed in their costumes for the night: they were all Madonna. Identical blonde wigs, red lips, black moles, and all those crosses on earrings, chokers, and chains. Only in L.A. could you find trained waiters nonchalant enough to serve gravlax and dim sum while dressed in bustiers and fishnet hose.

Holly was back from her last-minute run to the airport and she was working her way through the crowd toward me. Since Bruno had replaced her as our fortune teller, she made a very tall and very buxom Madonna. She actually looked quite pleased with her costume. The outrageous clothes were, after all, pretty close to what one would find in Holly's own closet.

Holly is our only full-time employee. She had helped with prep and cleanup at our very first party. She had been such a help, so efficient and so funny, that we ended up using her every chance we got. And by our first anniversary, we gifted ourselves by putting her on staff permanently. She answers the phones, whips up cookies, and fills in perfectly wherever she is needed.

Holly is a big girl, towering over me by more than half a foot. She's got pale, stick-straight hair that she gets chopped off above her ears while what's left underneath is shaved to the quick, giving her the effect that someone put a bowl on her head and just started trimming. She pays a stylist fifty bucks to get it to look that way.

''Madeline! There you are!'' She puffed as she came up to me. ''I kinda liked looking at all the arrivals.''

Holly is starstruck, and if Bill Murray ever showed up,

I was going to have my hands full trying to keep a six-foot-tall Madonna off of him.

"What's up?" I asked.

"Hey," Holly whispered loudly down to me, "is that Don Johnson?"

"He's just what you need." The star had had his ups and downs. I marveled at Holly's inevitable choice in men.

One of our regular servers approached in full Madonna regalia.

"Alan?"

"The Material Girl himself."

He had brought me a Diet Coke, my addiction. Just give me caffeine and a half-dozen unpronounceable chemicals and I'm happy. And I don't want to hear about how bad it is for me.

I took a sip and watched Alan swivel slowly towards the guests, his tray laden with champagne flutes, his backside in full view.

Holly turned to me, concerned. "Do you think he looks better in that outfit than I do?"

Just then, my old friend Captain Hook walked up to take a glass from Alan's tray. He was talking to a short balding cowboy and an older man in a really marvelous Dracula getup.

"You won't believe what she said to me!" Captain Hook was saying to his buddies. "She said, 'Get rid of the BMW, it will bring you pain!' So how'd that fortune teller know I own a BMW?"

Short Cowboy had a laugh like a cough. "Do you know how many guys here must drive a beemer? Lucky guess!"

"No! No! Listen to this! She specifically said 850!"

"Lucky guess," agreed Marvelous Dracula. "You look rich, John!"

"I'm telling you, she said 'Mint green is an unlucky color. It means death!' So how'd she know the color? I'm the only guy in this town with that color. It's special order for Christ's sake!"

Short Cowboy was smiling broadly. He said, "Every

son-of-a-bitch in this town knows you drive that piss-green beemer. So the gal's done her homework!''

Marvelous Dracula said, ''Actually, I got one of those appointment cards to get my fortune read. Maybe I'll go see her. Who knows? Maybe she can tell me if I'm gonna get a friggin' wide release on *Blue-Eyed Black Belt*!''

The small group broke up.

Holly suppressed a giggle. I shared her thought. Bruno said he'd take care of it. It looked like Bruno's friend was doing a rip-roaring job of telling fortunes. But how did she know Captain Hook's car? And ''mint green means death''? What was that about?

Holly joined me on my final walk around the property to make sure everything was as it should be. As we crossed the path that bordered the garden, I heard a rustling and caught sight of ivy leaves trembling on the hill next to us at just about shoulder height. I stared hard, but only saw the surface of dark green leaves so thick that the hillside beneath them was not visible.

Holly noticed my body stiffen, and thinking to explain the noise, she said, ''It's just the rats and stuff.''

I swallowed and said, ''Let's go check the buffet tables.''

I guess you have to be born in Los Angeles to take the rats for granted.

Chapter 4

To give the grounds of the estate the proper Halloween atmosphere, we had spent quite a lot on the decorations: on simulated death and dying, wrecks and rotting, skulls and skeletons.

The branches of the handsome old trees on the property had been blown with "cobwebs." Baby spotlights were positioned to pick out the witches and goblins lurking behind boulders and hedges.

The estate was wired so that miniature speakers emitted moans and groans as guests walked by, tripping the infrared beams that activated holographic images of ghosts projected into the night sky. Just then, Holly and I could hear a trail of moans coming up around the corner of the house towards us.

Lily Huntley was dressed as Rapunzel. She was accompanied by someone who was totally done up as a frog. I did some mental measurements, dismissed the idea that the frog could possibly be Bruno, and relaxed a little.

Lily wore a shimmering floor-length gown that was cut very low in front, exposing her rather small chest. A magnificent hairpiece extended her famous waist-length hair almost to the ground in an elaborate arrangement of braids and flowers.

"Oh, good! Madeline, I'm so glad I ran into you. The party is thrilling, isn't it?"

I almost said, "So far," but caught myself and murmured, "So . . . kind!" instead.

"Could I make one tiny request?" She smiled impishly.

She could make big honking demands, for the money she and her husband were spending.

"Bruno's son, Graydon, is acting a little huffy because of the dead Elvis we have out in the lounge. See, Gray is dressed up like Elvis, too, and I think he's a little p.o.'d that the guy you got looks a lot more like Elvis than he does."

"Yeah. Your dead Elvis is great," commented the frog.

I glanced over at the dance floor, which had been laid over the tennis court. It featured a band dressed as dead rock musicians looking a little moldering: Hendrix, Morrison, Mama Cass. And in the tent that served as the bar lounge on the other side of the property, what could be more hauntingly perfect than an Elvis impersonator made up to look like he'd spent every year since his death in August 1977 rotting horrifically?

I couldn't think what Lily expected me to do.

"Should I remove our Elvis, then?"

I'd really hate to do that. Not having entertainment in the lounge would be a mistake. I knew Bruno's grown son, Graydon Huntley, pretty well. His sense of self-importance usually amused me, but not when it got in the way of my rotting Elvis.

"I know!" She perked up. "Madeline, why don't you go find Gray and tell him how tremendous he looks."

I had to smile. Lily sure knew how to work this family.

"Point out how much like the young sexy Elvis he looks."

"I'll say young," I promised.

"Great! See you at the buffet later." And she was off, trailing long blonde tendrils, followed closely by a five-foot, nine-inch amphibian.

Holly and I followed the path that led around the house to the immense flagstone patio where seventy-five tables had been set around the Olympic-size pool. There were striped silk canopies spread high over each of the three serving areas. We paid homage to the orange and black theme by covering one entire buffet table with shiny black platters of color-coordinated delicacies. Black blini served with sour cream and golden caviar, grilled Atlantic salmon over black linguini in a lemon cream sauce, and candied orange slices dipped in bittersweet black chocolate were just a few of the dozens of dishes that were being artfully positioned for maximum eye impact.

Holly whooped when she saw the effect we'd achieved with the pool, the large aqueous centerpiece of the dining area. We'd managed to produce a nice eerie smoke coming off its surface with dry ice. A few mechanized sharks circled, just below water, and on top floated a raft on which a real human skeleton in a day-glo orange bikini was catching rays by starlight.

Holly and I turned to the tables and checked a few of the black-edged placecards: "The Late Mr. Steve Allen," "The Late Ms. Brooke Shields," and smiled. Almost at once, I heard shouts. They were coming from the guest house which had been transformed, for the party, into our fortune teller's cottage. The man I'd noticed earlier, Marvelous Dracula, was staggering backwards out of the door. He was yelling, "No! That's impossible! Get away from me!"

I know parties. Shouting is almost never a good sign.

I moved quickly over to that end of the pool to see if I could help. He turned and almost bumped into me. His face, beneath the Dracula makeup, looked drained of blood. So help me.

"Is something wrong?"

He looked at me and seemed to calm himself down as if by will. Before him, after all, stood Glinda, the Good Witch of the North.

"Sir . . ." I tried to sound professional, despite my dozens of satin bows and pair of glittered wings. "My name is Madeline Bean, and my firm is running this party. If something has upset you, please let me know and I'll try to put things right.''

"It was nothing. It's that fortune-telling gal, that's all. She had me there, for a minute. But that's the fun, eh? She told me my karate picture was gonna open big, so that's good news.''

This man had been screaming a minute ago. Was he having a good time or was he scared witless? "So, you're okay?"

"It's just a Halloween prank, I guess. See, she told me I wouldn't *live* to spend any of the money that *Blue-Eyed Black Belt* is gonna make. Said I'd 'die in the arms of Suzanne.' ''

Die? She was telling all the guests they were going to *die*?

"The thing is, how'd she know the name of my picture? We changed the title yesterday. It hasn't been in the trades yet.''

He was referring to the trade newspapers, The *Hollywood Reporter* and *Variety*. But I was more worried about this thing about death in the arms of someone named Suzanne.

"Do you know anyone named . . . Suzanne?" I asked him delicately.

"My new secretary. Just started to work for me last week.''

"Oh," I said. I was thinking. How ever had this fortune teller gotten that kind of inside information?

"But don't worry, nothing personal going on with Suzanne. Anyway, not yet. Maybe not ever if I listen to this advice, eh?"

Marvelous Dracula looked unhappy, but no longer shocked.

Upon his demand, I pointed him in the direction from which we could faintly hear "Blue Suede Shoes," and watched him make for the nearest bar. Things were getting out of hand. One man was turned off his beloved automobile. Another was warned off a future mistress. What the hell was going on with our soothsayer?

I walked through the door of the guest cottage and found myself in its small living room. For tonight, it had been arranged as a waiting area. On the table, a sign showed the face of a clock. It read, ''Cassandra's next appointment will begin promptly at: . . .'' The clock hands were set to ten-thirty. Next to the sign was a working clock that showed the current time to be 9:13.

I called out, ''Hello!'' and walked back through a doorway that had been hung with beads, and down a tiny hall that led to the one large bedroom. The door was closed and a sign warned, KEEP OUT. I knocked at the door. No answer.

I tried the handle and it opened quietly. Like the rest of the property, this room had been totally transformed. Where a king-size bed usually awaited the Huntleys' overnight guests, we had placed a round table with a gold gauze cloth that fell to the floor. On the center of the table was a stand that held a crystal globe the size of a basketball. It cost $250 for the night from a prop rental house that claimed it came from *The Wizard of Oz.*

We'd hung pale green curtain fabric all around the room and on the ceiling parachute silk was draped to give the feeling of being in a gypsy's tent. The lighting was very dim and indirect, but I could see at once the place was empty.

In the kitchen, however, I had a start. In the center of the linoleum was another rat. A stiff rat. Maybe it was a prop. I didn't stay long enough to check it out.

I took one last look into the crystal ball room, and this time I noticed a long leather strap on the floor, just sticking out from underneath the draped table. I knelt down and pulled on it. A black leather knapsack came out. Our sooth-sayer must be a very trusting soul to leave her purse laying around.

I stood up, leaving the bag undisturbed, wondering what to do. Maybe just push it back under the table? I used the point of my silver Good Witch shoe to nudge it back under, but unfortunately, I just managed to dump some of the knapsack's contents onto the floor, while the bag slipped back out of sight.

My eyes were riveted to the odd assortment of items that had been disgorged: a tube of lipstick, a small glass vial of white powder, a card of birth control pills, and a .22-caliber pistol with a "Grateful Dead" skull carved into its ivory handle.

Chapter 5

*J*ust then I heard the gong sound out, announcing the start of the dinner buffet. I bent down, quickly scooped the contents back into the soothsayer's knapsack, gun and all, and shoved the entire thing into its hiding place. I decided that as crises go, six hundred hungry people descending on poor Wesley had just taken precedence over our weird Cassandra.

Outside on the pool patio, a mob was circling the buffet tables like they all hadn't had perfectly wonderful expense-account lunches that day. I'm a cook at heart. This is what I love to see.

It was my first chance to take a really good look at some of the incredible costumes that were being worn. After goodness knows how many hours spent in aerobics classes and tanning beds, many of the female guests were using the costume theme to show off their toned and tanned flesh. The effect was staggering. Just imagine the prettiest girl from every high school in America moving to L.A. and all showing up at the same party. The congregation of so many former homecoming queens always strikes me as surreal.

People were making their way through the buffet line. A fabulous body floated past me. She was dressed in an absolutely see-through gray unitard with tiny opaque patches where modesty weakly prevailed. She wore a pale gray wig that was all fluff and curls and her mouth was covered with a transparent surgical mask. Across her shapely behind were the letters that explained her concept. They spelled out "Smog." Since she had come up with a way to display her tight butt *and* an environmental message at the same time, I figured she had a great shot at winning one of the costume awards. Wesley and I were betting on the event, so I made a note.

She bent over a serving table in a highly revealing pose. I reconsidered. This woman was after much more than a measly "Best Costume" trophy. In an outfit like that, she just might land herself a big-time agent. At these industry parties, the boundary between socializing and pursuing one's career could be as thin as the dotted line on a C.A.A. contract.

The tables were filling up as I walked to the main house. I noticed the drunken shrimp was popular. It was a new recipe we were trying where the shrimp are marinated in tequila and lime juice before being grilled. I was making a note to tell Wes to reserve some shrimp for late-arriving guests, when I saw Graydon Huntley seating himself at a table nearby.

At thirty-four, Graydon is Bruno's second son. Bruno's firstborn, Bru, Jr., had yet to show up and I thought that was just as well. The Huntley clan had been difficult to handle when I had been catering for Bruno on his various shows. I suspected they hadn't improved with age. Of the bunch, it's Graydon who is mostly harmless.

From his large office at Bruno Huntley Productions, Gray spends the bulk of his busy day mastering Solitaire on his Powerbook and fills in the rest of his schedule by having his secretary set up tee times at Lakeside. His position as senior vice president was a gift from his father. Like most of Bruno's gifts, it was pretty much undeserved and way too generous. But rather than be embarrassed by his functionless title, or even grateful for his lucky stars, Graydon mostly felt annoyed he hadn't been made president of the company yet.

Graydon looked up at me and grinned, his mouth a little

too full of spinach/pumpkin souffle. "Hi, Mad-Woman,"
he said.

"Gray. How are you?" I smiled back.

"Cool. Nice party, huh?"

I wondered if he had forgotten it was I who was doing
the party. Gray knew I ran a catering business, but sometimes it was hard to guess what information slipped through
the sieve.

"Thanks, Gray," I said. "I'm loving all these costumes."

"Hey, what's with that terrible Elvis impersonator
they've got going in the back? Have you seen him? He
doesn't look anything like the King. Do you think?"

"Well, maybe the older, heftier version," I said. "Not
like the young Elvis. No, that's the Elvis everyone loves. I
think you were so clever to come as the early Elvis. It takes
guts to try to measure up to his sexy good looks, and
you've certainly got them." Guts I was talking about, but
of course Gray thought I meant looks.

"D'you really think so?" He perked up. Of course.

"Where's Carmen?" I asked.

"Oh, I don't know," Gray gave an unfocused look to
the crowd. "Somewhere. I just look for the beehive, that's
the easiest way to spot her."

I tried to imagine his dark pretty wife dressed in a giant
beehive costume, but it didn't fit her hot, smoldering image.

"She's dressed as Priscilla in the big hair days. She really looks fantastic! She's wearing this tight white sweater
and tight black skirt, and those real spiky high heels. She
looks so damn cheap!" He smiled.

Priscilla Presley. That was more like the Carmen I knew.

Just then my Motorola squawked. "I'd better get going,"
I told him. I took a step or two as I listened to the radio.

"This is Rudy. I've got a little situation down here at
the entrance. Guy wants in without a costume and he's
kicking up a fit! Please advise."

I pressed the speak button and told him I'd be right there.

Holly was working as a spare waitress and she came up to me.

"Trouble?" she asked.

"I'll deal with it. Could you tell Wes to save the shrimp?"

Rudy had been quite accurate. Standing at the table with him was a grown man actually kicking down the signs that were set up at the entrance. I walked more quickly when I saw he was starting to kick at Rudy. Was this guy crazy?

I got a closer look. It was Bru, Jr., and he saw me approach.

"Hey, Madeline! Get over here! This demented jerk is trying to keep me out of Dad's party. What load of crap is this, anyway?"

He had a face like his father's, only every place that it could have turned ugly, it had. He was a couple of years older than Graydon but his hair had turned completely gray, like his father's. His beard was also gray. It had been about three years since he and I'd last met, but on him it looked more like ten.

Bru was considered the black sheep of a pretty darkly-fleeced brood. After rumors of stealing cafeteria money from the studio where his dad had offices, Bru, Jr. no longer held a position at his father's production company.

Instead of keeping another unworkable son on the payroll, Bruno simply paid his eldest son's bills and got him out of scrapes. But it wasn't like Bruno to just hand Bru an allowance. He had to get something in return for his cash. So he traded in humiliation. He made Bru come begging. Because Bru, Jr. could never seem to keep a job, they played out this sad ritual on a monthly basis.

"Hi, Bru," I said as I walked up to him. He stopped kicking stuff for a minute and started threatening and whining. For the Huntley boys, this is standard operating procedure.

"Let me in this minute or I'll tell Dad!"

"We have some extra costumes here for special guests,

Bru. Why don't you look them over and pick something before you go in?"

"That's bullshit! I'm not wearing any fucking costume!"

"Okay. No problem. Let him in, Rudy."

I started to turn away, but Rudy was angry. After putting up with all of Bru's insults and attitude, he hated seeing him get away with it. I saw what was coming and sighed. It's a guy thing.

"I thought Mr. Huntley said no exceptions to the rule, not even for his family." He did not open the gate.

"That's true, Rudy," I said, "but let's let Mr. Huntley, Sr., deal with this now."

I looked at him, kindly, but quite firmly. It's a boss thing.

Reluctantly, Rudy lifted the gate, and as Bru walked past he viciously yanked at Rudy's troll mask and broke the elastic that was holding it in place.

Rudy looked stunned. Bru took the mask, threw it in the dirt, and started stomping on it, ripping the delicate rubber features. Then he looked straight at Rudy and said in a low voice, "You'll never work in this town, pal. Never. I've seen your face. I can make it happen. Pack up and move back to Minnesota or wherever you came from. You screwed with the wrong guy!" Then he walked away, never looking back.

Before I could say anything to Rudy, I heard an unfamiliar voice speak up. I hadn't noticed earlier, but another guest had arrived late and apparently witnessed Bru's vitriolic speech. He now addressed Rudy in a shocked voice.

"Young man, I cannot believe what just happened. That man is not going to ruin anyone, I can assure you. That loud, obnoxious man cannot himself get a job in this town.

"Let me introduce myself," he continued. "I'm Jacob Dunmaster."

Rudy looked up in disbelief. Dunmaster was one of those legendary casting directors that no struggling actor could get in to see.

"Here's my card. Please call me Monday morning. I'm

sure there is something I can find for a handsome boy like yourself."

Rudy grinned. "Gee, thanks Mr. Dunmaster. This is great!"

"Nonsense, young man, I think I know talent when I see it." He eyed Rudy's pecs and delts. "And, please, call me Jacob."

At this point, I thought the conversation might actually be getting, well, romantic, and I took my leave quickly. In Hollywood, romance can be an odd mixture of desire and advantage, and really, who was I to judge? I just want everyone to be happy.

By the time I got back to the patio, the dinner was in full swing. The party was loud, as all good parties are, and I was starting to feel a bit of pride as I surveyed the scene.

A small combo was playing jazz in the background, and as the last song ended, the bandleader announced, "Your attention please, as tonight's host saves your hostess!"

I hadn't expected this. It must have been something Bruno sprung on the band leader and all I could do was gape in astonishment as a spotlight was moved from the band to focus on Bruno Huntley standing on a platform next to the house. Bruno was dressed as a young and handsome Prince Charming, in purple tights and gold cape. He wore a wig in the style of a long blond pageboy and he was looking up at one of the second-floor windows.

The Huntley estate was of Spanish design, and standing out on a wrought-iron balcony was Lily. She had somehow attached an even longer extension onto her floor-length hair, and she threw this blonde rope down to the ground. Bruno smiled and hammed it up, and then actually began to climb! It was a trick, of course, but it did look like he was climbing up her hair.

The crowd went almost silent, and then there was furious whispering, and then laughter.

Bruno seemed to love the crowd's response and he hauled himself all the way to the balcony. As he climbed over the rail, someone yelled, "Just like Jack Palance at the Oscars!"

He called down in his loud, hoarse, General Patton voice, "Friends! I am glad you could join Lily and me for this little get-together. Enjoy yourselves! What is life all about if not friendship and love?" And then he kissed his wife. The crowd had, most of them, been involved in making T.V. shows long enough to recognize an Applause cue. They cheered.

Wesley approached and could barely contain a snort. " 'Friendship and love!' I need a drink!"

Wes had been stewing all day about old problems he had with Bruno. Being this close to the man seemed to bring up his rancor.

I looked at Wes, all dolled up in his Wizard of Oz getup, and had to smile. What he needed was a distraction.

"Is there champagne in the kitchen?" I asked him.

"After you."

We walked to the kitchen door, eavesdropping on our way. No one had anything nice to say about the host, I'm afraid.

After pouring tall drinks into some regal Baccarat crystal flutes, Wesley proposed a toast. He always did this midway through a party. It was a Wesley Westcott tradition.

"Let's hope the worst is over and the best is on its way!"

The bubbles were the tiny, expensive kind and we felt indulged. As we sipped the wine, I tried to see if there was anything else going on with Wesley that might be putting him off-balance. He hadn't seemed quite himself all day.

"Everything okay at home?" I asked.

"Sure. Mal is fine. Although she may not forgive me since I've been working such ridiculous hours." He looked at his watch.

Mal was Wesley's beloved springer spaniel. He was so attached to her, he'd actually gotten her name tattooed on his left wrist.

I looked at the kitchen clock and figured now was a good

time to find our fortune teller. I still had to tell her to cool it with the dire personal predictions.

By this time, most of the guests had finished their espressos and were moving off towards the dance tent. There was just enough time to get to the soothsayer before her next appointment.

I opened the door to the guest house and walked back to the fortune-telling room in the rear. The door stood open and a pretty young woman was just sitting down at the table. She wore a beautiful silk gypsy dress, much nicer than the one I remembered renting for the occasion. Her shiny black hair was pulled up into a ponytail, tied with a green paisley scarf. She had beautiful skin and wore gold hoops in her ears. With dramatic black eyeliner emphasizing her upturned eyes, she really looked the part.

"Hi, I'm Madeline Bean," I said as she looked up.

"Yes. I know." Her purring, deep Brenda Vacarro voice was unexpected.

"How's it been going?"

"Not bad." She looked at me with eyes that were a little too green. Contact lenses, probably.

"Thanks for filling in here on such short notice. You've been very effective."

She smiled without revealing her teeth.

"Maybe too effective." I smiled back. "I've been hearing from a few of your customers that your predictions may be a little too Stephen King for the room. Perhaps you could use some other words besides, oh . . . say, *death*."

"Mmmm," she murmured. She still looked me straight in the eyes with her disconcerting emerald greens.

"By the way, where are you getting some of that stuff? Knowing the model of cars and the names of secretaries?"

"Oh, that." She paused.

She was extremely self-possessed. She wasn't stalling so much as pausing for dramatic effect. These actresses!

"I guess the stars tell me," she finished.

"The *Star*?" I asked. It was a popular rag that gave the *National Enquirer* a run for its money. Was she saying she'd read all these personal facts in the tabloids?

"No." Another pause, eyes still gazing at me. "The stars . . . you know, the cosmos!" She smiled sweetly.

"Come on!" I laughed. She was joking and I had been buying her whole otherworldly act. She was good.

"Ah, a disbeliever! You should pay attention to my predictions. The stars show good things in your future."

"Uh-huh," I drawled. I liked hearing her do her spiel. Whoever she was, Bruno had found us an interesting soothsayer.

She gazed off into the distance. I was disappointed to see she didn't even glance at my expensive crystal ball.

"Yes. I see a dark man. A new romance, perhaps? And a lot of money and . . . the stars say you'll leave this job."

Actually, I could use a dark man and a lot of money if they might be lying about, but the last prediction cracked me up. I'd been through hell getting this little career started. I studied cooking in San Francisco, and slaved myself out to work at one of the most food-forward restaurants in Berkeley. I peeled and whisked and kept an applewood-burning pizza oven stoked and then plunged into major-league debt to get my show on the road. I'd been racing against the clock to have a profitable year before I turned the big three-oh. The clock was winning.

"I won't quibble with your predictions about the man and the money, but I'm keeping my job. Good try," I told her.

"It's in the stars, Madeline, you can't avoid it."

"Anything else from the heavens?"

"A warning: watch yourself. The sun is dangerous."

Safe advice in L.A., the skin cancer capitol of the world.

She looked out across the cosmos and then focused back to me. "Something is going to happen tonight. Something terrible!" she whispered in her dramatic low rasp.

"Something worse than Bruno pretending to be Prince Charming?"

"Prince Charming?" She looked puzzled.

Well, at last my smooth friend was showing that she was not all-knowing, all-seeing.

"Just Bruno's subtle way of saying welcome to the party. He climbed up Rapunzel's hair and kissed his wife in front of the dinner crowd. Didn't you know?" Her omniscience was slipping.

"No." She seemed to be thinking about something else as she explained, "I took my dinner break alone, over in that building they use as the gym."

"Well, your next appointment is due soon. I just wanted to thank you for helping us out at the last moment. And if you can keep from freaking out the guests, so much the better."

"Mmm," she answered, mind still elsewhere.

Just then a bell rang from the reception room out front, and a drunk female voice shouted, "I'm a little late, is that okay?"

The beautiful gypsy snapped back to the here and now, moving past me and out into the corridor to greet her new arrival.

"I'm Madam Cassandra, and I have some fearful news for you, Ms. Summers."

"Bad news? Oh no! Well, you must tell me, my dear!" she slurred, following Cassandra into the little room I had just left.

I walked out of the cottage, astounded at how much people really do seem to like to hear bad news. Everyone except me.

Most of the dinner crowd had finished and moved on, but I could see Graydon, still at the table he'd been at all night. Next to him was his hot little wife, Carmen. Also there were the latecoming host and hostess of the party, just starting to eat, I realized with alarm. I moved towards their table.

"Are you just getting around to dinner?" I asked, eyeing their untouched plates. The pumpkin ravioli in sage sauce had been sitting in a warming tray forever. It would taste terrible.

"Let me freshen up your plates. This food may have been waiting a bit too long."

"Okay," Lily agreed, not really paying attention to my last words, since Bruno's tone had gotten more aggressive in the background. She turned her attention toward her husband.

"Exactly what are you saying, Graydon?" Bruno demanded.

If there was anything this family loved to do more than fight, it was to fight in public. I took the two plates and left quietly. Not that anyone noticed.

In the kitchen, Wesley was supervising the cleanup. He looked at me and asked, "How many are still eating?"

"Just a few," I answered. "Do we have any fresh food for the Huntleys? They've waited until every item on their buffet has run out or gone cold," I complained. It was nicer when the hosts, who were paying the tab, after all, had the meal of their lives.

"Not to worry." Wesley proceeded to arrange two perfectly beautiful plates with fresh food from the kitchen.

I took the hot plates quickly back to Bruno and Lily. As I approached their table I could hear that the volume had been turned up another few notches in the conflict between father and son.

As I silently slipped the plates down onto the table, Bruno was on the verge of shouting. His face looked mean. He said, "You imbecile! You had no right to tell the network we'd have the sketches to them by Tuesday!"

Oh. Work.

"D-a-a-d!" Gray whined loudly. "I told them maybe!"

"You have no . . . fucking . . . right! Got that? Do I have to write it down?" Bruno was choking on his anger, spitting out each word.

"I told you . . ." Gray tried to tell him again, this time louder—the Huntley way!

I left the table quickly. In my days of working for Bruno, I'd heard him berate and undermine his kids' efforts many times. I'd also heard him overpraise them and overpay them for absolutely awful performances. He had unwittingly trained them to be unfit to do much of anything. And it appears that they were still at it.

I could see the other Huntley brother, Bru, Jr., approaching, drawn by the fight. And I decided to get the hell out of there.

The party had moved into its final phase; after-dinner drinks were being served at all three bars, and tables of miniature desserts were being set up at the dance tent. The rest of the party should wind peacefully down.

I looked at my watch. It was only eleven o'clock, but I was exhausted. And as I walked over to the tent, I couldn't help feeling a tingling of dread. What was it the soothsayer had said? "Something is going to happen tonight. Something terrible."

I was getting the itchy feeling that there was still time for something truly terrible to occur.

Chapter 6

*W*esley and Holly and Alan and I were standing together outside of the dance tent. Strains of "You've Got To Change Your Evil Ways" provided a soundtrack to our conversation.

It was almost midnight and the party was going on like mad. People were found clutching one another in various deserted areas around the grounds. Important guests were raving about the food, and most everyone was feeling the effects of the drink.

We started the ritual comparison of war stories from the night's event. This kind of banter was our comic relief. After three sleepless nights hammering every single detail in place, and then charging through these last intense hours coercing all those details to work, we were ready for a break.

As was our custom, we tried to outdo each other for most scary moment in the party, best save of a crisis, most important movie gossip overheard, and so on.

"Did you talk to our soothsayer?" Holly was asking Wesley.

"Yeah. She told me my life would soon be in jeopardy."

"Oh, dear," I muttered. Death again.

"I live in L.A.," Wes said. "Tell me something I don't know."

We laughed. In L.A., you either develop a great sense of humor, a great sense of denial, or you move out of town.

"But she did have some good news about you, Madeline. She said that Arlo would propose soon. Don't give up hope!"

I groaned. Why does every fortune teller take it as a given that unmarried females are hungry to hear those words?

"Want to know when Arlo will pop the question?" he teased.

"No."

"Yes!" insisted Holly.

"Stay out of this."

To change the subject, I offered, "Did I tell you? The Huntleys were fighting right after dinner!"

"See," Wes jumped in, "I told you everyone enjoyed the party. The Huntleys love a good fight. The louder they fight, the closer that family feels."

"What do you mean the Huntleys were fighting after dinner?" Holly demanded. "I saw them after dinner and they were definitely not fighting."

"Where?" I asked her.

"I was upstairs in the house, bringing dinner plates to the staff and the little boy. I opened the door to this room that I was sure was the Nursery, and I'm afraid I accidentally walked in on Rapunzel and Prince Charming . . ." She paused for effect. ". . . *doing the deed*."

"No!" the rest of us hooted.

"Oh, yes!" Holly was loving this. She had waited quietly while we were doling out our best party stories, holding back her aces.

"Not doing . . . it?" Good old Wes.

"Well, I couldn't just stand there staring at them, could I? I just opened the door, spotted the pair on the floor . . ."

That got another hoot out of our crowd.

"On the floor!" from Wesley.

"Gotta give the old boy credit," from Alan.

Holly said, "Hey, do you want to hear?"

That quieted us down.

"He was on the bottom, and the two of them were cov-

ered with all that fake hair she had on. He was kinda writhing and moaning. You know, the usual.''

In our exhausted state, the mental picture was way too
much to deal with. There were some soft ''Oh, god''s and
shakes of heads.

''I don't think they even knew I was there.''

''Bruno probably likes an audience,'' Alan offered.

''Okay! Enough!'' I commanded.

''Well, anyway, they sure weren't fighting when I saw
them,'' Holly finished, giggling.

''I didn't mean that Bruno was fighting with Lily—''

I never got to finish my thought. Instead, I was interrupted by a strangled, animallike wail. It came from inside
the tent and was followed by other screams, other voices
shouting.

All of us ran the ten feet or so to the nearest entrance to
the dance tent. We pushed quickly past others who, like us,
were drawn to the screams. At the center of the dance floor,
a tight knot of people had formed around someone who
had apparently fallen.

Oh, lord! Someone taken ill or worse. My brain began
to solve this unknown problem. There must be a number
of medical doctors on the guest list. Someone would help,
I prayed, as I pushed my way to the center of the crowd.

The screaming had stopped for a moment, which I took
as a positive sign, but now it started again. As I moved
closer to the trouble, I heard the sounds of violent retching
and coughing that were punctuating the screams of pain.

The band had stopped playing, and as I almost reached
the person who had fallen, I heard the man in front of me
whisper to his date, ''Don't look!''

Of course, I had to.

It was Lily who was standing over Bruno, shrieking. It
was Bruno who was lying on the floor, writhing and convulsing. His body arced backwards. It didn't look like a
heart attack. More like a fit.

Wesley and Alan were right behind me, and I heard them
trying to move the people back.

My eyes were glued to Bruno's face. It was contorted, agonized, dying. I reached out for Lily, who was now sobbing, but no longer screaming.

Bruno's mouth was frozen in a painfully wide-open grimace, and with each sob from Lily, he actually seemed to grimace harder. It was horrible. His face strained, like he was trying to gasp for breath, but he was taking nothing into his lungs. Something stronger than he was seemed to be strangling him from the inside.

I heard a voice above the crowd's whispering and crying. A man was shouting, "Let me through! I'm his doctor! Move aside!" It was Bruno's golfing buddy, Dr. Cary Epstein.

Lily was still sobbing in my arms. I told her, "Lily, it's Dr. Epstein. Don't worry, he's here!"

But Lily was not hearing me. Her face was blotched with red and her eyes were swollen. Her mascara had streaked her face with dark gray smudges. I'd never seen her looking a mess. Nobody had.

The doctor moved to Bruno's twitching, arcing body, and yelled, "Somebody help me hold him down."

No one moved.

"Would somebody . . ." the doctor started to ask again, but he was thrown off-balance by Bruno's seizures.

Lily looked wild-eyed at the crowd. "Somebody, please!" she shrieked. "Somebody help!"

At each of her cries, Bruno's body jerked and arched into almost a complete backbend. It was beyond grotesque.

I looked around and saw Alan moving people back.

"Alan!"

I caught his attention and he moved in to help subdue Bruno.

This was the most horrifying thing I had ever seen in my life. And it got worse. Bruno started to speak. That is, he tried to speak. It came out in a racked, choking whisper, like someone trying to form words on the inhale, desperately trying to drag in air at the same time. I couldn't make out any words.

"What's he saying?" Lily demanded, hysterical. "What?"

She pulled away from me and fell to her knees at Bruno's side. The doctor was trying to look in Bruno's eyes as Alan held him down. Bruno finally noticed Lily and he got even more agitated. Again and again, his fierce, gaping mouth grimaced horribly, as he struggled to catch a breath of air. He simply couldn't.

And then he just stopped. Brown eyes open, distorted mouth gaping, long body rigid in a contortion one moment and frozen deathly still the next.

Alan let go of Bruno's shoulders and Lily started howling, "No, no, no, no!" and threw herself on top of Bruno's body, crying, her fake hair covering him in disarray.

Holly, who had been standing there right beside me, reached out her hand and grabbed my elbow. She put her other hand over her mouth and said, "Oh my god!"

I turned to comfort her, and then I remembered. Holly had just described walking in and seeing the two of them in exactly this position. Bruno stretched out on the floor, with his young wife astride him.

It doesn't get much creepier than that.

Chapter 7

*P*anic.

Since the doctor was attending to Bruno, I raised my voice and shouted above the whispered, weeping, "Oh my god!"'s and the worried, "What's happening?"'s.

"Everyone, please stay calm." I had to repeat it a few times just to get their attention, and soon the guests started to quiet down if only to hear what was going on.

"The Huntley family would appreciate your cooperation at this time. Could you all please clear this area and move to the patio where coffee and drinks are now being served."

There was movement.

I radioed the bartenders who were stationed near the patio so they would be prepared for the crowd. Wes and Holly hurried from the tent to set up a makeshift dessert and coffee buffet there. Soon only the immediate family gathered around Bruno on the floor.

I got a squawk on the radio and moved away a few steps so I wouldn't disturb them as I spoke into it.

"Rudy here." He sounded slightly out of breath. "I'm having a situation at the front gate."

"What is it?"

"Somebody called the paramedics, so I sent them up to the tent. And somebody else must have called the cops, because they just arrived and they're kinda bent out of shape. They don't want no paramedics touching nothing 'cause they heard the old guy's dead anyway."

"Cops are coming up?"

"Yep."

"That's dandy."

A clutch of Huntley offspring and ex-wives were arguing near the body. I wasn't really surprised. When were they not?

The giant frog stood off to the side. It must have been the same man I'd seen earlier with Lily, only now he'd taken his mask off and I thought I recognized him as one of Bruno's employees.

Dr. Epstein was kneeling next to Lily. She was sitting on the floor a few feet away from the body. Her white dress was streaked with blood. Bruno must have cut himself with all his tortured banging against the floor.

Lily was holding herself. No tears. Not a whimper.

Two men, dressed in L.A. Fire Department paramedic uniforms entered the tent. The doctor rose and conferred with them. I could hear him say Bruno had died at 11:59 p.m., after suffering an acute onset of seizures. I noticed that aside from feeling for a pulse, the paramedics left the body alone. Police. Control freaks.

I slipped out of the tent. Just ahead on the path I saw two people approaching, dressed in street clothes. It struck me. Here were two people who were not wearing costumes and did not have invitations. Poor Bruno; dead for fifteen minutes and already his wishes were being ignored. It seemed, in this new universe, it no longer mattered what Bruno Huntley wanted. And at that moment I realized that there were a great many people whom Bruno had bullied and managed and overpowered and outshouted that might now find themselves throwing off their masks and sighing in relief.

"Are you the police?" I asked, to start the conversation.

The man who spoke to me was tall, certainly over six-two, and I'd place him in his early forties. He was accompanied by a woman officer, and as they came into the light, I immediately recognized her.

Lizzie Bailey was about the most stunning-looking

woman I'd ever known. When we'd first met, I hadn't been living in L.A. for very long. Even the cops, I'd thought then, look like movie stars.

"I'm Lieutenant Chuck Honnett and this is Officer Elizabeth Bailey." He looked at me and took in my silver tights and the glitter sprayed in my hair. "You have a body here?"

"Actually, it's the owner of this house. Bruno Huntley."

In the context of this tragedy, it felt odd to hear the sounds of prerecorded moaning coming from the speakers and see the holographic ghosts that were projected in the trees.

Honnett followed my gaze.

"Quite a party going on. You Mr. Huntley's daughter?"

"No." Both Officer Bailey and I answered at the same time. Then she smiled her cocky smile at me.

"This is Madeline Bean, a friend of mine. She doesn't always look so . . . fluffy."

"My catering company is in charge of this party, so I . . ."

"You took charge. Fine. You okay?" Honnett asked.

"It was pretty grim watching Bruno convulse and die like that."

"You know him pretty well, then?" he asked.

"I've worked for him on and off for a number of years. The family's in there." I nodded to the tent. "With the body."

Honnett didn't seem in such a hurry to see Bruno. He kept talking. "Possible poisoning was what we were told. That right?"

"Maybe." I swallowed. It sounded horrible. "His doctor was with him when he died. He said . . ."

"I'll get the doctor's statement in a minute. I just wondered if you've already cleared up the food from the party? Make sure your people don't dispose of anything, okay?"

Was he implying Bruno died from food poisoning? From *my* food?

"Lieutenant, six hundred healthy guests ate the same . . ."

"Mrs. Bean, I never suggested . . ."

"Call me Madeline." I could interrupt, too.

Honnett smiled at me, calm as a bowl of oatmeal. "All right, Madeline. This is the beginning of what looks like a hellacious investigation. There were what? You said maybe six hundred people that had opportunity? Motive we don't know yet. And the usual way that nasty people get their victims to eat poison is to hide it in their food or drink. So we need to stop all the cleaning up. That way we can hand our diligent forensics people the bloody nightmare of trying to pin down exactly what dish of spaghetti or whatever was dosed with poison."

"Oh." Maybe I overreacted.

"It's okay, Maddy," Lizzie said. "We're going to need to speak to all of your staff. Can you arrange that for us?"

"Sure."

I was no longer in charge of this party. I felt relief, along with something else. I guess it was anticlimax. Instead of the thanks and congratulations I always gave our workers at the end of a great evening, I now had to round them up to await police questioning.

Lieutenant Honnett turned to enter the tent. Lizzie stayed with me.

"I didn't know you were with Homicide," I chided her.

We had first met years ago, both working on a film of Bruno's. Lizzie, working on her off hours from the department, headed up location security and I did the food.

"This is a big break for me. The call came in and I heard it was at the Huntley place. I told them I'd been here before and had worked with Huntley in the past. So they gave me a chance."

Lizzie was good at making the most of her opportunities. In a system that had historically been slanted against young black females, she always seemed to find a way around.

"I could use your help, Maddy. Can we get together and talk this one through? How about breakfast tomorrow?"

"Make it lunch." I knew I'd be exhausted, but I was intrigued to hear anything she might have to tell me about this case.

"Meet me at Chez Nous in Toluca Lake at twelve. That give you enough beauty sleep?"

I took the path to the patio to see the last of the unhappy guests being rounded up by officers. Wes walked over to me.

"Where have you been? Is he dead? Half the guests are convinced it's a giant hoax just to get them to leave the party and stop drinking Huntley's booze. Isn't that terrible?" Wes suppressed a smile. It's hard not to succumb to gallows humor, especially for us.

"Wes!" I warned him.

"Tell me what's going on."

"He's dead and it may be poison and the police want all the plates and trays and food to be left as is. No cleaning up. They want to sift through all this trash for clues."

"Hmmm." Wes and I surveyed the scene.

Of course by this point, all the cleaning up is pretty much done. We like to be able to leave the premises of a party by one o'clock. The late crowd could then serve themselves drinks all night, if they wanted, on into the a.m.

I looked around. Instead of the trays and plates and glasses that had been there a few hours ago, there was now a line of trash bags, about sixty or so, and a few dozen crates of china, glassware, and silverware to be picked up by the party rental people.

"They're going to hunt through all that?" Wes asked, dubious.

We eyed the fifteen hundred pounds of trash and dirty dishes.

"Wesley, when did we lose control of our Halloween party?"

"I remember exactly. It was the day we agreed to work once again for Mr. Bruno Huntley."

Chapter 8

I woke up very late Saturday morning, warm and safe beneath my old postage-stamp quilt, with its tiny stitches holding together hundreds of faded, patterned, one-inch fabric squares.

Oh, yeah. The party. Last night. Bruno Huntley was dead.

Dr. Epstein said he'd never seen anything like what killed Bruno. If it was poison, he said maybe it could have been strychnine. The actual cause of death was asphyxia. Bruno couldn't breathe.

I flashed on the vivid picture of Bruno's body twisting and squeezing the very breath out of him from the inside. All that pain, his trachea and stomach and lungs in spasm after spasm without letup.

I pushed my head deeper into the pillows and tried to drift back to sleep.

Memories of last night would not switch off.

My hand ventured out from under the quilt and made an unerring swipe for the remote control on my bedside table. I turned on my twenty-seven-inch Toshiba and flipped through the stations until I hit PBS.

Julia Child was trilling on about sesame oil and a wok. I had seen this episode before. I knew the recipes, but I was struck by the sound of her voice, so confident, so optimistic. I feel like that when I'm cooking, too. I sat up in bed and began to feel a little better.

Maybe that was the key to Julia's popularity. It wasn't about food so much as it was about her gusto for life. Julia could whisk just about anything into a pleasing outcome. My goodness, if this large pleasant lady could master the intricacies of a forbidding French dish, not even looking at what she was doing half the time, all the while talking and smiling at the camera, couldn't we all master a little problem of our own? Especially if we paid attention.

Somebody had killed Bruno Huntley. And my normal happy denial seemed to be deserting me. Most days I do a pretty fair job of hiding from the pain of living on the outside edge of the twentieth century. But last night, I'd run screeching into something ugly and evil.

Julia Child was talking to the camera, giving the impression she was looking right at me. She said, "You just have to roll up your sleeves and get started!" Julia. So safe. So familiar.

I wanted to get started. I pushed aside my quilt and stood up.

I sleep in the smallest bedroom of a three-bedroom house in the hills just north of the 101 Freeway, in an old neighborhood in Hollywood named Whitley Heights.

My house is California-style Art Deco: a lot of geometric angles, a lot of rounded moldings and coved ceilings. When I first found it, it was a wreck. Still, it suited my needs, it had a romantic history, once having been owned by a long-forgotten silent movie star, and its dilapidated condition just barely allowed me to afford it. I use the downstairs for my business and the upper floor as my home.

Two of the upstairs bedrooms now serve as my living and dining rooms, with the added advantage of giving me extra closets. When dressing, I may walk through to the living room to find my belt and then move into the dining room to retrieve a silk blouse. In this way, I promenade around my upstairs apartment and call it exercise.

On this Saturday morning, I showered quickly and then walked into the dining room, looking for clean jeans.

This room was actually the middle bedroom. But now,

my small dining table is surrounded on three sides by walls, lined to the ceiling with clear pine bookshelves. On them I keep my overflowing collection of cookbooks and travel guides and mystery novels.

I've rigged up an old-fashioned dumbwaiter connecting this room to the kitchen down below. When I invite a friend to dinner, or more often, read a book while dining alone, I pile all the food on a tray down in the kitchen and push a button that transports the whole thing up one floor to this dining room above.

As I pulled a pair of faded Levis out of the dining room closet, I noticed the silver clock on one of the bookshelves. I'd have to get moving or I'd be late meeting Lizzie.

I moved into my living room, looking for my boots. This was originally the master bedroom and so it has the most space and best windows. I looked under the sofa, pulling up its linen slipcover. No boots. Facing the sofa are two thirties-style down-filled chairs that I rescued from a friend's garage. And in front of the fireplace, the bare wood floor is covered with a Chinese hook rug.

I opened the closet. No boots. Under the chairs, ditto.

Marching down to the opposite end of the hallway, I entered my tiny bedroom, which has just enough room for my old iron bed and the pine dresser that holds my T.V. No sign of my boots there, but the sweater I wanted was in the dresser, and as I bent to close the middle drawer, there was Julia Child in my face.

"Don't be afraid to really get in there and stir!"

I pulled the thin black sweater over my head and nodded soberly at Julia's advice as I walked into my bathroom.

There they were. My favorite black ankle boots were tucked near the claw feet of the tub. As I pulled them on, I noticed the crumpled costume I'd worn at Bruno's party discarded only six hours ago in a heap near the hamper. Impossible to escape from last night.

I tried to do something with my unruly hair as I picked up the bathroom phone and dialed Arlo at home. Naturally, he wasn't there.

I left a message. "How ya doing? My party went great except for the part at the end when Bruno got poisoned. Call me."

I dialed his office number and got voice mail. I had already used my best material on his home machine, so I told his voice mail to call home for messages and hung up. If we were true to our usual pattern, we'd probably hook up around Tuesday. It was okay. Who had time for passion these days?

I scooped up the satin gown with the sparkling silver netting and took it with me as I descended the curving grand staircase that brought me into the office area below.

Downstairs, I'd had to modify the kitchen by knocking down the walls to the breakfast room and a small laundry room and butler's pantry. Now it was large enough to cook industrial-size meals, and more importantly, to pass the city building and county health code regulations that made cooking there for the public legitimate.

What used to be the formal dining room was now an office that Wes and I shared. Holly had a small desk set up in the entry hall, and we used the living room to hold meetings and entertain clients.

As I came down the stairs, I was surprised to see Holly already there. It was eleven-fifteen, earlier than she normally liked to make an appearance on a day we didn't have a party scheduled. She claimed to keep "rock 'n roll" hours.

"Hi." She smiled at me. I handed her the Good Witch ensemble and told her about my date for lunch.

Holly followed me through my office into the kitchen. I opened the refrigerator, grabbed a Diet Coke, and asked if she'd had coffee yet. She shook her head, and her long uneven white-blonde bangs spiked into her eyes.

"I can't get over what happened," Holly said, with gusto.

"I know." We both shook our heads at each other.

I set about making her an espresso. I get my espresso beans from Torrefazione, a wonderful shop in Seattle that roasts their own. "If he was really murdered," I said, "what I keep asking myself is who killed him?"

"That dude was a genuine jerk. It could have been anyone."

I protested. "Not just anyone could commit murder!"

"Oh, sure they could, if they're ticked off enough."

I was measuring the correct amount of ground espresso beans into the Pasquini. But I stopped.

"Could you kill someone?"

"Of course." She stared at me. "You never know about people. What secrets they have, what pain they're in . . ."

"But to actually buy some poison, and put it in the stew, and then sit back and wait for the poor sucker to die in agony?"

"Oh, sure. I imagine that's the best part."

"Holly!"

"No, really! A lot of people hated that old guy. What's amazing is he wasn't killed a long, long time ago."

"Holl." I smiled and shook my head at how simple she seemed to think life was. "There are lots of despicable people in this big bad world. But justice isn't so black and white! People don't just get fed up one day and . . . and kill them."

"Hmmm." Holly sipped her cup of caffeine and arched a colorless brow at me. "Too bad."

I laughed. She was teasing me. And then we heard the faint tinkling of our front doorbell.

I looked at my watch. It was getting late and I had to leave in order to meet Lizzie.

Holly noticed my look. "I'll get the door," she said. "You can sneak out the back if you want."

How could anyone as thoughtful as Holly think herself capable of murder? I stood at the sink and downed the last of my Diet Coke. And as I was rinsing the glass and feeling around in my purse to find my sunglasses, Holly popped her head back into the kitchen.

"You still here? This is kind of odd. The person at the front door is the maid for the Huntleys. Weird, huh?"

"Their maid is here?" That stopped me.

"She says she'd like to talk to you and it's important."

Intriguing. I took off my sunglasses and put down my purse. "Take her into the living room and, Holly, call over to Chez Nous and leave a message for Lizzie Bailey I'll be late."

She nodded and disappeared.

The living room had a very high arched ceiling and a wall of French doors that open out onto the patio. When I entered, I saw the woman's profile as she stood looking out at the view.

"Hello, can I help you?" I asked.

She turned to face me. It was Rosalinda, the Huntley's nanny. I noticed one of my cream-colored business cards in her hand.

"Missus, I am Rosalinda Luquin, maybe you remember me?"

"Yes, of course. My name is Madeline. Please sit down."

Rosalinda stood where she was and looked at me uncertainly. Then, she moved over to a straight-backed chair and sat down. I waited while she decided what to say.

"It is about Mr. Bruno. Oh, what a terrible thing. My poor Babalu, *pobrecito*, this morning they tell him about his daddy and he is very upset."

I murmured something sympathetic, but couldn't imagine what any of this had to do with me.

"Mrs. Madeline I will tell you the problem," she said. I looked up. She was small and thin and looked to be around thirty. She had thick dark hair, cut short, and she was dressed up, wearing a silky purple dress and heels.

"There is something wrong with what Mr. Bruno say. I am very worried, you see. It is wrong."

"What did he say?" I asked her.

"Let me tell you. For the time of the party, I sit in the house with Babalu. I watch him in the Nursery. And that nice lady, the one who answer the door for me right now, last night she bring up the food for our dinner, for Babalu and for me, too.''

I nodded. That would have been Holly.

''My Lewis, he go to bed maybe at ten o'clock and then I sit and watch the party out of the window. At eleven-thirty, I think everything is pretty quiet, so I go outside to look at the party.''

That was right before the murder. She might have seen something. ''Then what happened?''

''I walk around and I see all the pretty things. Oh, it is such a beautiful party, I think. And I walk to where the music is playing to maybe take a look at the people all dressed up so nice. So that is why I was standing near to the . . . *carpa*?'' Unable to find the correct word in English, she tried the Spanish one.

''I'm sorry?''

''Oh, the *carpa* is . . .'' she shook her head. She started again, ''Where the music is playing and all the people dancing. You know?''

''The tent?'' I asked.

''The tent. Yes!'' she said firmly. ''I was near to the tent and I hear the shouting, very loud shouting. So I go very fast to see what it is. And I see it. I see it all! Poor Mrs. Lily is crying and I hear Mr. Bruno. He is choking. But he is talking! Talking, Mrs. Madeline, and saying a terrible thing.''

''What did you hear?''

She shook her head, but then she went on. ''He is talking about a curse! Like a witch could make.''

''A . . . curse? Are you sure?''

She whispered, ''And then he say . . . he happy. He die and choke on these words, 'happy, happy.' '' She shuddered and started weeping. ''Missus Madeline, I cannot sleep. There are bad witches in the house. They make a curse on Mr. Bruno and he die! I cannot say these things to Mrs. Lily. She is all the time crying. The police . . . for me it is not too good to talk to the police. But I have to tell some-one.'' She looked up at me. ''Yesterday, you say to me you would help me. You remember? At the sink? And your friend, he told me to come to you. And I have your address . . .''

Yes, Wesley had handed her our card after that disgraceful scene in the kitchen.

"And your house, it is not too far away. I see I can take a bus. I know you are a smart lady. Maybe you can tell the police what is the problem. It is a witch that killed poor Mr. Bruno.''

"Yes, well . . .'' I looked into her serious eyes. Who was I to dismiss her culture, her superstitions? Yet, somehow, I didn't think Honnett of the LAPD would think much of this witch theory.

Her English was serviceable, but I was pretty sure she had misunderstood Bruno's last words. A curse? Bruno Huntley using his last gasp of air to say he was happy to die? Jeez, I hope she misunderstood him.

Chapter 9

I felt that my luck was changing. I found a great parking
spot right in front of Chez Nous and did a masterful job of
parallel parking my old wagon, backing in only once and
then straightening up and throwing it into park.

I drive a 1991 Jeep Grand Wagoneer, a big black four-
wheel-drive buggy, with a ton of room in back to hold
oversize platters and insulated chests and cases of booze.
It is huge and fearless. Without even blinking, I could probably drive it straight up the side of Mount Wilson.

The Wagoneer's got a lot of chrome and those kitsch
woody panels. I think it's funny, an irreverent antichic
choice in a town that worships gods named Lexus and Saab.
At least that's what I tell everyone who wonders how I
could drive a car that gets about six miles to the gallon.

As the hostess looked up at me from her podium, I spotted Lizzie, already seated at a far table. Chez Nous is a
trendy neighborhood bakery that was close enough to the
studios of Burbank to do a good morning business in croissants and decaf cappuccinos. On the weekends, it was filled
with the junior studio executives who lived close by.

The main room is casual, with small tables clustered
along a wall of multipaned windows. The effect would
seem a little more French countryside if the windows did
not look out onto busy Riverside Boulevard and the 31
Flavors across the street.

As I approached Lizzie's table, I was startled to see she

was not alone. Sitting with his back to me was Lieutenant Honnett, a man with whom I did not get off to a flamingly good start the night before.

"Sorry I'm late, Lizzie."

"I had company. You remember Lieutenant Honnett?"

"Sure," I said, not quite sure at all what he was doing here at our girls' lunch out.

"Sit down, Miss Bean," Honnett suggested. He had a homely handsome face, strong-featured, and thick dark hair starting to show gray, which he wore kind of long. His tanned, weathered skin was testimony to a lifetime's blatant disregard for sunscreen.

I sat down. Lizzie smiled. No one spoke.

Finally, I said, "So . . ."

I don't do well with silence. I mean to work on that. Unlike the Navahos that Tony Hillerman writes about, who can spend happy hours sitting in silence, I can make it maybe twenty seconds, tops.

"So what's up?" I tried again.

Honnett set down his cup of coffee and smiled.

"I told Liz here that I'd be visiting you this afternoon and she invited me to join you gals for lunch. Hope you don't mind." He spoke with a solid self-assurance. "I have a few questions I wanted to put to you, Miss Bean."

"Shoot," I said. Perhaps that wasn't the best choice of words when speaking to a member of the LAPD.

I wished I'd taken the time to put on mascara. When I'm in a hurry, I have a tendency to just sort of let the whole makeup thing go. And I was still embarrassed remembering last night. I had been defensive and flustered and dressed like a fairy.

I looked up at him, waiting. Honnett had honest, penetrating blue eyes. But he didn't look at me straight on. Maybe he was afraid he'd scare any skittish lambs by giving them a direct gaze. Hey, Chuck, I can take it.

"Let me tell you what we know," Honnett started, still not looking at me directly.

He was squinting at a small spiral notebook. "We know

that at around midnight last night Bruno Darren Huntley, Sr., died, witnessed by a couple of hundred friends. The M.E.'s office thinks he was poisoned with strychnine. We have to wait for the toxicology results. Meanwhile, the contents of his stomach revealed that he dined sometime near 10:00 p.m. on shrimp, crab, mushrooms, cheese, and rice. Alcohol was also found in his blood. Sound familiar?''

''Well, actually Lieutenant, I don't often hear my ingredients list read back to me from an autopsy report.''

Chuckling, Honnett looked up at me and flashed me his big blues. The restaurant was uncomfortably warm. I must tell the waitress.

''You happen to observe Mr. Huntley eating last night?'' he asked.

''I helped get him his dinner.''

Lizzie stopped buttering her croissant and looked up.

Honnett flipped his little notebook back a page. ''This was a buffet dinner where folks helped themselves. That right?''

''Yes. But by the time Bruno and Lily got to the buffet everything had gone cold. I wanted them to have something better than that, so I went to the kitchen and got them something fresh.''

''You got it yourself? From what? The pots on the stove? That sort of thing?'' Honnett looked at me with those zingers. I think I was developing a crush on a cop.

''No. Wesley was in charge of the kitchen last night—Wesley Westcott—so he put the food on their plates, if that's what you're asking. But I was standing right there, watching him. It came from the same pans as all the other food for the party.''

Were we really talking about the wonderful dinner that Wes and I had worked so hard to prepare as if it was now suspect? It was just impossible to believe. After all, no one but Bruno was sick.

''And did you or Mr. Westcott bring the plates of food out to Bruno Huntley?'' Honnett asked.

''I did.''

Silence, again, as Honnett wrote in his notebook.

Our waitress brought me a menu, but I was feeling flushed. I asked for iced tea.

Honnett said, "Just a few more questions. Did you know of any reason for Westcott to want to harm Bruno Huntley?"

"Wesley?" I think my voice squeaked. I looked over to Lizzie for some sort of explanation. "What's Wes got to do with this?"

"I understand that he works with you in your cooking job . . ." Honnett started.

"He's my partner and my friend." I thought the lieutenant's tone had edged right past self-assurance and on into arrogance.

"Yes, of course, he's your friend. But witnesses told us Westcott was trying to get Bruno alone all night. Westcott was described as very angry. Perhaps you noticed this yourself?"

I felt a pinch of tension at the base of my neck.

"We also learned that Bruno Huntley had fouled up a business deal that left your friend Wesley in financial trouble. So isn't it true he had a pretty good reason to want to kill Huntley?"

Maybe Wes did have his own grievances with Bruno. Who didn't? But could the police honestly believe that Wes was involved in Bruno's death? I was speechless with anger. I hate being speechless. It doesn't happen often.

"Mr. Honnett," I said, purposely ignoring his title, "you're a moron. There were six hundred people at last night's party who had better reasons to kill Bruno Huntley than Wes did. All of them!" I noticed that the couple at the next table had looked up.

"You may be right about that, Miss Bean." Honnett was calm as he signaled to the waitress for a refill.

I could be as calm as he could. We sat together in silence, everybody sipping something. I thought about the time when Bruno was proposing to Lily, six years ago or more. Back then, Bruno was looking to buy Lily something "significant'' as a wedding gift and he cast his eye on a parcel of property located just above his own. It was virgin canyon, but there were rumors that a land developer was interested in turning it into eighty gated mini-estates.

As it happened, Wes knew the guy who inherited the land and was looking to unload it. He arranged a private sale to Bruno for five million, and Bruno promised Wes a finder's fee of one percent. Let's just say that it was one of the many times Bruno matched to a millisecond the moment he forgot his part of the deal with the moment he got what he was after.

Wesley tried to get Bruno to pay him the fifty thousand dollars he was due. Months went by. Then years. But at the point when Wes finally got an attorney and had papers served, Bruno suddenly calls our office about his huge Halloween dinner with a budget of a $250,000!

We knew all the top caterers were making bids. Ours if we wanted it. A chance to become stars overnight. The message was clear. Take Bruno Huntley's friendship and patronage and forget about that nasty little real estate business.

It was one of those decisions where you couldn't figure out what to do the harder you tried. I said let's pass. Wes said, no, let's do the party. He could always proceed with his lawsuit after the party, if he didn't get his money.

But Wes would never kill Bruno. Never.

And then I realized that Lizzie must have told Honnett about that land dispute. Lizzie knew the story. Lizzie. A real pal.

Honnett seemed to be keeping an eye on me as I thought things over. He shot me a cool glance with his razor blues. I'd had it with the silence. It was probably some cheap cop trick to get a chatty ''gal'' like me talking. I also gave up on calm.

''Are you arresting Wesley?'' I asked in alarm, staring straight into his goddamn blue eyes.

''Arresting? Why, heavens, it's too early . . .'' Honnett started.

"No, Maddy. Nothing happens that fast." Lizzie looked upset.

What was she saying? It might not happen "that fast" but it could still happen?

Shit! I had to find Wesley.

Chapter 10

I was standing in the street next to my car, pulling the keys out of my shoulder bag. I felt a hand on my arm. My heart was still pumping adrenaline, and I swung around fast enough to throw Lizzie off balance.

"What?" I asked fiercely. Everything was said. I looked at Lizzie a moment to make the point and turned back to my car.

"I have to talk to you. Please, Madeline."

I opened my door and climbed up to the driver's seat.

Lizzie stood outside my car, talking about giving her a chance to explain. Please, she said, it wasn't what I thought.

What I thought was: I was becoming way too involved in the murder of a man I really didn't know, or even like, that well. I had that "uh-oh" feeling of standing in quicksand. And I didn't think Lizzie's climb to be top cop was compatible with my health.

Lizzie gave up. She ducked around behind the Grand Wagoneer and then, before I knew what was happening, she opened the passenger-side door and jumped in.

"I'm not getting out til you hear what's going on. You don't have to say a thing. I know you must be steaming. You figure I told a few tales out of school. Jeez, Madeline, what could I do? I didn't tell Honnett anything that he couldn't have found out with a few phone calls on his own. And he knows we're friends. How would it look if I hadn't told him that stuff about Wesley and Bruno's property? Like I was covering up for you guys. And then he'd wonder why. It would make Wesley appear more guilty, see?''

"What do you want from me, Lizzie? I gotta go.''

"Not yet. There's a lot more. You should know that no one is figuring you to be involved. Anyway, the theory is that Wesley got into a snit over the money deal that went south. Unfortunately, he had motive and he had opportunity.''

"Liz, come on!'' I was furious.

"Hey, I don't think Wesley is the kind of guy who would kill. But the way things look, Bruno picked a damn inconvenient time to die and Wes has got some explaining to do. That's what happens in this big bad world when a creep you hate goes and gets himself murdered right under your nose, eating your own goddamned food!''

"You're turning out to be a big help.''

"Maddy, I want to help. Okay?''

"Well, tell me about things that don't point to Wes,'' I suggested. We'd see where the line in our friendship was really drawn. I knew I was pushing her to betray some cop secrets.

"You gotta promise to keep this stuff confidential. See, we've got witnesses who say Bru, Jr. was asking Daddy for money at the party. A hundred thou. Know what Big Daddy told him?''

"Bruno turned him down?''

"Bingo.''

"Okay. So now you're starting to make sense. Bru Huntley has always had money problems.''

"Yeah, I guess since the Menendez murders, it's the fashionable way to inherit.'' She grinned at me, daring me not to smile, too, at her tasteless joke.

"So why hassle Wes? There's got to be more against Wesley than you're letting on.''

The line that appeared between Lizzie's brows told me I was right. I was getting that sinking feeling again.

"Wes had been complaining to everyone that Bruno

cheated him out of a fortune. How does that look?''

"It was only fifty thousand."

"Pocket change, right? Sugar, do you know what most of us cops make a year? And, then Wesley knows about poisons . . ."

"That's ridiculous!" I said. "Where'd you hear that?"

"Wesley majored in pharmacology up at Berkeley. When he was doing grad work he taught a course on poisons. You knew that."

I'd known about the chemistry degree. But after Bruno's death last night, Wes didn't say a word about his knowledge of poisons. Why had he kept that quiet?

"Here's another part of the puzzle. Witnesses heard Bruno say something to Lily as he was falling. Something about 'Mal.' "

"Mal?" I looked at her sharply.

Lizzie nodded.

"Bruno could have an enemy named Mal."

"Or he could have been talking about Wesley's dog, Mal."

"Why would he be talking about a dog, Liz?" Then I remembered Wes and that silly tattoo. Was Bruno trying to identify his murderer by drawing attention to the name inked on Wesley's arm?

"What did Bruno say? Exactly." I tried to hide my distress.

"Mal or Moll something-or-other. They said it sounded like 'Mal Fee-so.' But no one heard him that clearly."

"It just doesn't make sense."

"He was dying, honey. What makes sense? Anyway, I didn't tell Honnett about Wesley's dog."

"Thanks."

"He'll find out about it, sugar. Wes better have a lucky star. This thing is thick."

"Yeah." I was deep in thought. A small Toyota wanted my parking space and was hanging back, waiting me out.

"I better go," Lizzie said, and she opened the door. "Just remember, I'm really not out to hurt you, Madeline.

I promise." And she hopped out of the Grand Wagoneer.

I worked at pushing away the overwhelming fear that wanted to grab me and hold me down and smother me. I punched the buttons that opened all the windows and the sunroof. Warm air poured in.

Sure, this looked bad. But it was just some nasty problem and I fix problems for a living. I'd get to work. I'd talk to Wesley. This whole mess would be over in fifteen minutes.

I yanked the car away from the curb. In my rearview mirror I could see the patient Toyota pulling into the spot.

Chapter 11

*M*y car phone has a feature for frequently called phone numbers. With the touch of a button, it automatically dials for me. I usually enjoy hearing the electronic arpeggio of rapid tones speeding through their drill. Today, the joy had gone out of my electronic gizmos.

One ring. Come on Wesley, answer. Two rings. I was pretty sure he'd be home. Three rings. Please, just ans . . .

"Hi . . ."

Damn!

". . . this is Wesley Westcott. Leave a message at the beep."

"It's me. It's ten after one and I have to talk to you, like, *now*. Call me in the car or at the office."

What if they had already arrested him? Would they move that quickly? I was driving in the direction of home, but I changed my mind and headed toward the Huntley place. I had a few questions, and the sooner I asked them, the better.

I pushed a button. The electronic notes played their tuneless tune. One ring. I could drive home faster than I'd get the call through. Hmm. Maybe I better slow down.

"Madeline Bean Catering, good . . ."

"Holly! Thank god you're still there. Is Wes in?"

"No. Is something wrong? You sound kinda . . ."

"Holly, everything is wrong. I've got to find Wes and he's not picking up his phone. Go over to his apartment

66

and knock. Wake him up if he's still sleeping. It's important.''

"Calm down. It's okay. He called here right after you left for lunch. He asked if you'd please do the Fryman brunch tomorrow? He's gone away for a while to unwind.''

I had that seasick feeling when you realize all your problems are not going to be over in fifteen minutes. "What do you mean he's gone? Where gone?''

"He wouldn't tell me. Wes said he'd never get any rest if the whole world could find him and drag him back.''

My voice got very tight. "Did he actually say those words, Holly? Think. That he thought people might try to drag him back?'' Wes was running. What did this mean?

"What's going on? Why are you so upset? Tell me something!''

"At lunch, I met up with people who really need to get some things straight. I have to find Wes, that's all.''

"Oh. Sorry.'' Holly didn't get it. Just as well.

"I'm on my way over to the Huntley house. Just in case Wes should call again, tell him I have got to talk to him. It's urgent. Tell him I love him and I want to help.''

"That's a pretty odd message.''

"These are pretty odd times.''

My old Grand Wagoneer had no problem climbing up the steep driveway leading to the Huntley house. Once I got up to higher ground, I had to find a place to park amidst several unfamiliar vehicles. Looked like the cops were still at it, picking through the remains of the party. It was a big job.

As I hopped down from the driver's seat, Lily opened the big mahogany front door and ran to me. I had hoped to avoid the grieving widow. No such luck.

"Madeline! Thank goodness you're here. It's been unbearable, all these people in my trash. Can't you make them stop?''

"I don't think so. They're cops. Better to just go away and not be bothered by all this . . .'' I gestured at the cars and strangers milling about.

"I can't leave. They told me I couldn't leave. I wanted

to take Babalu and Rosa and go somewhere quiet, where we could rest. But the detective told me last night to stay put.'' Lily sounded strung out, frazzled. She was not used to being in charge.

"I can't believe they would force you to endure all this when you just lost . . .'' I didn't actually want to say it. Lily didn't notice my delicacy.

"My husband was murdered! Right at our own home! And now they think I did it! Can you believe that? Me!''

"No, Lily, they can't!'' My mind raced. Could it be true that the police suspected Lily? Maybe they had lots of suspects. Of course. They wouldn't tell me everything. Maybe they just went around throwing accusations and the first person to panic and run . . . Oh dear. I just had to find Wes and bring him back before anyone got wind that he'd split.

Lily walked me up the front steps and into the house. As we approached the kitchen, sounds of male voices grew louder. Lily stopped and shook her head in a tight little shudder.

"I can't go in there. My kitchen has never looked like that . . . I . . .'' Her tears formed little rivulets that looked like they knew the quickest path down her pale cheeks.

"Why don't I come and see you later?'' I suggested.

Lily just stood there, mute and in tears. After a few more awkward seconds, I pushed open the swinging door, leaving Lily weeping in the hall.

In the kitchen were four men and a woman, all sifting through dirty dishes. They had dozens of cartons of dishware and glassware open all around them, and they were examining each plate, each knife, each goblet. It was ridiculous. Everything had been rinsed and packed up the night before, in preparation for return to the party rental shop.

"Has anyone told you all that stuff was handled by my cleanup staff and rinsed off hours ago?'' I asked the room.

One of the men looked up. "Who are you?'' he asked.

"The caterer for last night's party. My staff cleaned all this up and stacked it long before Mr. Huntley's . . . uh . . . death. I don't see what you could possibly hope to find in all that.'' I looked down to see hundreds and hundreds of dirty salad plates, bread plates, dinner plates spread over every counter, and even on the floor. No wonder Lily couldn't face it.

''Well, what we have here is a case of murder by deliberate poisoning,'' said the man who had spoken up, ''and so far we haven't been able to find out what food was dosed. We don't usually get ten thousand possible plates,'' he noted, exaggerating only slightly, ''but this investigation is standard procedure.''

He had been looking at me pretty closely, taking in my tight jeans, my long curly mop, held back with a ribbon. He had that look like he was going to get talkative. I've seen it before.

''My name is McGee, Richie McGee. I'm heading up the team of criminalists on this investigation.'' He held out his hand.

I shook it. ''Madeline Bean,'' I offered.

He was a tall, bony, youngish man. His light hair was already in mid-retreat. He'd be bald by the time he was thirty-five.

''Are you sure the poison was in his food?'' I had to ask.

''No, Madeline.'' First name. Yep, he'd get talkative. ''But that's the usual deal. We're going with the assumption that all the symptoms were consistent with strychnine poisoning. We'll know for sure in about a day when we get the toxicology reports. With strychnine, the onset of severe convulsions can begin anytime between ten to thirty minutes after ingestion. But usually by fifteen. So that means whatever Mr. Huntley was eating or drinking at approximately 11:45 p.m. was pretty heavily dosed with poison.''

''Oh,'' I said. That was all the encouragement McGee needed.

''We've asked around. No one remembers seeing Huntley holding a plate at that time. But, there were desserts set up on tables, and a lot of dirty dessert dishes left all over. We spent most of our time out there in the early hours this morning, dusting dessert trays and plates and forks for prints. None matched the deceased. We bagged quite a few for the lab, but I doubt we found anything.''

"Bruno didn't eat desserts. No sugar," I said, thinking aloud.

"That right?" McGee seemed interested. "There was alcohol in his system. We don't have the lab tests back yet, but the strychnine could have easily been put in a drink.''

"Easily?" I asked.

"Well, yes. From a covert standpoint." McGee moved closer, taking me into his confidence. I could see this man as a twelve-year-old, reading Ian Fleming under his blanket by flashlight.

"Most folks know that strychnine is used in commercial rat poisons. But get this! In its pure form, strychnine has a peculiar, bitter taste. Did you know that? It's not a very popular poison, from a murderer's standpoint, because strychnine pretty much tastes like poison. Heh-heh.'' McGee grinned, looking way too into this. I think he thought we were flirting.

"So you're saying that if strychnine had been used to poison Bruno, he should have been able to taste it.''

"Right," McGee looked at me. Then pulled out his note-book and started writing. "Odd, isn't it?''

"And if it wasn't in his food, which you seem fairly sure of after all this . . . investigating,'' my slow gaze took in the mess on the floor and the kneeling officers who had stopped shuffling through china, "then it was likely in something he drank.''

"You know anything about his drinking habits?''

"Well . . .'' Actually, I did. But I wasn't sure how help-ful I was prepared to be to the police who were looking for evidence to lock up Wesley. "Bruno was fond of brandy.''

"Brandy?" McGee snapped his finger at a short, red-haired officer. "Harold, get me the list of liquor!''

I had perched on one of the pine bar stools at the kitchen's large center island. McGee took the list from Harold, came over to my end of the island, and showed it to me.

"Did your company supply the liquor for the party?"

I nodded.

"Do you see anything missing?"

I looked over the list. It was an inventory of all the bottles that had been used to set up the three bars. I went over the list slowly. They were the right quantities and the right brands. They had listed the number of bottles of mixers, and they, too, seemed okay. Some of the bottles were listed as empty, some partially filled, and others unopened.

I looked again to see if the amount of booze that had been consumed seemed appropriate to that stage of a party where the majority of six hundred guests were blotto. I couldn't find anything suspicious and told McGee so.

He seemed disappointed. "We sent every last bottle to the lab. It will take some time, but we'll find out if any of them contain the strychnine. I just thought if you had any suspicion, we could have the lab test those bottles first. Like that bit about Huntley drinking brandy. I've made a note to have them test the bottles of Courvoisier and the Remy Martin first. Who knows, it might save us some time." He beamed at me.

I figured I'd gotten as much useful information from Richie as he could provide, but you never knew when you'd need more. I smiled back.

Just then, a young man poked his head in the swinging door.

"TerryRents pickup?" His voice squeaked.

"Right here," said McGee, still grinning into my eyes.

The TerryRents boy blankly looked at the counters, the sink, the floor.

"Ten cents extra for packing. Per item," he informed us without blinking, and then started racing through the plates, stacking them in boxes faster than the thought that was racing through my mind: that the cops should really pay for this mess.

McGee handed me his card. "If I think of something else

I need, could I give you a call?'' Right question, wrong cop.

We traded cards. After all, I just might need an update on what they found in those bottles. But I really didn't think so.

McGee and his troops left the kitchen, leaving me alone with the TerryRents kid. He was screeching the words to ''Love in an Elevator,'' plugged into his headphones, and at the rate he was packing plates and silverware, he was going to be three hundred dollars richer in about an hour. I went out the back door, looking for Rosalinda.

She was sitting in a patio chair, watching little Lewis as he stood on the first step of the large pool, his thin legs immersed right up to just under his knees. He was kicking and splashing. Rosalinda was sitting close enough to save him from disaster, but far enough to avoid most of the water droplets as he splashed.

The day was warm and fine. It was the start of November, but the series of high pressure systems that had been dominating the West Coast had pushed the temperature up into the low eighties for most of the week.

Rosalinda watched me cross the wide lawn and walk along the flagstone patio until I reached her. The area had been returned to its regular appearance. All the rented dining tables and chairs from the night before had been moved out and replaced with heavy wrought-iron furniture. The chaise lounges and armchairs sported thick cushions with wide stripes of forest green and white. I sat at the foot end of a chaise next to Rosalinda and she smiled at me.

''I need to talk to you about what you heard last night. About Bruno's last words.''

Rosalinda nodded. Little Lewis was just beyond earshot, and with the splashing, he couldn't hear what we were talking about.

''Tell me again, if you would. What did Bruno say?''

''He say, 'happy, happy.' And he talk about a curse. He don't say it too clear. He choke, you understand? Then he say 'happy' again and he die.'' Rosalinda crossed herself.

''Rosa, is my daddy happy?'' It was Lewis. He was now standing right behind her.

"Oh, Babalu!" She turned and hugged the boy. He held on, his arms wrapped around her neck. "There, there," she said.

"I love you, Rosa." The boy's voice was almost lost as he spoke into her dark hair.

"Go, play," she told him, with a final hug. He let go and skipped back to the pool step. He sat down at the pool edge and swung his legs over and began, again, to kick.

Rosalinda turned to me. "Do you know why Mr. Bruno would say these terrible things, Mrs. Madeline?" Her eyes were troubled, like they were earlier.

"No. And I'm confused. Someone else heard Bruno talking and they said it was something quite different. They told the police Bruno said a name. He said 'Mal.' "

"But Mrs. Madeline, that is what I hear! Mr. Bruno he say, '*maleficio*.' '*Maleficio*' it mean a curse like a witch would make. The other people, maybe they do not speak Spanish. They do not know what they are hearing. I know. He say '*maleficio*' and it make me so scared I cannot sleep."

My breath quickened. "What else did Bruno say? Tell me the exact words."

"He say, '*Feliz, feliz! Maleficio.*' And then again he say '*feliz.*' It is just the same like I tell you over and over again."

But it was, of course, completely different. Rosa had misunderstood. In Spanish, the word for happy is *feliz*, and so she'd thought Bruno must be saying he was happy. But her words about a curse jogged my memory. Bruno had not been happy to die. He must have been talking instead about Los Feliz, these hills where he lived.

According to legend, a curse was placed on Los Feliz a century ago. Today, the Curse of Los Feliz is no more than a tall tale told to neighborhood children by the few parents who are even aware of it. I now believed that as Bruno fell dying on Halloween night, he must have used his final painful breaths to speak of this long-forgotten curse.

But why?

Chapter 12

*B*ack at my house, I left the Wagoneer in the driveway. I let myself in the front door, and found a note from Holly. "Gone to Western with the costumes. Be back at 5. How about dinner? P.S. No word from Wes."

I had to find him. For one thing, I needed his help in sorting through all the information that was coming at me.

I was fuzzy on the details of the Curse of Los Feliz and I couldn't remember where I'd heard about it. Wes might know. I dimly recalled us talking about it back when Wes was handling Bruno's land deal. Yes! That was it!

Hell. Just as I manage to get Wesley out of the Calphalon he seems to land in the fire. Where was he?

I walked into the kitchen, flipped on the light, and immediately felt the stiffness that had clawed at my neck all afternoon start to ease. This kitchen always had that effect on me.

The shiny tiled walls, grouted checkerboards of white on white, were clean and practical, while the dull gleam of brushed stainless steel on the Viking range and the Traulsen refrigerator were pure industrial luxury. Through the glass doors of the restaurant refrigerator, ceramic bowls of red peppers and yellow crookneck squash and bunches of bright green cilantro were on display. My kind of art. The worn butcher block and old marble counters were discards from a turn-of-the-century Pasadena bakery. I loved the feel of the warm wood and cool marble. My studio: where I could invent recipes, create dishes, nourish body and soul.

I craved comfort food, so I decided to make polenta. The old-fashioned way. Call me a masochist.

Preparing polenta is a simple affair, really. Three commonplace ingredients and a few easy techniques. But it's the merciless hand-beating of the cornmeal and water and salt that has for centuries given Sicilian housewives triceps of steel.

I pulled down a favorite old French copper stockpot, deep and heavy, put it over a burner, and waited for thirteen cups of salted water to come to a boil.

Time to find Wes. I pulled a tall stool up to the counter next to the stove. I dialed his mother in Arizona.

"Madeline? What's wrong?"

I heard the concern in Doris Westcott's voice. She lived alone in a huge, new Southwestern-style home on one of those unnaturally perfect golf courses they've built in the desert all around Scottsdale.

"I have to find Wes. It's nothing to worry about. Just some business stuff. Do you know where he is?"

"Well, he called here about an hour ago, honey. I thought he sounded upset. Have you kids had a fight?"

"No, no. Nothing like that Mrs. W." I couldn't be sure, but I suspected that Wes's mom thought we were a couple.

"I think I know where you can find him."

"Great." I felt a rush of relief.

"Perhaps, dear, it would be best for me to try to get him and that way he can call you . . ."

"Well, thanks, Mrs. W. I don't want to put you to any trouble. Maybe you could give me the . . ."

"This isn't some sort of lover's quarrel?"

"No." She had a lot to learn about her son, I sighed.

"Okay, honey. We'll work this out."

My water was boiling and here's where things can get hairy, polenta-wise. I had learned the traditional trick of adding the cornmeal by the fistful, letting it trickle between almost closed fingers in a fine golden stream, while whisking constantly, to prevent lumps.

I found my container of stone-ground yellow cornmeal and measured out four cups. Then I shook my clenched fist over the pot as I sifted and whisked, sifted and whisked. And I thought about what I hadn't disclosed to the police.

It's just that everything kept pointing to Wes. Like the idea I'd been toying with of the poison being slipped into Bruno's brandy. I knew Bruno's drinking habits a little better, in actual fact, than I had led on to old Richie McGee.

Bruno did drink only brandy after a meal, as I'd reported, but it was a waste of time for the police to test the bottles from the bar. Bruno would never have touched the brandy intended for his guests. Only the very best of the best Armagnac would pass his lips. And I was beginning to believe it just may have killed him.

Bruno had become fascinated by the 1962 vintage Armagnac from Larressingle, one of the oldest firms in Gascony. Naturally, this kind of spirit costs a bundle. The Larressingle was $150 a pop, and Bruno boasted that he'd cellared a dozen cases. It was his habit to keep a bottle locked in his private liquor cabinet in the butler's pantry. Bruno, with a large staff and a small child, had liked the idea of locks and keys.

If the poison was in Bruno's brandy, it had to be from that locked-up bottle of Larressingle Armagnac, vintage 1962. I recalled that for last night's party, the ring containing all the keys to the house, including the ones to the wine cellar and the liquor cabinet, had been given to us early in the day. And they had been held by Wes.

The polenta was getting thicker. Careful whisking had kept the cornmeal smooth but now the real work began. I turned the heat down to medium-low, switched to a wooden spoon, and began to stir.

The phone rang. Mrs. Westcott.

"Madeline, this is odd. I was sure Wes said he was staying at his favorite hotel . . ."

"The Ritz-Carlton in Laguna?"

"Yes. Well, I called and tried to get him, like you asked. But it turns out I was wrong. He did tell me he was staying at his favorite hotel, Madeline, but he wasn't at the Ritz-Carlton.''

Where are you Wesley? I changed the phone to my right ear, and shifted my wooden spoon to my left hand. That felt better.

''Thanks, Mrs. W. I'll find him.''

Wasn't I the woman who always met a challenge? Didn't I profess to love a good mystery? Well, here was a chance to prove I was up to it. Maybe Wes had registered under a false name, or maybe . . .

I remembered Mal.

''Ark Animal Hospital,'' a young woman's voice purred in my ear.

''Yes, great. This is Madeline Bean, and my partner, Wes Westcott asked me to check on Mal, his springer spaniel. Could you tell me how she's doing?''

''Just a moment,'' she said and she put me on hold.

A dull ache had seized up my left arm and, while I listened to ''Raindrops Keep Falling On My Head,'' I switched sides again; phone to left ear, spoon to right hand. I looked up at the clock. I'd only been stirring for ten minutes.

''What was your name again?'' the voice asked.

''Madeline Bean.''

''Mal is fine, Miss Bean. But Mr. Westcott told us you wouldn't be picking her up until tomorrow. Is that still your plan?''

Yowza!

''Uh, yep. That's right.'' So Wes had brought his dog to the vet to have her boarded while he was away. I felt a flush of victory. It sounded like Wes had been planning to leave Mal with me. I always looked after her when he traveled.

I figured a bit further. When he called earlier, I had already left the house for my lunch date with Lizzie, so he took her to the kennel until he could reach me. That made sense. I was sure if I had been home he would have told me everything. Wesley wasn't running away from me. So no need to panic.

"By the way, did he leave a number where you could reach him in an emergency?"

"555-2010," she read to me quickly.

That was my number.

"Any other notes?"

"That's all that's on the card," she said sweetly. This call was just about over.

"It's just that I've got to find Wes . . ." I was running out of anything rational to add, and just began to blither. ". . . and he is supposed to call me, but I may be out when he does, and it's about Mal's special food . . ."

"You just wait a minute. I'll ask Francine. She was here when Mr. Westcott brought Mal in." And once again I was listening to "Raindrops." Considering the extra effort I'd just inspired, I must make a note to stop trying to sound so competent all the time.

The polenta was a thick, sticky, golden mush and weighed a ton, but I kept at it. I was entering a kind of Zen state of stirring.

"Miss Bean. You know what? Francine says Mr. Westcott was going to the desert. How about that? See, we don't really have any room for last-minute boarding, especially on a weekend like this. But Mr. Westcott said how it was he had this urgent business in the desert and how you'd be picking up Mal as soon as he could reach you. So Francine said yes. Does that help you at all?"

The desert. In California, that meant Palm Springs. Quick switch of hands, phone to right, dialing; spoon to left, stirring.

"This is Rita. What city, please?"

"Rancho Mirage," I said rapidly. "The Ritz-Carlton?"

After noting the recorded number, I dialed it and asked for Wes. I was betting that a man who loved the feel of Ritz-Carlton towels after a dip in the pool in Laguna Niguel would find them just as plush while drying off on the outskirts of Palm Springs.

"Mr. Westcott? One moment, please." I heard the line connect and ring through to a room.

I grinned. I had done it. Tracked him down and it had only taken thirty-five minutes. Not bad.

"I'm sorry, there's no answer. Is there a message?"

"Could you connect me to the health club?" I countered. Faint victory if I couldn't get him on the line. I knew my quarry. I'd track him through his favorite little luxuries, even if I had to be transferred all over the damn hotel. I was going to nail him.

"Spa," a deep male voice answered.

"Does Wesley Westcott have a massage scheduled today? This is his . . . wife."

"Umm, yeah. He's here now. He's in room two with Theo."

"It's an emergency. Please tell him it's about Mal and get him to the phone right away."

"Just a moment, Mrs. Westcott."

I waited, listening to Chopin—it appears I'd earned a muzak upgrade—and counted the strokes I was stirring in the polenta. I had gotten to thirty-three when Wes's voice came across the line.

Victory.

"Wesley Westcott get dressed. We have got to talk."

"Madeline! I've left messages. Where have you been?"

"After my brush against the thorny backside of the law, I have been trying to figure out who the hell killed Bruno Huntley."

"I'm standing at the spa reception desk wearing a sheet. I'll call you back . . ."

"Oh, no you don't. I've been through hell trying to find you and I have fifteen more minutes of stirring polenta, so park it in a chair and tell me why you ran off."

"I was trying to keep you out of this mess." He sighed. "You have permission to remind me to keep my mouth shut. Ordinarily, talking about what an asshole Bruno is can be a popular conversation starter. It's just that I was dishing the man at a rather bad time."

"Wesley!" He had that familiar tone. He was not taking any of this at all seriously.

"Well, how was I to know he'd get popped off last night? Do you think I'd go around trashing the man if I was planning to murder him? It's ridiculous."

"I know, Wes. But leaving town so suddenly only makes it look worse. Now they're going to think you ran away. I'm scared."

"Well, honestly! Would I kill anyone? The police are so immature!" he groused. "Granted, I was annoyed at the bastard for ripping me off on that old land commission. But how would his death get me my money? It's not logical."

His tone of voice changed. "The towels? I'm not sure I can help you." He was speaking to someone at the spa.

"Wes." I giggled. "Are you really sitting there in a sheet?"

"Hey, did you turn down the heat on the polenta? You want the cornmeal to taste toasty, not bitter."

Wes and I could argue recipes for days, but on polenta we were both a bit old-fashioned. No instant mixes, no shortcuts.

"Leave me alone about the polenta. Look, I need you back here to help me figure this out. I've come up with some clues . . ."

"Oh, good. Clues!"

"Yes. But, oddly, they all seem to lead to you, my friend."

"Me? Like what?"

"Like the strychnine that was used to poison Bruno? I'm getting an unsettling feeling it was put into the bottle of Armagnac that Bruno kept locked up for his special night-caps."

"In the Armagnac? Are you sure?" Wesley thought it over. "That would make certain sick sense. The killer had to know that sooner or later Bruno would take a drink from his precious bottle of Armagnac."

"Sure. Everyone close to Bruno knew how he'd pour himself a snifter of brandy after dinner. And by poisoning that one bottle, they could be pretty sure they'd only poison him." It had been Bruno's inconsiderate habit to offer no one else a drink from his private bottle.

"Interesting," Wes drawled.

"Then, assuming we're right about all this, the poison must have been placed in the Armagnac bottle some time after he took his last drink on the night before the party."

"Of course."

"But, Wes, it was right after that Bruno gave his entire key ring to you."

"Hmm." He paused.

"Wes?"

"I'm thinking."

"Good idea."

"Keep stirring," Wes chided me.

"Wesley!"

"I did lend the keys out to several people. And I'm sure Lily must have her own set of keys. And, for all we know, someone else might have made a duplicate of the liquor cabinet key at any time."

"Of course, you're right. But tell me, who did you give the key ring to?"

"Well, I lent it to what's her name, the soothsayer, so she could lock up the guest cottage when she took a break. And then Alan needed the key to the wine cellar. I gave him the entire key ring when I asked him to get more champagne."

"I don't expect it could be Alan," I reflected. He'd been an employee of ours, off and on, since we'd started. However, lately, his acting career had been fairly active. We'd not seen him for months until this party. But now that I thought about it, I remembered that Alan had worked on one of Bruno's soap operas and been let go. Could he have a grudge big enough to kill the man? My head swirled. It was impossible to really know a person's heart, if they meant to keep it hidden.

"Anyone else have the key?" I asked.

"Well, not exactly. But . . ." Wes's tone changed to

deep melodrama. "I did unlock the liquor cabinet for Carmen Huntley at one point in the evening."

"What! When? Why?" I sputtered.

At that moment, Holly walked into the kitchen. "You sound like a journalism student," she offered.

"I'm on with Wes. Could you start a salad and take out the chops?" Then, back into the phone, "Wesley, what about Carmen?"

"It must have been around 11:20, because I was about to go meet up with you and Holly. Carmen swiveled into the kitchen on those six-inch heels and said Bruno had sent her for something or other. I just unlocked the liquor cabinet door and left her."

"Carmen Huntley was in the liquor cabinet, Wesley."

Holly stared at me and then looked at my arm, dragging itself around in determined circles in the pot. "Want me to take over?" she whispered.

I smiled, shaking my head no, and picked up my stirring pace.

"Got to go," I told Wesley. "Get back here this instant. We've got work to do and I've got a load of questions."

"You're probably right," Wes sighed. "Save me some of that polenta. Don't let Holly eat it all. After it cools, maybe I'll slice it and fry it up in butter with some nice crimini mushrooms."

"We've got portobello."

"Perfect. And some ripe plum tomatoes and onion . . ."

"Get back here, Wes. I'm worried the police are building a case against you. We may have to prove you are not the killer."

"Killer?" Holly's eyes went big. She had finished a salad of mixed field greens with a simple vinaigrette and was now putting four lovely lamb chops on the grill of the Viking range.

I removed my pot from the flame and turned half of the thick and sticky mush out onto the marble counter where it would cool, perfect for Wes to slice later. The rest I spooned into an old green bowl. It poured out like whipped cream that's been beaten into stiff peaks. I added about four tablespoons of butter, grated in some fresh Parmigiano-Reggiano and beat it some more until the polenta was smooth. Then I tasted.

It had a rich corn flavor with a slightly bitter edge that was a perfect match for the cheese and butter. "You've got to taste this, Holly."

Holly tasted. She made that face like she was falling in love.

"We need to find the guy who killed Bruno Huntley, Holly. It may be the only way to keep Wesley out of jail."

I walked back to the grill and flipped the chops.

"We've got work to do. I need to talk to Alan, and that girl who did the soothsayer bit, and I may even talk to Carmen Huntley, what the hell?" I served the lamb with the polenta onto brightly colored Metlox plates and we sat down to eat.

"Maddy, if anyone can find out who killed Huntley, you can."

I grinned at her. Maybe I could.

But first, dinner.

I put a vivid yellow plate down in front of my assistant, and watched her mouth form into a satisfied smile. This girl did love to eat. She started to cut into one beautiful lamb chop, grilled medium rare and dusted with rosemary.

"Killer!"

For once that day, I figured someone was using that word in a purely complimentary way.

Chapter 13

There were still a few little things I needed Wes to clear up. Like, what was this rumor that he's some kind of poison expert? And, how did he figure into the Curse of Los Feliz? I checked my old Hamilton watch with the scratched crystal. Since he was driving in from Rancho Mirage, it would take him at least another hour to get to my place. I swore.

Nobody had ever accused me of sainthood. Patience was sorely missing from my inventory of fine qualities. I became aware of the sound of my tapping foot.

For the moment, I was alone. After helping me clean up the dinner dishes, Holly had to go meet her latest guy. So I grabbed my notebook computer and walked out through the french doors of my office into the back courtyard. I arranged myself on a large wooden chaise lounge, with the computer in my lap and a Diet Coke by my side, and I started a journal of the events that surrounded Bruno Huntley's murder.

First, I typed the heading "Enemies and Suspects." I stared at the blank, vivid blue screen. This was no use. Everybody could be on that list. I backspaced through the heading and tried again. I typed "Motives" and considered.

Money was always a popular motive. Who stood to gain the most? I figured Lily would come into a chunk of money. Also, Bru, Jr. and Graydon. I made a note to find out to whom Bruno had left his estate. Not too tough. With the gossip mill in this town, that news would practically be broadcast on "Entertainment Tonight."

I thought I heard the doorbell ring, and I jumped up to answer it. Maybe Wes had been speeding. I reached the entry hall and opened the door. Standing in the small circle of low-watt yellow light was Arlo.

Arlo and I hadn't been seeing each other that much lately, and suddenly finding him there made me miss him, with a sharp, inward hurt.

He had wavy brown hair that seemed to be getting longer, I noticed. His compact body was super slim. Despite my reputation in the kitchen, this guy was strange in the ways of the palate. He would only eat certain foods, cooked certain ways, and in certain combinations. Serve him meat and fruit in the same meal and he'd have a cow.

Send me to a shrink for a year, but I kind of dug the way he was so uninterested in food. Or better yet, save your money. I was always being patted on the head for my cooking. Maybe I just wanted a man who saw me for something other than the obvious.

Arlo walked through the door and tossed his black sports coat down on my desk as he detoured past my office. I padded in my stocking feet behind him. He hadn't said a word, yet. It was his offhand, familiar way of picking up where we'd left off a few weeks ago.

Another of Arlo's appealing traits is that he is really funny, and I can actually feel myself revving up, just to keep up with him in conversation. A night with Arlo is a terrific mental workout. I find it stimulating, tiring, hysterical.

"Arlo?" I was trailing him as he made a straight path to the kitchen and found a bottle of Scotch. He clinked some cubes in a water glass and started pouring.

"Hey." He finished pouring and looked up. "You look great."

My jeans, by now, bagged at the knees, and I hadn't bothered to put on any makeup. You had to love a guy who thought you looked great. Maybe he'd been missing me, too.

"I've been leaving you messages all over the place," I said. "C'mon and join me outside."

Arlo followed and sat on the edge of my lounge chair.

"So. I leave you alone for a few weeks and you go and kill one of your clients. You should have asked my advice. I'd have said don't do it."

I smiled. "Is that why you haven't returned my calls? Are you afraid you'll be connected to my crime spree? By the way," I added, "are you sure you really want to drink that?" I nodded to his glass, which was tipped up to his mouth.

"Didn't you wonder why I poured my own drink?" he countered, grinning.

"Hmm. Not smart enough. 'Cause the poison used on Bruno was most likely slipped into the bottle. *L'chaim*!" I smiled and toasted him with my glass of Diet Coke.

"You vixen! What were you thinking of? Don't you know poisoning clients does not promote positive word-of-mouth for a caterer?"

"Duh!"

"But, hey. A guy doesn't praise your warm goat cheese with walnuts and toast, he's got it coming."

"Not a jury in the country would convict me."

"Well, not an L.A. jury, that's probably true."

"To my town!" I toasted, and we both drank again.

"Hey, you." Arlo moved in closer and put down his empty glass. I put down mine. "This courtyard is pretty damn private, you ever noticed?"

"Uh, Arlo," I bent to move my computer off the chaise while trying to catch a quick glance at my watch at the same time. I got a face full of denim shirt. It smelled good.

"No, I'm up here, sweetie," he coached.

A kiss.

"Thanks for reminding me. Only, Arlo, we can't. Wes will be here any minute and . . ."

Another kiss.

". . . it's kinda important we get him off the hook with the police."

My sweater was being lifted and I was definitely in the mood to have it off, but the timing of this thing was distracting me from the present tense.

"Arlo," I tried again. "There isn't time."

He stopped. He sat back down and the wind chilled my semiclothed body as he pulled away.

"Get out your Filofax, cause this is the only time I've got open until I turn in my script on Thursday." It was hard to tell when Arlo was mad.

"Well, Thursday is not good. I'm teaching a little class in sourdough that night." It had been weeks since I'd last been with Arlo, and I was not all that anxious to put my sweater back on. With our schedules, it was now or never.

"Get back here," I ordered, pointing to my bare chest, shivering, "and I'll see if I can squeeze you in without an appointment."

Arlo smiled a slow, appreciative smile and got back there. It was always a little easier to be wittier than he was when we were having sex. I think it was all that blood rushing away from his brain.

I'll admit, it was hard for me to focus. There was the unpleasant thought that maybe, what with Arlo's modest eating pattern and all, he might actually weigh less than me. I tried to put that out of my mind.

And then, what was that noise? Wes did have a key.

"Is that the door?" I asked. By now we were pretty much out of our clothes.

"You've never called it that before." A joke.

A new thought: What if the motive isn't money? What if it's revenge? That's going to open up the possible suspects.

As Arlo pressed a trail of kisses on my neck, he was inadvertently mashing me into the hard wood of the chaise. I adjusted my position and gasped. That's better.

My mind couldn't stay away from the problem. So, maybe if Wes and I could come up with a real case against the real murderer, I could go see that Lieutenant Honnett and get him to . . .

"Ah." Even as scattered as my brain was, this was beginning to feel very good.

Where was I? Chuck Honnett. Yeah, Chuck Honnett. He was a big one. He had to weigh, what, 210, maybe more. Hey, what was I thinking about? And of all times.

At some point I noticed Wesley, inside the house, discreetly tiptoeing away from the french doors. So much for privacy. So much for timing. So much for my fabled skills of concentration.

But just as I was about to give up, Arlo whispered to me, "Think Peeping Tom would like to join us?"

"Unlikely. I'm afraid we can't even inspire the guy to keep peeping."

"Oh, yeah? I can rise to that challenge!" Laying on me, propping himself on his elbows, Arlo wove his fingers through handfuls of my hair, pulling it back off my face. "Can you?"

Ah. A challenge.

With great effort, I put the murder on mental hold. Then I flipped Arlo over until he was on the bottom, with his behind smooshed into the wooden slats, and I was on top. No big trick. Hell, I outweighed him.

He chuckled up at me, instantly aware of the increase in attention he was suddenly receiving.

"Want to kiss my door?" he offered, innocently.

But I had another idea. It was way better after that.

Chapter 14

It was nine o'clock. Arlo and I were slowly putting on this (a stray gray sock) and that (a white silk camisole); retrieving articles of clothing from here (atop of a potted hydrangea) and there (scrunched under the leg of the chaise). The aftermath.

For some time, we had been aware of certain lights and movements from behind the quickly closed curtains of the industrial kitchen. Wesley, no doubt getting a head start on prep for the brunch we were doing tomorrow. Sixteen guests. No sweat.

Arlo put his arm around my waist, and in the pale patio light I leaned against him.

"Erica thinks the first two acts suck," he told me as he disengaged from our hug and finished buttoning his shirt. Erica Moss was the star of Arlo's sitcom, "Woman's Work."

"She's nuts," I said. "You know, this poisoning business worries me because the police maybe think Wes did it."

"No kidding? Wes?" Arlo went back to his original thought. "Anyway, I figure if writing the script in the first place didn't send me screaming down Lankershim Boulevard, rewrites every night until 2:00 a.m. should do the trick."

"You need a break, Arlo. Maybe we could get away."

"How about after my next taping? We could leave Saturday. The show will be down the next week, so I could manage maybe a three-day weekend in Santa Barbara.''

''I have this murder thing, remember? I don't know if I can wrap it up in, oh, the next four or five days.''

''You underestimate yourself.''

''It is my first murder.''

''Well, let me know.'' Arlo looked toward the lighted kitchen window. ''But for tonight, maybe I should leave you and the murderer to work out your problem with the law.''

''Maybe that's a good idea.''

I walked with him through the office and on into the entry. At the door we held each other, content. I could now get on with working out the puzzle of Bruno's death. Arlo seemed equally happy to get back to his place. Knowing him, he'd be up all night fiddling with his script problems in his usual workaholic haze.

Back in the kitchen, Wesley was at the sink, elbow deep in romaine lettuce. He was washing and drying and tearing in preparation for tomorrow when we would finish off the salads with Caesar dressing at the home of our clients. He had also started the garlic marinade for the chicken breasts. They'd soak in the flavor all night so they'd be ready to grill fresh and top the salads at the client's home in the morning.

''I hate this.'' Wesley waved his hand over the pan of soaking chicken. A stickler for tradition, he believed Caesar salad should be adorned only with anchovies and croutons. Adding chicken had become a restaurant lunch fad and it was, regrettably, a favorite with our Sunday brunch clients.

''Didn't a great man once say, 'We can make it taste good but we can't make them have good taste'?'' I quoted to him.

''Ah, my favorite author. Me.'' Wes smiled.

''I thought Charlie the Tuna said that.''

So far, the conversation had skirted the recent activities on the patio. It was his way. No matter how outrageous the situation, he strove to hit just the right note of nonchalance. It could be infuriating.

"Ahem. Notice anything going on when you arrived?"

Wes took the radical shift in subject without dropping a leaf of lettuce. "I had no idea you actually still had a sex life, what with your and Arlo's busy schedule. What happened? Did his series get cancelled?"

I shot him a look.

"You know," I said, "the best thing about an established relationship is that it's comfortable. It doesn't need to take up every minute of your time."

"Judging from recent events, I'd say your relationship is so 'established' it only requires . . ." He looked at his watch. ". . . about forty-four minutes."

I looked at my watch, defensively. "Fifty-four minutes."

"Maybe," Wesley offered, "the best part of being in love isn't bringing a tender encounter in under an hour."

I shook my head, defeated.

"Just a thought," Wes said, kindly.

"I'll figure this relationship business out one of these decades. I hope."

I checked the salmon, which had been curing in a pound each of sugar, fennel seed, and kosher salt, and a couple of ounces of whole black peppercorns. I had weighted it down with a heavy griddle and left it in the refrigerator for the past forty-eight hours in a perforated pan. I would finish assembling the caramelized onion tarts with marinated salmon and cream tomorrow, but as I worked on the various components, I filled Wes in on my day.

Wes only interrupted me twice. The first time was to explain that while he knew all about the chemistry of poison he was not actually an expert at poisoning people. It was true he had T.A.'d a class on biochemistry that covered toxins. He could probably diagram the strychnine molecule, if pressed. But he had no practical knowledge of how to poison a man, whatsoever.

His second interruption struck a somewhat more unsettling note. He inquired if I had begun to develop some sort of "thing" for Honnett.

"Thing?" I huffed. "Thing! Tonight, of all nights, you choose to question where my heart lies?"

"It's not necessarily about the heart, my girl."

"I would never even think of it!" I knew I sounded defensive.

"It's not necessarily about the mind, either."

But all that said, I still couldn't get past this overwhelming feeling of anxiety about the murder. And it was abetted by the realization that Wes was not, somehow, taking his situation seriously enough.

He just kept saying everything would work out fine. He explained that the police, bumbling as they were, were bound to bumble onto the right suspect in a short time. That's why he'd thought why not ride out the first few days of their investigation in the splendor of the Ritz. If he just kept a low profile, he seemed convinced, it would all blow over.

"Surely, they are not going to arrest me without finding the poison. Obviously, I do not now have, nor have I ever had, poison in my possession. And, the motive they ascribe to me is not exactly faultless. I needed Bruno alive to pay me back. When they find more hard evidence, it's sure to lead them to someone else."

"If they're actually looking for more evidence. They may just sit tight thinking they have all the evidence they need to take you in."

Wesley smiled. He still seemed too jaunty to be fully appreciating the mess he could be in.

"And who's going to help me grill the blasted chicken if you're in jail?"

Wes gave me a hug. "There, there," he said. "I'd never leave you in the lurch with all this uncooked poultry."

"Look, maybe we better work this thing out ourselves. If we could come up with any other leads, perhaps the cops would move on to torment someone else."

"Believe me, I'm all for getting the cops off my back. Where do we start?"

"How about the Curse of Los Feliz?"

"Oh, that old curse," Wesley mused.

"With your incredible memory, I knew you'd have the details. Can you tell me?"

"Do you have a spare hour? It's kind of fun. I first heard about it back when I was helping Bruno get that land he wanted to purchase behind his house.

"You remember Denny Steigitz, don't you? That guy with the weird hair who played drums in that jazz group I used to go watch on Sunset? Anyway, the deal was that his grandmother owned this property up in Los Feliz and one day he tells me he inherited it all and did I know a real estate agent to help him unload it. He thought it might be worth a million."

"Right. And then I suggested you get in touch with Bruno." It had just been one of those coincidences. I'd begun catering the cast lunches on one of Bruno's soaps and I had heard he was interested in that property. "But what about the curse?"

"Well, after I got involved, God forgive me, with helping Bruno get the land he wanted, I heard from the title insurance company that the parcel had been part of this old legendary Curse of the Felizes. I always appreciate a bizarre story, so I looked it up. You want to hear the whole thing?"

"Naturally."

"Long version or short?"

"Long." After all, if Bruno Huntley died talking about this curse, something in the story might shed light upon the murder.

"Here goes. Let me take you back in time. It's the late 1770s, and an ambitious Spanish soldier named Jose Vicente Feliz was appointed to be the military escort for the first Spanish settlers who went up the California coast, eventually founding San Francisco. By being in the right place at the right point in history, and by not getting his party massacred by hostile natives, Feliz got his toe in the door of the new land.

"A few years later, the Spanish governor of San Francisco sent Feliz south to keep tabs on the folks who were settling a little burg which today is our fair city. Another fortuitous job transfer. As the years went by, the Spaniard, Jose Vicente Feliz, became a big man in a California that was governed by Spain.

"At that time, all this beautiful land was like giant party favors for the rich and powerful. The map was being divvied up into enormous estates, called "ranchos," to be granted as gifts to those who had done service to the Crown.

"In 1802, twenty-five years after he first came to California, Jose Vicente Feliz is granted his own rancho and he settles down to a kingly life. Actually, the neighborhood we know of today as Los Feliz was only a small portion of his great property. Originally, Rancho de Los Feliz was close to eight thousand acres. And it was touted as being some of the prettiest and richest land in all California: pastureland, rugged hillsides, mighty oaks, the works.

"After securing his fortune, Jose Vicente leaves the wealthy property to be passed down in his family, from generation to generation. And, eventually, it comes into the possession of a relative named Don Antonio Feliz.

"The terrible Curse of the Felizes dates from the day, in 1863, that Don Antonio died of smallpox. It was also the day the Feliz family lost their beloved rancho."

"Wesley, this would make a great miniseries. Go on." I kept working as he spoke.

"So here's the back story. It seems this Don Antonio is a bachelor and lives with his sister. Her name is Soledad and she has a daughter, Petranilla, who lives there, too.

"Well, Don Antonio gets smallpox and they decide to send the girl, who is only seventeen, away to protect her from the deadly, contagious disease. Soledad stays."

"Are you getting to the curse part?" I asked, slicing

extra thin slices from the salmon, and interlacing them with sleeves of plastic wrap.

"Pipe down. You're interrupting my flow!" he complained, and then resumed the story in that radio drama voice of his.

"Soledad stays behind to nurse her brother. On his deathbed, Feliz gets a couple of visitors. It's this powerful, influential guy named Don Antonio Coronel . . ."

I arched my eyebrow in question.

"Yeah, the names are kind of confusing, but stay with me. Anyway, Coronel was there in the bedroom with Feliz, who's sick as a dog, and he thoughtfully brought along his lawyer, Don Innocante, who entered the sickroom leaning on a fancy walking stick.

"Here's where it gets dicey. The two visitors draw up a will. The lawyer, Innocante, reads it aloud. Remember, Don Antonio Feliz is dying of smallpox, feeble, maybe unconscious. So the men fasten Innocante's walking stick to the back of Feliz's head. And with their strength, they lower the stick, forcing him to nod his assent to the new will."

"Ooh. This is good stuff," I approved.

"So, guess what? Feliz dies, and surprise, surprise, Coronel was willed the ranch."

"What happened to the sister and her daughter?"

"I think Soledad got a few pieces of furniture. Her daughter, Petranilla, got zip."

"Bad luck, ladies. Could they take the will to court?"

"A little update on California history. Spain had been thrown out and Mexico took over for a while. By 1863, California has only recently freed itself from twenty-five years of Mexican rule, but the men who really run the place are this handful of influential Spaniards who helped settle the place. L.A.'s still a small town. And these big-shot Spaniards, Colonel and Innocante, know the judge. He upholds the new will and declares it legal."

"Are we up to the curse?"

"Yep. Petranilla would not be placated. She is major league pissed."

"You know teenagers."

"She unleashes the Feliz curse."

"Maybe they should have left her a little something. A painting, a vase?"

"I actually have an article with the word for word curse somewhere at my place," Wes said. "It was terrific. She goes on and on. 'Your falsity shall be your ruin! The Feliz family shall be your curse!' Stuff like that.

"She puts the curse on Coronel and the lawyer, Innocante, and the judge, too. 'One shall die an untimely death, another in blood and violence . . .'"

"Heh-heh-heh," I interrupted, affecting a nervous laugh. "Now why is this sounding a little too familiar?"

Wes and I exchanged a look.

"There's more. Petranilla curses away at them. The land would go bad, the cattle would sicken, the oaks would wither. 'The wrath of heaven and the vengeance of hell shall fall upon this place!' She cursed and she cursed and then she fainted. By the next morning she was dead."

"So what happened?" I had moved over to the stove to start the onion/fennel marmalade.

"Coronel was a smooth-talking, successful local politician. At first he gracefully explained away his sudden windfall. But then, he began seeing ghosts amongst the oaks."

"Wes, we projected ghosts in the oaks in Bruno's garden, last night."

"So we did."

We shared another look.

"But back to the nineteenth century. After experiencing all these horrifying, ghostly visions, Coronel decides to, all of a sudden, cede the entire property to Innocante, the lawyer."

"Wow!"

"It gets better. Time goes by and Innocante makes a very lucrative deal to sell the land's water rights. That evening, he gives a large party to celebrate his good fortune. He parties into the night, waving his walking stick."

"A large party in Los Feliz? Don't drag this out, Wesley. Was he murdered?"

"Shot and killed.

"After that, a guy named Leon 'Lucky' Baldwin buys the land. Isn't that a great name? You know, I'd like a nickname," Wes said, detouring off.

"How about 'Jailbird' Westcott?"

"Cute. Anyway, Lucky's rich and he spares no expense to make the Rancho de Los Feliz the most profitable and luxurious rancho in all of California.

"Can't you just guess what happened next? A guy named Lucky? A curse? Let's just say, nothing good.

"Pretty soon the cattle sicken and die in the fields. The dairy business is a disastrous failure. There is fire. There are grasshoppers. The vineyard is stricken by a strange blight. It's the seven friggin' plagues!"

"Go on."

"Well, with a run of luck like that, Lucky Baldwin goes broke. Eventually, he has to sell off the ranch to pay back the mortgage.

"The buyer, this time, is Griffith J. Griffith. Things don't get a whole lot better. Misfortunes continue to pile up. A huge storm in March of 1884 brings lightning down upon the oaks. Waves of water cascade down the hills onto the flatland. Ranch hands actually claim they see the ghost of Antonio Feliz riding the waves, later reappearing to dance the *jarabe* over the ruin that had been wrought."

"No! Wesley! You made that part up." I was laughing out loud. "That part about Don Antonio surfing that tidal wave from hell!"

"I swear. That's the legend, anyway."

"What happened after he hangs ten?"

"They decide to cut the dead oaks and sell them for lumber. But all is not proceeding without incident. Workers claim a spirit, calling itself Antonio Feliz, sometimes appears to them at a promontory known as Bee Rock. Ostriches, which are being raised on the rancho, inexplicably stampede at night."

"Ostriches? Stampeding ostriches in the night?"

"Do you want to hear the end?"

"Of course."

"Well, Griffith is so spooked, the story goes, that eventually he will only visit the property at midday. In the end, he bolts and donates a lot of the land to the city for a park. And that's Griffith Park."

"Amazing." Today Griffith Park contains hiking trails and a train museum and a couple of golf courses. The Los Angeles Zoo is located in Griffith Park, and I made a mental note to visit the ostrich enclosure the next time I visited.

"It was 1898 when Griffith got rid of the land. So one night soon after, the city fathers gather at the old Feliz adobe to celebrate the city's acceptance of the former rancho as a park."

"Uh-oh. I can see this coming. Parties on the property did not fare well."

"Right. The legend says that at midnight, a gaunt figure with a fleshless face appears at the head of the oaken banquet table and announces: 'Gentlemen, I am Antonio Feliz, come to invite you to dine with me in hell. In your great honor, I have brought an escort of subdemons!' "

"Uh-oh. Nothing like a bunch of rowdy, uninvited subdemons. It pays to hire bouncers."

"That's the lot. Makes a great ghost story. I've told it at a party or two. Griffith had been able to unload several thousand acres to land developers when he donated the park to the city, which accounts for the neighborhood of Los Feliz. In fact, I told the story to Bruno on the morning he signed his final escrow papers to purchase his new acres. He loved that legend, I can tell you."

"He wasn't frightened?"

"Not in the least. He said he hoped he'd see the ghost."

"I'm worried."

"Why?"

"Before, when I found out that Bruno didn't say the name of your dog, Mal, I felt relief. You know, I figured the police wouldn't be able to connect you to Bruno's last words. But now, since we know his last words were about this curse, it seems like it puts you back into it, somehow."

"I see your point."

"You told Bruno the story. You helped sell Bruno the land, and then got burned on the deal. And you could write a damn masters thesis on the details of the curse. The cops will still think Bruno's last words point the finger at you."

"Well, either me or old Don Antonio," Wes said lightly.

"Perhaps. But who are the cops most likely to arrest?"

Chapter 15

Sunday morning, as I stood in the shower, I kept hearing the chorus from "Big Time" going around in my head. I whipped my hair from side to side under the cool water, rinsing out shampoo and willing out the eighth replay of "My head is getting bigger."

I dressed quickly. A pair of white jeans and a chef's tunic with "Madeline Bean" embroidered in small black stitches over my heart. My fingers raced up to my neck over the tunic's double row of buttons, and then I shook out my hair. No matter how quickly I shower and dress, this is where my routine comes to a soggy halt.

I used the ConAir 5000, blowing and brushing for a good thirty minutes, thinking about whom I should call and whom I should visit in person and which technique might net me the most reliable information.

By taking the natural curl out of my reddish-gold hair, I had added a good five inches to its length. I neatly braided it down my back, where I could forget it.

I laced my white oxfords tight, and ran lightly down the steps.

Wesley was going to meet me at the Frymans' house, so I loaded the Grand Wagoneer with all the food for the party and made my way over to Santa Monica.

As I crossed Third Street, heading south on La Brea, I saw the Sunday morning people, true to their religion, lining up outside of DuPar's coffee shop at Farmer's Market.

I took Olympic west and experienced an unexpected calm. I had found a time of day and day of week when there was no trace of the usual, lurching crawl of east-west traffic.

It was another pretty day. Having been raised in the Midwest, I can still clearly remember the sharp cold and stinging winds of November. But here, with the sun winking through the palm fronds, I am admittedly dazzled by winter's glamorous Hollywood makeover.

I'm certainly no holier than any other shivering, midwestern soul who has finally found the comfort zone. I am sold on L.A., despite the smog, despite the traffic, despite the crime, despite the threat of brush fires and mudslides and earthquakes. What, me worry while the sun shines?

As I made the turn onto Fifteenth Street, I could see Wes waiting for me in the Frymans' driveway. He'd arrived early to set up the grills, and now he helped me unload the food and bring it into the kitchen.

Houses in this fashionable neighborhood of Santa Monica had been built in the thirties and forties on identical size lots, and tended to be of restrained middle-class proportions. In the late eighties, when prices scaled the dizzy peaks of real estate's Everest, the frenzy had pushed a modest, three-bedroom, two-bathroom home like the Frymans' upwards of three-quarters of a million dollars.

I looked around as I brought in a stack of colorful Metlox platters. This spectacularly priced home boasted a kitchen that measured eight feet by eleven feet. What did the realtors call it? Ah, yes. "Cozy."

"The guests are starting to arrive," Wes informed me, as he put some finishing touches on the buffet table he'd set up earlier in the small dining room.

"They're one hour early? Who comes to a party an hour early?"

I picked up my pace as I began preparing circles of puff pastry, first brushing them twice with a raw egg wash. When baked, this would give the tarts a nice glazed finish and prevent the hot topping from soaking through and mak-

ing a soggy mess. I inverted a second baking sheet over
the one holding the puff pastry circles, a trick to prevent
the dough from rising too much and keep them a uniform
height. How perfect a dish looked on the platter was part
of the job. Moving fast, I popped the pastry trays in the
oven.

"Did you see the *Times*?"

Bruno's murder, having taken place so late on Friday
night, had only received modest coverage on Saturday. But,
gathering steam from the outrage of the entertainment community, many of whose leaders had been inconvenienced
at the party, it made front-page news in the Sunday *Times*.

"You wouldn't believe the calls we've been getting."

I was letting the machine pick up the messages, which
seemed to be mostly curiosity mixed with excitement on
the part of our clients and acquaintances.

Wes told me he had been treated to an early morning
interview with the police at his apartment.

"Seems they aren't arresting me just yet."

"Thank god!"

"They are content to simply harass me and insult me
with their suspicions and attitude. Typical."

I asked lightly if it was the good detective Honnett that
did the asking. Honestly, I can't even mention the guy's
name without Wes giving me a look at his smug face.

Apparently, it wasn't Honnett, so maybe they were putting Wes on the back burner, after all, and instead focusing
on Lily. I was too scared to feel complacent about Wes's
chances.

Wes had been up early, baking. He put out a platter of
warm pecan pumpkin muffins alongside an antique silver
rack of buttered, oven-toasted raisin cinnamon bread. The
Guatemalan coffee had been brewed. And the host was
pouring the mimosas I'd prepared, so the blasted early
guests were fine for a while.

I had eighteen minutes to wait while the tarts baked and
I couldn't stop thinking about all the people I needed to

talk to. I took my cell phone out of my bag and walked outside. My first call was to Lizzie.

"Bailey." She answered like a cop.

"It's Madeline. I'd like to see a copy of the coroner's report on Bruno."

"The autopsy report? Why? It's not fun reading."

"Are the police still convinced that Wesley was involved?" I asked her.

"Look. I'll see what I can do. I know I owe you. But no promises."

"Thanks," I said. I was getting over being totally pissed at Lizzie. If she came through with the information I needed, I might just be big enough to forgive her.

Wesley had come outside to get the chicken started and was listening in to my side of the conversation while fussing with the controls on the gas grill.

"What next?"

"What we need to do is track down the people who had access to Bruno's liquor cabinet." So far, I figured we were the only ones who suspected that Bruno was poisoned by his own precious bottle of brandy. We needed to move quickly. I dialed the number we had for Alan.

I got his machine. As I started to leave a message, Alan, groggy-voiced, picked up his phone.

"Hi. I was kind of just getting up," he explained.

"It's about the night of the Halloween party. Do you remember when Wes asked you to go down to the wine cellar for more champagne?"

"Sure."

"Tell me about it."

"Let's see. It was about ten, ten-thirty. After dinner. And people were still asking for champagne. Wes told me to go downstairs and bring up another two cases, just to be safe."

"The cellar was locked so Wes gave you the key, right?"

"Yeah, he handed me a key ring with the wine cellar key marked. I carried up two cases of Domaine Chandon.

End of fascinating story. Hey, Madeline, what's this all about?''

"I wish I knew. So you gave the keys back to Wesley?''

"What's the deal? Are they missing? I think I tossed them to Holly. She was hanging around the kitchen. She'll tell you.''

"Sorry to trouble you, sleepyhead. Go back to bed.''

I looked at Wes. "I don't know where this is getting us. Holly had the keys.''

"Wonderful,'' Wes said, dryly. "Keep investigating, Madeline, and let me know when you've managed to pin the murder on Arlo.''

I heard the faint ding of my kitchen timer and moved back inside to deal with the tarts. Each flaky puff was removed from the parchment-lined baking pan and placed onto a bright turquoise platter, where I spooned hot onion/fennel marmalade atop each circle. The baked-on double egg glaze was holding. Wes and I had a little bet on how long this dish could sit on a buffet table.

I quickly phoned home for messages and found two. An attorney was requesting my presence at the reading of Bruno Huntley's will. My, my. I guess I would be one of the first to find out who got what.

Then I heard Lieutenant Honnett's deep bass on my machine, sounding polite. He had a few more questions.

Our brunch host and hostess peeked into their kitchen. "Everything smells wonderful,'' Brenda said.

"Wonderful!'' her husband boomed.

"Everyone's here. So we can begin the brunch whenever,'' Brenda said brightly.

"Whenever,'' offered her husband, beaming.

I smiled my reassuring caterer's smile as they ducked back out of the tiny kitchen.

Wes was slicing the freshly grilled chicken. I looked at him and said, "Race you!''

Famous last words.

I quickly placed the beautiful, pink slices of gravlax over each mounded, steaming tart.

Wes was tossing together the Caesar salad more quickly than was absolutely safe. I saw a crouton go flying.

I took a plastic squeeze bottle, filled with creme fraiche, and drizzled a pattern of fine white lines, like lacework stars, over each salmon covered tart.

Wes was nimbly arranging the chicken slices in a chevron pattern over the enormous wooden bowl of salad.

Like a maniac, I sprinkled finely chopped chives over the top of my tarts and looked up.

Wes was nonchalantly checking his watch.

Bastard!

Maybe I should just let the cops have him.

Chapter 16

I stopped off at my house to change out of my cooking clothes. It was just past one o'clock, and I still had a few Sunday hours free before I had to be at the Huntleys for the four o'clock reading of Bruno's will.

Stepping out of my chef's rig, I walked around the upstairs rooms looking for just the right thing to wear. I was aiming for something that would be appropriate for sleuthing and yet still strike the properly modest note for visiting with relatives of a murdered associate—a fashion challenge that would give both an editor at *Vogue* and Miss Manners pause.

A short black knit dress came off the hanger and I slipped it on. From white to black. I looked in the mirror and decided that the outfit would do for Bruno's gathering. Maybe the dress was a little short, but such are the advantages of not being a member of the actual family of the deceased. Opaque black tights were my concession to modesty.

Rummaging through my drawers, I found a red silk scarf to tie around the end of my long braid. After all, let's not be morbid.

I moved from bathroom to bedroom to dining room, tying a quick knot in the scarf, and searching for my black boots. Instead, I found my notebook computer under a cushion of the living room sofa.

I flipped it open and punched a few keys, looking up the

list of names I had jotted down the day before: Alan, Carmen Huntley, Soothsayer—the people who had access to Bruno's key ring. With a sigh, I added Holly's name to the list.

Graydon's wife, Carmen, was likely to be at the reading of the will later. I'd try to chat with her there. Holly I'd see tomorrow.

That left the soothsayer. I didn't have her name jotted down. And, as I thought about it, I didn't think I'd ever actually heard her name. I'd have to call Wes and get it.

I went into my bedroom to find the phone, and there were my boots. Honestly! As I stepped into them, I dialed Wes and he answered at once.

"Hey, do you have the name of the girl who did the soothsayer thing?"

"Hmm." Wes mulled. "She didn't sign in like our other staff people. And I don't think she ever really introduced herself to me. She just walked in wearing that terrific gypsy costume and asked for her instructions."

"That's odd."

"A little. But since Bruno had chosen the girl himself, I never gave it a thought. I was glad to have the soothsayer thing handled. In retrospect, everything seems ominous."

"True."

We both thought for a bit and I walked with the phone back to the living room and plopped on the sofa.

"Wes, did she get paid? Don't we have to get name and address-type information for payroll?"

"That's right, we do. But she never turned up to collect her money. I figured maybe she was just too upset about the murder. After all, she did know the victim, didn't she?"

"Ooh, Wesley, she sounds really suspicious. Mysterious soothsayer. Nobody knows her name. And don't you remember? She's the one who kept predicting death."

"Hey, I'm all for the soothsayer doing it, Holmes. Sure, she was maybe the only woman in Hollywood still on good terms with Bruno, doing him a big favor at his party, but don't let a few inconvenient facts spoil that plot you're cooking up.''

"Yes. Well. I still think she was too damn mysterious for her own good. And another thing. When I peeked into her purse at the party . . .''

"Maddie!''

"Accidentally! She had a gun.''

"Had you not heard, perchance, that the poor man was *poisoned*?''

"And she had this vial of powder, Wes. It could have been poison.''

"Or . . . Sweet 'n Low?''

"I'm serious!''

"Okay. Me too. But how do you suggest we find her?''

I'd find her, all right. I signed off with Wes, and fiddled quickly with the trackball in my computer and brought my Rolodex up onto the screen. A few seconds later I had Rudy Torgensen, my favorite bouncer, on the line.

"Rudy, this is Madeline Bean. At the party Friday night, do you remember the woman who played the part of the fortune teller?''

"Pretty. About five foot seven or eight. Real thin and long black hair. That her?''

"Good memory. I'm trying to find her—she never got paid—but I don't have her name and address in our records.''

"Sorry. I didn't talk much to any of the girls, you know?''

"Yeah.'' I knew. "There is one other thing, Rudy. After Mr. Huntley got sick, I asked the parking guys to keep a list of all the guests and what time they left.''

"Now that you mention it,'' Rudy said, slightly startled, "I think I got that list in my jacket pocket.''

"If you checked the list, could you tell me which car was driven by our soothsayer friend?''

"I'll see.'' By the loud plastic bang that punched through the receiver, I figured he'd dropped his phone on the table, but he was back quickly.

"Good news. The guys wrote down the time everybody left and the name, if they knew it, on the checkout sheets."

"And the soothsayer? What was her name?"

"I can't tell you that. But the guys wrote down 'hot gypsy babe' and the time 12:22. That what you needed?"

"Well, yes and no. Thanks anyway, Rudy. I just really need to find her."

"Yeah, so she can get her money. Tough break for her, huh? Well maybe you could find her by running down her license plate."

Of course.

"It's 3BBP021. California plates. You know, the boys write all that stuff down."

As I dialed Lizzie, I said out loud, "I'll find this 'hot gypsy babe'!" Liz was at her desk. My luck was holding.

I dangled a worm. My security guard just happened to have a log of guests departing the Huntley party. But not to worry, I'd call Honnett about it.

Snap. She had a better idea. Why didn't she just run it down herself? Fishing was never this easy.

While I had her full attention, I hit her with my request. I needed a DMV check on a license plate so I could pay an employee.

"Well . . ."

"Tell you what?" I suggested. "If you take a second to run this plate, I'm sure by the time you get back to me, I'll have found Rudy's number for you. That a deal?"

"Deal."

I waited all of three minutes.

"His name is Perry Hirsh." She spelled it. "Lives at 792 North Bedford."

"Beverly Hills?"

"Flats." Lizzie put on her bored, snob voice, and we both burst out laughing.

"Okay, girlfriend." Lizzie got back to business. "I showed you mine, now you show me yours."

I gave her Rudy's number.

''By the way, Lizzie, they aren't really serious about Wesley as a suspect any more, are they?''

Lizzie's voice got quiet. ''You just keep doing your best to find out the truth, honey. It don't look that great.'' And she hung up.

Chapter 17

*N*estled into a block of gracious traditional homes, the ungainly, ugly-modern box of a house at 792 North Bedford loomed large. Instead of the lush landscaping of lawns and ferns and flowers which fronted neighbors north and south, this gray monster had a poured concrete yard, broken up by thin lines of gravel.

I walked up to the front door and rang. As I waited, I pulled at my thin knit dress, gaining about a quarter-inch in length, feeling a quarter-inch more respectable.

I needn't have bothered. The door was opened by a woman wearing a black bikini top and baggy denim pants, sporting an even, buzzed off, eggplant-colored crew cut. This was not my soothsayer.

"Hello. My name is Madeline Bean and I'm looking for a woman who worked for me a couple of nights ago."

"Doing what?" An eyebrow arched.

"It was sort of an acting job. At a party."

"A hooker? You some sort of Beverly Hills madam?" she asked, not in the least surprised.

"No." I decided to start again. "Is Perry Hirsh here?"

"There is no one by that name at this address," she huffed. Then, the door was shut in my face.

Wait. The hooker scenario she was having no problem with. It was mentioning the Hirsh name that pissed her off.

I rang again. No answer. Shit.

I walked across the driveway. There was a tall, gated

chain-link fence that stretched out from the far side of the garage. As I approached, two horrible dogs snarled into my view, and headed straight for me. They seemed agitated, growling and yipping, and with a chill I realized they were pit bulls.

I didn't back up. The chain link was reassuringly between them and me. But they threw themselves so fiercely against the gate, that the metal links clanked hard at the impact, and for a moment I thought the latch might give.

Belatedly, I backed away, startled, adrenaline rushing.

Just what was I doing, anyway? This was probably an old address from the DMV. No Perry Hirsh. No soothsayer. I would have to start over. I turned away.

Once again, the growling and snarling got louder behind me as again the dogs hurled their tough bodies at the gate, mindlessly barking as they careened off the steel wire. And mixed with the wild animal shrieks, some other noise. A metallic jingle and clank. I spun. It was the latch. The deep iron "U" now hung loose off it's mount.

The dogs hadn't realized it, but the gate was now unlocked. One slight push and it would swing open. I started to run.

Their fierce barking and shrieking picked up. My retreat had only heightened the animals' sharp instinct to chase this rabbit down.

I rushed to my car, fumbling to open the door.

In the middle of a quiet Beverly Hills Sunday afternoon, I was fleeing two vicious attack dogs. What was going on?

Once again, the dogs threw the full force of their bodies at the gate, and this time, out they poured, charging fast the few dozen strides across the driveway up to my Wagoneer parked at the curb. Hysterical, blood-lustful barking grew unbearably loud as they flew straight at me.

Frantically, barely inches from their teeth, I managed to dive into the truck and shut the door tight. I gasped in relief, sucking in lungfuls of air.

Safe.

Then a blur filled my front window, and then another.

Both savages had jumped upon my hood. Their enraged duet, a high-pitched, unending "RAH RAH RAH RAH" of barks, held me frozen as they eyed me through the glass. Their exposed fangs dripped with foamy saliva as they screamed with frustration and clawed at my windshield. The left wiper blade came partially off and the dogs, shrieking and growling, tore into it. Shreds of black rubber stuck to their sharp white teeth.

I screamed at them, "Bad dogs!" in my most commanding voice.

They could care less.

With their hard, muscled bodies lunging at my windshield, I started to imagine the pit bulls shattering the glass, actually breaking through, and, what then? Landing in my lap?

I kept stealing glances at the house where they belonged, but no one was coming to my rescue. And then I heard a heavy thump above me. One of the pit bulls had leapt from the hood to the roof! I looked up in horror. I'd left the sunroof slightly ajar when I'd parked, to keep the car cool.

Now, the drooling jaws of a seriously disturbed attack dog growled through the sunroof. The opening was about three inches, just wide enough for him to get his snout down into the car and huff bad dog breath down on my hair, snapping a little too close to my head.

I shrank further down to avoid him. My trembling hand still clutched my keys and, awkwardly, I managed to find the ignition. Then, bam! I punched the right button and the sunroof suddenly began to close.

The startled animal finally shut up as he tried to pull his face out, but his snout had become stuck in the tight grasp of closing metal. I slammed "open" and the dog jerked his face out of my sunroof. I hit the close button fast. If he'd been annoyed before, he was now prepared to kill.

He flew back down onto my hood to face me, hoarse from barking, jaws snapping, teeth clicking loudly on glass. How long would my windshield hold up to this renewed double assault?

"*Really bad dogs*"! I tried again.

My attempts to humiliate them were pathetic. I knew what I had to do and shuddered. See, I love animals. But I stuck the car in reverse and punched the gas.

Two surprised dogs skidded off the hood of my car. But one of them still clung onto the grill, caught by his paw, somehow.

Shit. He was shrieking in a horrible, hurt, high wail. That was just about as far as I was willing to go in the line of cruelty to animals. I was freaking.

Just then, a car came up the street from the opposite direction. I watched it left-turn into the driveway. Somehow, the driver didn't seem to notice me, or the fact that I was under attack by two killer dogs, one of whom was attached by his claws to the front bumper of my car.

The young man drove his white Bentley through the open gate. At once, my two snarling companions pulled themselves free and chased after him.

I put my car in drive, intent on getting the hell out of there. But as I passed, I spotted the garage door closing after the Bentley. The license plate read 3BBP021.

Perry Hirsh.

I put my foot on the brake. I backed up. I parked. I waited until I was sure Hirsh must have latched the gate, then I got out and walked up to the front door.

On the third ring, the testy young woman appeared and said, "Come in."

I followed her into a large entry hall. Then, without a word, she walked away. Nervously, I looked around for some sign of the family pets.

"Excuse me?" I called after her. "You don't have any Milk Bones on you?"

I stood in the entry and studied the large living room off to the right. Everything was chrome and black leather and didn't look like it was designed for comfort. There was a lot of art, though. Large, colorful, frightening canvases.

"You need me?" The man who had just arrived in the

Bentley stared up at me. He was maybe my height in stocking feet. But I had the boot advantage.

"Are you Perry Hirsh?" I asked.

"So who are you? My girl says a hooker. You trying to get me in trouble with my girl?" He smiled at me, but it was not a friendly smile.

"I'm a caterer, Mr. Hirsh. I am looking for a woman who worked for me at a party the other night, playing the part of a gypsy fortune teller. Do you know her?"

"Who? Some gypsy? You gotta be kidding. Go home, Miss Caterer." He started to turn away.

"The woman I'm looking for was driving your car. The plates match the ones on your Bentley."

He stopped and turned toward me again.

"You got good legs, you know that?" He smiled his unfriendly smile.

"The woman I'm looking for? I owe her some money."

"Yeah? How much?"

"A hundred and fifty."

"Dollars?" he sneered.

I was lost. "Know how I can get her the money?"

"No. I don't know any lady who makes a hundred fifty a throw. Not my style, babe. But if you're going, like, door to door, offering to party for the same rate, maybe I'd be, like, interested. What do you say?"

He was young and full of himself. He was overdressed, wearing a tan silk shirt and black suit. His dark hair was short and gelled and looked untouchable. His manner was pure punk bullshit. This might have to go in the books as the all-time low in men I'd attracted.

"No, thanks. But if you should think of the name of this woman, please give her my number." I handed him my card. He sniffed it. I cannot imagine why.

I turned to leave. As I reached the handle on the mammoth front door, he called after me.

"Great ass!"

In retrospect, I think I preferred dealing with the dogs.

Chapter 18

I was stressed. With the weird encounter on Bedford Drive behind me, I pulled a right on Santa Monica and headed the Grand Wagoneer towards Century City. I could stop at the shopping center and grab a Diet Coke at the outdoor food court. Then, maybe fill in the time until the reading of Bruno Huntley's will with a little window shopping.

I made the left into the mall parking structure, and cruised the aisles in the underground lot. Behind me was a dark Taurus.

As I circled, looking for a place to park, I began to get the itchy feeling the Taurus was tailing me. In my mirror, I could just make out two men. The driver, a young guy, was looking this way and that, apparently on the lookout for an open spot.

I tried to focus on the big picture. After all, everybody in a crowded parking lot is following everyone else, like rats in a maze, looking for a nice cheesy spot to deposit our twenty-odd-thousand dollars worth of metal. Be cool.

A white Volvo wagon was pulling out directly across from the escalators up to the mall—a prime spot. I slowed down. Naturally, so did the Taurus behind me.

The Volvo moved off ahead of me down the lane. Testing my paranoia, I decided to pass up the empty spot.

I checked my rearview mirror. If everything was normal, I expected the Taurus to pull into the empty spot. But he didn't. My stomach clutched.

My car phone was useless in an underground garage, but I picked it up anyway. No dice. Panic was making my neck hot. I kept telling myself they weren't interested in me at all. But I just had to get out of there.

Following the EXIT painted on the pavement, I turned up an aisle. Suddenly, a red Camaro backed out of its space, blocking me. I waited. When the Camaro finally cleared the space, I was startled to find the gray Taurus, no longer behind me, but now coming down the aisle towards me from the opposite direction.

Squinting to see through the Taurus's windshield, I felt sure I'd never seen the driver or his friend before. Was this some traffic misunderstanding? Had I cut them off accidentally?

The Taurus sped up, crossing over into my lane, coming directly at me. Already, a few cars were waiting behind me, so I couldn't back up. With the Taurus bearing down on me, I slammed on the gas and pulled forward into the space that the Camaro had just vacated.

The Taurus flew by, just swerving in time to miss the car that had been patiently waiting behind me. I breathed heavily to the sound of cursing car horns and screeching tires. Jeez! L.A. could be a scary place. People did not always behave rationally. Especially in cars.

I tried to back out again, but now the line of vehicles waiting for spaces had me literally blocked in my spot.

Through the herringbone rows of parked cars I could see the Taurus recklessly swinging around the parking structure. Shit! Were they coming back for me?

I darted out of my car, dodging traffic, and ran for the nearest escalator. Rushing past a couple who were about to step on, I mumbled, "Someone may be following me."

They looked back, but the garage seemed quite normal.

I moved up the steps faster, and emerged onto the open air shopping level. Out in the sunlight, I walked quickly past Bloomingdale's, turning my head every few seconds to see if anyone was behind me. Where was a security guard when you needed one? I galloped past Häagen-Dazs and turned left, hoping when my pursuers emerged from the escalator, I'd already be out of their line of sight. If, that is, I was actually being pursued and hadn't just gotten in the way of some whacked-out parking lot warriors.

Why would anyone want to follow me? All I could think of was that ugly house and those wretched dogs. Could Perry Hirsh be behind this? Did I stumble, in my first try out of the box, on the conspirators who had killed Bruno?

Set out on the sunny mall sidewalk were large ornate pushcarts selling T-shirts and inexpensive jewelry. I rushed past. Ahead of me was a store for the Metropolitan Museum of Art and, just beyond that, was another escalator coming up from the underground parking garage.

Emerging from below were the backs of two heads. As they ascended into view, I stared. Two young men. I froze as they stepped off the escalator, tall muscular men, who turned and looked straight at me. Were they the ones? Was I nuts?

Still frozen, I kept staring at them, looking for any sign of recognition, readying myself to bolt. But their gaze swept over me and around to the shops. They moved on ahead of me, in the direction I had been going.

With nerves now completely on edge, I trotted backwards past the museum store. If they kept going, I was just insane. If they stopped, I was in big trouble.

The two men stopped.

They stopped! Spinning around, I pinballed off the corner of a building and ducked into the nearest open door. Laura Ashley.

I moved through the large Victorian boutique, breathing hard, inhaling the scent of Floris perfume, reassured by the civilized, lace-collared calm of the store. I turned, still backing up, and thought I caught a glimpse of men standing outside the plate-glass window.

Pushing deeper into the store, I grabbed a handful of dresses from the nearest rack and held them up to shield me from eyes that might be peering into the shop. With this armload of merchandise, I moved further into the depths of the store, disappearing into a dressing room, the perfect "Women Only" sanctuary. At once, I felt safe.

The dressing area was divided into private alcoves by pretty little sprigged curtains, peach and apple green on white, that hung from a system of brass railings. There was a woman in the next curtained dressing stall talking to her pre-teen daughter. They were trying on frilly white petticoats and purple velvet dresses and giggling. I passed them as they emerged from the their stall to look at each other in a three-way mirror placed in a common area of the dressing room.

With nervous, jerking motions, I tore off my black dress and black tights. Feeling every beat of my heart, I slipped into one of the Laura Ashley dresses I'd brought with me.

In the mirror was a little milkmaid in a cheerful cotton print dress. I seemed to be awash in a bright red field that was heavily landscaped with tiny white flowers. It was several sizes too large. I tore the braid out of my hair and shook out the red scarf that had been tied at the bottom. I then fastened it, kerchief-style, over my head. I checked the mirror. A nice look for a sixteen-year-old. Make that a six-teen-year-old virgin from Berne before the war.

My black boots. They were a dead giveaway. Then I noticed a pair of white Keds that had been kicked off by the mother in the next dressing stall. She and her daughter were still standing outside their cubicle in front of the three-way mirror, admiring themselves.

Grabbing my wallet, I pulled out enough cash to cover the cost of the dress and left it in a pile on top of my abandoned black clothes. I quickly patted myself down. I yanked off the price tags and added them to the pile. Luck-ily, this outfit wasn't equipped with one of those plastic devices that set off alarms.

I stuck fifty dollars into my beloved boots, and scooted them under the curtain into the adjoining dressing room. Then I stepped into my neighbor's Keds and walked con-fidently out.

I scanned the store. Where were they? Outside? By my car? A figment of my imagination?

I'd make a run for it. Maybe I could get to Bloomies, I

improvised, and flag down a security . . . As I approached the register, a woman with her black hair cut very short backed into me. A pudgy baby wriggled in her arms while she tried to hang onto two huge Laura Ashley bags.

"Can I give you a hand?" I offered, smiling, as I slid my hand through her bags and tugged.

"Well . . ." she looked up and took in a gayly dressed milkmaid with a red babushka. The little flower-print seemed to put her at ease.

"Are you parked close to here?" I forced myself to smile while my nerves jangled into overdrive. We left the store.

"This is really too kind of you."

"No problem," I said, just as we passed my two stalkers, standing outside about twenty feet from the entrance, surveying the people leaving the stores. With my distinctive hair entirely covered by the scarf, and my slender silhouette obscured by yards of gathered cotton, I ducked my head closer to my newest friend's ear and said something to make her smile. As I had hoped, the men didn't pay close attention to two ladies and a baby, all dressed in floral prints.

"Where are you parked?" she asked me as we descended one level on the escalator.

"Actually, my car is having some trouble, so I'll probably just call a cab."

She looked concerned.

"Don't worry."

The baby smiled at me and said, "Dam!"

I smiled back at the little guy as we kept walking.

"He doesn't really talk, yet," his mother explained. "He just makes sounds. That's his latest."

"Kids are great. He's so beautiful!"

The mother smiled an I'm-zonked-in-love-with-my-baby smile. "My name's Martha Cummings. Can I drive you somewhere?" Bingo!

"Which way are you headed?" I tried to sound normal.

"East. Over the hill in Glendale."

"That would be great. I'm going to a friend's house in

Los Feliz,'' I explained. By this time we were at her Mercedes, getting junior into his child safety seat.

As my new friend Martha pulled the Mercedes smoothly out of her space, those same two awful men came crashing down the escalators, looking here and there and then straight at our car. Jolted by fear, I turned quickly, jerking my back to the car door so my profile could no longer be seen.

I was near panic, unable to bear not knowing whether they had spotted me or not. Were they running up to the car? Were they . . . ?

Martha was picking up speed, approaching the exit of the structure. Near panic, I shot a glance out my window. The men were on the run, just ten feet behind us! Up ahead, the traffic signal changed to yellow. The men were gaining on us. Martha, oblivious to the danger, hit the gas pedal just as the light turned red, making a smooth right turn. As our powerful car sped off, I couldn't bring myself to look back. So I missed seeing their expressions as the bird got away.

One thing was finally clear. Those men were, most certainly, after me. Totally unclear was just about everything else.

Martha made pleasant conversation as her baby fell asleep in the back seat and she insisted on driving me all the way to Bruno's house. I gave her directions up the winding streets, and she had to slow down to squeeze past the many cars that were crowded around the Huntley property. With all the press coverage Bruno's murder had elicited, hopeful reporters and curious sightseers kept a constant vigil near the house. The neighbors were probably furious.

"This is where that murder happened, isn't it?" she asked me as the house came into view. "I saw it on 'Eyewitness News.' It was that producer, Bruno Huntley, right?"

"Yeah. Actually, they're reading his will in fifteen minutes."

"And you're invited? Wow."

"A fortune teller predicted I was going to come into money. Unfortunately, I do not believe in fortune tellers."

We smiled as she pulled to a stop. "Was that why those men were chasing you back at the mall?"

"Excuse me?"

Man, had I underestimated this Martha Cummings woman! Not only had she realized what was going on back in the parking lot, but she had most efficiently gotten us out of there.

"Will you be okay?" she asked as I opened the door.

My thanks seemed weak compared to the huge favor she had done me, but she just waved cheerily as she drove off. Thank God for these cool, invincible supermoms. I was now convinced they could do anything.

At the foot of the driveway, a police officer chatted with the crew from the Channel 5 news van which was set up for remote reports with the mansion in the background. My name was on the officer's list. As I walked up the steep driveway, I heard the segment producer from Channel 5 ask, "Who's that?"

The cop said, "Nobody."

The door was answered by Graydon. He looked surprised. "What are you doing here, Maddie? It's a bad time to come for a visit. The family is a little busy right now. Why don't you come back some other time?"

"I was invited here, Graydon. By the attorney."

He stared at me.

"So, may I come in?"

"I guess," he floundered, and I walked in right past him.

Lily was in the hall and when she recognized me, she stopped. Her mouth dropped open and she stared hard.

"Madeline!"

I'd be explaining myself all afternoon. "It seems the family was not expecting me. But I got a call from the attorney and . . ."

"I'm glad you're here," she said, graciously.

And as she regained her composure, I realized she wasn't shocked I was there for the will. She was startled speechless by my damned cheery red cotton tent ablaze with daisies!

Chapter 19

"**W**e're waiting for Bru," Lily explained, as she led me away from the front door and down two steps into a large study.

"I would have thought he'd be right on time." Bru, the older son, always needed money.

"Yes, well . . ." Lily looked around, but we were quite alone in the study. "The thing is, it was Bru who insisted that this awful will business be done today. He was adamant. He kept phoning the attorney and demanding to know what was in his father's will."

"Being here today . . . I hope I'm not making things harder."

"I'm glad you're here. Honestly. I've never made many women friends. Well, not any, actually. And with Bruno . . . gone, I don't know if I can trust the women in the family. I'm scared."

"Of what?"

"Of Bru, when he hears his father's bequests."

I turned to look at her. She was all alone. Without Bruno to fill up the mansion with his booming personality, she seemed lost.

"It'll work out."

She shook her head weakly and let out a tight, nervous whinny. "When they find out . . ." She sighed. "Bruno did not include his first family in his will. Lewis and I get everything."

"Are you sure, Lily?"

She nodded and held her breath, like she was afraid to let it out for fear she'd sob. "Bruno told me. I begged him to be fair, but . . ." She shuddered. "They'll crucify me. The boys will tear at me and never stop. I can't face it, Madeline. I don't want the money, really I don't . . ."

"Hey, calm down, calm down. There." I had moved over to her and put an arm around her shoulder.

Just then, Graydon came to the door of the study and whined, "Hey! Everybody is waiting. Let's go. Let's go!"

We followed him out through the foyer and across the entry hall to the large living room. The cathedral ceiling was striped with heavy oak beams.

As we crossed the intricately inlaid hardwood floor, I became hyper-aware of the sound of Lily's heels. They alternately clacked on the mahogany and then went silent in the scattered oriental rugs. Clack-clack, muffle, clack-clack, muffle.

Sitting in a deep brown leather chair across from the fireplace was Bruno's attorney, Mark Baker, trim, tiny, and bald. On the two large sofas flanking the fireplace spread the family.

Bru, Jr. and his mother, Rosemary, sat on one side. Bru was not in an attractive mood. He was smiling, showing sharp teeth, and fidgeting. He and his wife had separated recently, and so she, of course, would not be included today.

His mother, Rosemary, sat stiff-backed against the down pillows, once again in the home that Bruno and she had shared long ago. I had met her once or twice in the past. As Bruno's first wife, she'd earned the beach house in Laguna Beach, a black Eldorado, and a reported ten grand a month.

It sounded generous, unless you believed the rumor that Rosemary had been forced to revoke her share of Bruno's production company in the settlement. It was a company that she had helped build and today was worth countless millions. But of course, twenty years ago, who'd have guessed it would be worth so much one day? Only Bruno.

Rosemary's mostly gray hair was cut extremely short and made her seem older than just late fifties. She had a fierce, gaunt expression, with sharp cheekbones and small black eyes, and she had a nervous habit of pressing her thin lips together, as if she were continually blotting her coral lipstick in place.

Sitting to her right was Gray's wife, Carmen. In contrast to her mother-in-law, Carmen looked soft and young and a little lost. She had a curtain of shoulder-length hair, very black and very straight, which beautifully set off her perfect olive-colored skin, perfect white teeth, and perfect oval face. At this moment, all of Carmen's facial perfection was cast downward, gazing at the hands in her lap.

Her husband, Graydon, having led us into this cozy viper's lair, now moved next to Carmen and sat down. It made a tight fit on the brocade sofa, this family portrait of sharp expectancy with the four of them on that one piece of furniture.

Across the massive oak coffee table, on a matching white sofa, sat a slender, red-haired woman. Second wife, Deborah, present and accounted for.

Bruno decided to leave his first wife and then teenage sons soon after meeting Deborah at the Asp Bar. He'd moved to a stage in his life where the most important qualities he could hope for in a woman involved the length of her legs. So he found Deborah, an appropriately-legged, party-happy female bartender. In the ten delirious months before they wed, Bruno spent not a single sober evening. One short year later, they too had divorced.

I looked at Deborah more closely. Her skin was very pale. She wore a white suit and, except for her bright hair, seemed to blend into the overstuffed furniture.

Her successor, Lily, sat down at the opposite end of the sofa, making wifely bookends to the untouched cushions between. I took a chair to the side, noticing that Bruno had selected a brunette, now graying, a redhead, certainly not natural, and a blonde.

"Is that it, then? Can we get started?"

Mark Baker ignored Bru's rudeness and simply opened his briefcase and got out his paperwork. He pulled a pair of reading glasses out of their Gucci case and placed them gently on his nose. He was not hurrying.

The room was silent.

"There is generally no urgency to the disclosure of a family member's last will and testament, and I really much prefer to handle these arrangements in my office."

He stopped and looked right at Bru.

"However, in this case, I have acceded to a personal plea from the family to make the contents of Bruno Huntley's will known to those who are most affected. As there was mention of each of the persons attending here this afternoon in the document in question, I am satisfied that this group reading of the will is in the best interests of all parties."

No one moved.

"I will read from the document dated September 27, 1997:

'I, Bruno Darren Huntley, being of sound mind and body, do hereby bequeath my estate in the following manner:

To my first wife, Rosemary Jean Herritt Huntley, the mother of my sons Bruno, Jr., and Graydon, I leave $1,000. The alimony checks stop here. I guess I can count on at least one person to feel grief after I'm gone.

To my second wife, Deborah Lee Baines Huntley, the mother of no offspring of mine, I agree to pay off all your credit cards and start you back at square one.

To my present wife, Lily Pamela Goldman Huntley, I leave the remainder of my estate, including the house and properties on Winding Oaks, all cash, assets, land, and all my holdings in and revenues from Bruno Huntley Productions. Lily, you have been the shining light in my life and the best thing that has ever happened to this ornery old man. I wish I could be there with you forever, but we both knew that wouldn't be the case. Take good care of our boy Lewis and remind him what a great man his daddy was.

To my sons, Bruno Darren Huntley, Jr., Graydon Herritt Huntley, and Lewis Gordon Huntley, I have already given you the greatest gift of all: You have my genes. That should be more than enough. Go out and make your fortunes!

The only condition on the above bequests is as follows: I fully expect to live a good long time and take care of my family as I see fit. However, if after my death it can be proven that my wife, Lily Goldman Huntley, was disloyal to me during our marriage by having had an affair, then she and her son Lewis shall be barred from inheriting from my estate.

Since I expect there may be some interest in pursuing this possibility by the older boys, I give you one month to prove Lily was unfaithful. Prove it in that time, and the estate is to be divided equally between Bruno, Jr. and Graydon Huntley. But fail to prove any infidelity by that deadline and Lily inherits absolutely. The law firm of Baker, Barrison, and Ludd will act as arbitrators in this matter.

Let the month of investigation give you all a chance to have your fair say. I am confident that you shall find out for yourselves that Lily has a sterling character. After that time, she's to be left alone.

I trust that my lovely wife will soon have all that I have gained in my lifetime at her disposal. But, while I think of it, I should just give those antique copper pots I bought from the kitchen of Windsor Castle to Madeline Bean. They cost me $27,000 and, Lily honey, you don't even boil water.'"

Mark Baker had been speaking in a soft, leathery voice, and as he came to the end of the document, his dry voice could barely be heard. He looked up and surveyed the scene.

"So, like, is that it? What do we get?" Graydon was never the brightest light on the dimmer board.

Lily was staring straight ahead, measuring her breaths. Carmen, across the coffee table, was in tears. That was a surprise. She was actually sobbing.

Her husband, Gray, having gotten it at last, looked stunned. But that's awfully close to his usual stupefied expression.

To his left was his mother, Rosemary, who was looking sharply to her left at her more dangerous son, Bru. He, however, was smirking.

And the second Mrs. Bruno Huntley, the redheaded woman on the far side of Lily, seemed to have relaxed. All her credit card debt wiped out! By the look of her Manolo Blahnik pumps and Armani suit, I'd say she did okay this afternoon.

"He felt guilty," she said, with wonder in her voice. "The old bastard must have felt guilty for not giving me the most precious gift of all, his kid." She laughed. "So I got the consolation prize."

Mark Baker seemed to want to get the whole affair over with.

"If there are no questions, I have copies of the will for each of you. You may wish to seek your own advisors, of course, but . . ."

Bru interrupted, "I take it this is all legal and everything?"

"Of course it is," Baker nodded.

"Then it's just one of Dad's weird jokes, right?" Bru asked.

Baker looked at Bru with distaste.

"Yeah, wouldn't it be just like Dad to have us all tear around proving that Lily was in bed with just about everyone in Hollywood. Kinda funny, don't you think?"

"Certainly not!"

"But it is funny." Lily spoke up and the rest of the

chatter died down. "It's really hilarious if you get the joke." Her voice edged up. "Because Bruno knew I'd never been with anyone but him. Never."

The room grew still as Lily blurted out more. "You'll go running around trying to ruin me and my reputation just to get his money. I expect that. But you won't be able to do it. Bruno is setting you all up." Lily stood up. "Thank you for coming, Mark. And now, would the rest of you please leave my home."

"You're not getting away with this bullshit!" Bru hissed at her. "It doesn't go down like that!"

Rosemary stood up, tapping sharply at Bru's leg. "We're going. Bru! Gray!" Her stern voice brought her sons to attention. "What can you expect from a pathetic old man who cared more about proving his virility than he did about taking care of his flesh-and-blood sons!"

As the strained party broke up, I could see ex-wife number two conferring with Mark Baker, perhaps the quicker to pay off her tab.

In the main hall, I tried the handle on the powder room door, opening it on a very startled Carmen Huntley. She was just standing there in the tiny garnet-colored room, staring at herself in the oval antique mirror, dissolved in tears.

Well, I had hoped to talk to her sometime in private. I stepped in and shut the door.

"Carmen! Guess the door was unlocked." I smiled at her. She blinked fat tears down her perfect dark cheeks. "I've been meaning to ask you something."

They say timing is everything.

"What are you doing here?" she sniffed. That could mean anything from what was I doing at this family disaster of a will reading to just a simple inquiry as to why I was invading the privacy of her restroom needs.

"I have a few questions about the party. Did you see Bruno drink cognac that night?"

"Yes. I got him a glass of his Armagnac after dinner."

Simple as that.

"You got it yourself? From the liquor cabinet?"

"Yes."

"What time was that, Carmen?"

"I don't know. Maybe eleven-thirty." She stared at me.

"Were you with Bruno while he drank the brandy?"

She nodded.

"Did he seem okay?"

"Of course he was okay! I didn't poison Bruno. Is that what you think? We just talked." More tears and more sobs.

"Care to tell me about it?"

"He and Gray had been fighting at dinner, so I wanted to see if I could smooth him over, you know?

"I found him at the dance tent. He said, 'Carmenita, go get me my Armagnac like a good girl. Then we can talk.' "

She turned back to the mirror and dabbed a handkerchief gently under her eyes, perfectly catching the tears while protecting her mascara. "So what was I to do? I had to tramp all the way back to the house like a waitress. Your partner had the key, so I unlocked the cabinet and poured the drink. Just the way Bruno likes it."

"How's that?"

"In a Baccarat brandy snifter, filled about a third . . ."

"That's right." She had jogged my memory. He had liked to warm it between his hands, and then just nurse it forever.

". . . and warmed against my thigh," she finished.

"Excuse me?"

"You knew Bruno pretty well, didn't you?" She looked at me through thick black lashes. Although her makeup had been carefully tended, her huge dark eyes were red from crying.

The door opened abruptly, and Deborah seemed startled to find Carmen and me chatting in the loo.

"Oh, dear," she offered.

"I've got to go." Carmen stepped out into the foyer.

"Me, too." I tried to follow Carmen and keep up our

conversation, but she was quickly back at her husband's side.

What had she meant? Was she having an affair with Bruno? With her husband's father? My God, had she reason to kill him?

Still, something seemed off. If she'd poisoned Bruno, would she have admitted to handling the deadly drink?

I wasn't under many illusions about Bruno's character, but I didn't want to believe he'd been having an affair with his daughter-in-law. I wanted to believe he was happy with Lily, but then what was this horrible game he was playing with the will? Surely he knew the obscene lengths to which his sons would go to prove Lily was a tramp. And what was the point, if all the time, Bruno was fooling around with Carmen?

I needed fresh air. I moved to the front door to let myself out. On the steps to the driveway, I saw the attorney stepping into his Rolls Royce. He stopped and turned to me.

"Ms. Bean. I hope you realize that Mr. Huntley meant for you to take possession of the cookware, regardless of the outcome of the other bequests."

"How could Bruno do this?" I walked up to Baker. "I mean, how could he put Lily through this kind of humiliation?"

"I gathered that Mr. Huntley was amused by the circus atmosphere that this provision in his will would provide. I have drawn up a good many odd documents for Mr. Huntley in the past. This was just another way for him to make his presence felt, but you shouldn't let your own kind feelings for Mrs. Huntley stop you from taking your property, Ms. Bean."

"I'm really shocked that he would mention me in his will in any way. It's truly odd. We weren't that close."

"That wasn't the impression he left with me. Mr. Huntley spoke of you with affection. Why, he even told me he considered you as his 'backup.' "

I stared at him, not wanting to get it.

"I hope I didn't just reveal a confidence that should have

been covered by attorney/client privilege,'' he said, trying for a droll smile. ''But, in the circumstances, I would have thought you'd be flattered.''

''What did he mean by 'backup'?''

''It was just a little joke, naturally, but he did say that if Lily didn't work out, he considered you as his best candidate for wife number four.''

Chapter 20

A silver Mustang convertible, with the top down, pulled up the driveway. From behind the steering wheel, Lieutenant Chuck Honnett stared at me. I felt my stomach jump.

He stepped out of the car.

"Ms. Bean, don't you look nice!"

I smiled, and then noticed that I was wearing that three-sizes-too-large red sack. Hey, maybe this was a look I should try on purpose.

"So are we starting over?" I asked.

"Might be an idea."

"I've been thinking about you."

"Want to confess?"

I smiled. He was tall and in the late afternoon sunshine, he looked better than I remembered.

"Woman at your place said I'd find you here. Do you have a minute?"

"I could use a ride. How about a lift back to my car?"

"Get in," he offered, holding the passenger door open. I could not remember the last time a man held the door open for me. "Where you parked?"

"Century City."

That gave him pause. "Must have been a long walk."

He pulled out into the street and eased his car toward the west side of town. I liked the rush of the wind in my hair, racing away from the Huntley house. I liked noticing that Honnett was speeding.

"You better call me Madeline."

"All right."

"And I'll call you . . ." I thought a moment.

He had many helpful suggestions. "Lieutenant? Sir?"

"Honnett." I smiled. Out the window, I noticed the neatly tended homes in Los Feliz give way to blocks of Hollywood sound stages and postproduction facilities.

"Well, Honnett, about this murder . . ." I took a deep breath. "Why Wesley?"

"Maybe you could pass on some advice to your friend. We cops tend to know pretty quick when a man is lying."

"Lying? Lying about what?"

"About where he was yesterday." He looked over to catch my reaction. I was reacting to his blue eyes.

Honnett looked back to the road and turned west on Santa Monica. "Day after our murder, your Wesley vanishes. See our side of it? Here's a guy on the scene has a beef with our victim, and right after the murder this guy disappears. Under the circumstances, we take an interest."

I didn't like how it sounded.

"Here's a tip: if you should ever want to hide out, use cash. We track people by where they used their charge cards. This morning we got a lead. Westcott used his American Express card yesterday at the Ritz-Carlton out in the desert. So why did he insist he was at home all day yesterday?"

I didn't say anything.

"Know what I think? He ran. He got out of town fast and then maybe he cooled down and had a chance to think. Or maybe someone called him out there at that fancy hotel and warned him to get his butt back into town. I don't know yet, but we'll have the hotel phone records soon and check it out."

I nodded, working hard at looking unconcerned. I was wondering just how quickly the police would find the spa attendant who took an emergency call from "Mrs. Westcott."

Honnett took in my unconcerned nod and shot me a nonchalant look. There was so much subtle acting going on in that Mustang, someone should have called Scorsese.

"Westcott made a classic mistake, trying to bluff his way through an interview with the police. Most folks improvise badly. See, a killer can't stick to the absolute truth. Otherwise, he'd be confessing, wouldn't he? So we investigate his story, and we catch him here and we catch him there and pretty soon we've worn down his story and just plain catch him. It's simple, really."

"Don't innocent people ever lie to the police?"

"Yeah." He smiled. "Sometimes they do. That's what makes the whole thing interesting."

"It's a real science, huh?"

He didn't seem offended by sarcasm. I liked that in a man.

"Look, we haven't found out how the poison was administered, so no fingerprint evidence to match to the killer's. And we haven't been able to link Westcott to any source of strychnine. So far. What I'm saying is, if you've found something that could clear your friend, now's the time to speak up."

"I may have figured out how Bruno took the poison," I said, tentatively.

"That would be helpful. Lord knows our guys are clueless even after sifting through every goddamned piece of china in the state."

"Bruno kept a private decanter of Armagnac."

"That's a fancy kind of brandy?"

"Right. He kept it locked up in a liquor cabinet. I think he was given a glass of Armagnac just before he died."

As I was talking, Honnett picked up his mobile phone and called in the information to someone at his office.

"What makes you think the Armagnac was poisoned?"

I explained my theory and he nodded.

"Okay. So who could have tampered with it? Who had the keys to the liquor cabinet?"

When I didn't answer immediately he said softly, "Oh, no. Not Westcott?"

"So what? Lots of people used those keys. Or maybe the poison wasn't put into the decanter at all. Maybe someone poured strychnine straight into Bruno's glass. Just because Wes had those damn keys . . ."

He let it pass. "So how did you find out Bruno drank this special brandy that night, right before he died?"

"Carmen Huntley. She said she got it for him."

"That's Huntley's daughter-in-law, right? The beauty."

He had no trouble remembering the lovely Carmen. Ah, well. "She brought a glass of Armagnac to Bruno at around eleven-thirty p.m."

Honnett thought that one over. "They close?"

"Well, don't be shocked." I looked over and saw a man who may never have been shocked by anything in his life, and that included the O. J. verdict.

"Go ahead," he drawled, "shock me."

"I think Carmen and Bruno may have developed the kind of intimate in-law relationship you only hear about on 'Jerry Springer.' "

Honnett gave me a questioning look. "Sleeping together? How do you figure?"

"Well, she's crying too much. She's making odd remarks, intimate, sexual. And she gave me this . . ." How could I explain it? ". . . this . . . look."

"A look, huh?"

"Clearly, she had a much better chance to poison Bruno than anyone else at that party. She gave him the brandy, and now she has a motive!"

"Assuming Carmen and Huntley were lovers?"

I nodded.

"If people murdered everyone they'd gone to bed with, this town would be empty."

I was getting kind of down, I had to admit. "So all this stuff I found out is just a big fat zero."

"No. Absolutely not! I'm going to check out everything. That's what I do."

Honnett was close to the Century City Mall. Just in case those guys were still hanging around, arriving with a cop seemed like an excellent precaution. I directed him down into the underground parking structure and over to my car. By this time, the lot was pretty deserted.

He pulled his convertible into the space next to my car and turned off the engine. We sat there. Suddenly, it felt like maybe there might be more on his mind than just the murder investigation. I don't know. It was an eleventh-grade kind of feeling. Was he going to make a move?

I did what I used to do in high school. I didn't open the door of the car and say goodbye. I just sat there.

"So, this was good," he said. "We had a pretty productive talk, right? I mean without you having to storm off."

"Everything out in the open. Much better," I agreed.

"People don't like the police."

"That's so true."

He smiled. Perhaps he hadn't expected me to agree with him so quickly.

"So, thanks for the information. We'll check out everything from our end, of course."

"Of course."

"And if you should come across anything else . . ."

I was getting the old heave-ho. I bent down to get my purse and a bullet sang through the air and embedded with a crack in the glove box right in front of me.

Honnett was shouting to get down and another shot rang out and hit the Mustang. As I flattened myself on the floor, I could hear a car race by.

I crouched as low as I could, hands covering my head. An open convertible does not give one a secure feeling in a bullet storm. Over the pounding of my pulse, I could hear Honnett's footsteps as he chased after the car that had gone flying by. Boom-boom-boom. I heard more gun shots, much louder, maybe coming from Honnett's gun, echoing in the underground acoustics. Then, a car's tires skidded.

Footsteps running. I peeked up. Honnett, fully adrenalized, was coming back to see if I'd been shot.

"You hit?" he shouted, still thirty feet away.

"I'm fine," I shouted back. "Tell me. Was that a Taurus?"

He stared at me.

"A gray Taurus?" I asked him again, urgently.

Honnett was still breathing hard. "You know those guys?"

"Not really."

"Everything out in the open, huh?" His voice was back to its casual drawl. "Lady, I was just about to ask you out on a goddamned date."

He was going to ask me out. That high school crap really works!

Chapter 21

It was well past ten on Sunday evening as I stepped out of Parker Center, the downtown headquarters of the Los Angeles Police Department. It had taken four hours to describe where I'd been and who'd I met while looking into Bruno's murder.

My talent for collecting rumors, scandals, and guesses was acknowledged by the cops. That and the fact I'd managed to annoy someone to the point where they'd shoot at me. What they wouldn't acknowledge was my certainty that the attack had something to do with Bruno's real murderer. My 'instinct' doesn't count, they said. This proof thing's a bitch.

I was asked to check mug shots, but I'm lousy with faces. Honnett had looked at me with something like disgust and asked for the third time, "Are you positive you don't know anything more?" I informed them about my visit to Perry Hirsh. They took notes but looked bored.

On Sunday night, the deserted downtown streets seemed like canyons between all the gleaming, empty office towers. As I stopped, virtually alone at a four-way signal, my car phone beeped. It was Wes, worried. Where was I?

Where was he?

"I'm at your place, you know, pacing."

"I'm okay. Just got hung up with a little police business."

"Madeline, are you in trouble?"

I thought, "No, you are," but I said, "I'll explain when I get there. I'm on my way."

"Wait. You just got a call from Graydon Huntley, of all people. He sounded upset. He wants you to come by and talk to him."

"That's odd."

"Definitely, but never mind that. I'm dying to know what happened with the will. Did Bruno leave you all his money?"

"Alas, no, but we did get his pots from Windsor Castle."

"Hey! Not too shabby! Think Graydon wanted them?" Wes snickered.

"No. But he might have been happier if his father had left him a little more than he did."

"What did Gray get?"

"Remember Petranilla?"

"Zip? Absolutely nothing? Oh my."

"I think I'll just go on over to Graydon's and find out what he wants. Did he leave his address?"

Wesley gave it to me and offered to stick around so we could talk later.

It was almost ten-thirty when I pulled up in front of a high-rise on Wilshire. The name "Wilshire Heights" was inscribed in the brown granite at the base of the building and a sign, advertising "Luxury Condominium Living," promised several one- and two-bedroom units were still available starting "in the low $400,000s."

I pulled my car around the corner and found a space to park on the side street.

There was no one at the guard desk in the lobby. Security maybe had to take a leak. It happens. I waited.

After a few minutes I just leaned over the desk and picked up the intercom handset. I leaned a little further and tried to read the list of extensions for each of the condos. I had just about gotten to Huntley.

"Can I help you?"

I looked up to see the security guard. "I'm here to see Graydon Huntley."

"May I?" he asked, as he and I traded places, me handing him the phone and moving, he sitting at the desk. He seemed polite, no matter how inappropriate my behavior. A lone woman was simply not a security threat to this man.

The guard announced, "Mr. Huntley is in Apartment 2203. Please go right up."

I rode in the carpeted, mirrored elevator alone. I looked up and found there was also a mirror on the ceiling. Head back, I studied my face. Somewhere, I'd read that this is what you would look like if you had a facelift. As you look up, gravity smooths your wrinkles. On my youngish face, there wasn't that much difference.

The door opened on eleven, admitting a woman in her sixties. I quickly returned my head to its normal, upright position. It appeared that this woman had gone way past the looking-in-mirrors-on-the-ceiling phase. She'd gone all the way to her nearest surgeon and done the deed. If you didn't mind a mouth pulled into a tight line, her face looked pretty good.

I got out on twenty-two and quickly found 2203. Before I could knock, the door was pulled open and there was Graydon Huntley, eyes swollen and nose red.

"Hi," I said. "I hope this isn't too late. I just got your message."

"Maddie, come in." He tried to smile, but it didn't look right on his teary face.

Inside, I looked around and saw a modern condo with a remarkable view of the whole Wilshire corridor, two parallel rows of sleek high-rises dotted with lights. I'd always wondered who lived in these expensive buildings. Rich widows and New Yorkers is what I'd always thought.

"Come on into the living room," Gray offered. I walked toward the enormous view and entered a room done in gray and white. The white carpet and stark white walls seemed cool. The leather sofa and chairs were in a dark gray. There were tables made of glass and some black and white photos on the walls that were quite nice.

The apartment was more tasteful than I had expected. In

surprise I said, "What a nice room, who decorated it?"

Graydon let out a loud snuffle and then just started sobbing.

"Are you all right?"

"I'm miserable. I want to kill myself. I'd like to just end my life right now!" He kept on sobbing, his nose running, his eyes wet with tears.

"Is this about the will, Graydon?" I was clearly at a loss. Why had he sent for me? True, we had known each other for several years, and I'd been one of his father's pets. For some reason that made him treat me as if I were part of their family drama, but I wasn't.

"No! I mean, well, yes. It's Carmen. Carmen left me." Fresh sobs and groans accompanied the announcement.

"Is that why you called me, Gray?"

"Why did she leave? Why? I know she loves me. I know it. So why did she go?"

He expected comfort. Unfortunately, I could only wonder why Carmen had married him in the first place.

Graydon was a big, gangly, happy guy most of the time. He didn't go in for deep thoughts. I could only think that it was a blessing that his father kept him employed, subsidizing his lifestyle, because Graydon had no real usable skills. Still, that could be said for many successful network programming executives, so perhaps I was being unduly harsh in assessing Graydon's long-term prospects now that his dad had left him high and dry and possibly without employment.

"Graydon, I know that Lily has control of your dad's company now. Has she fired you?"

He looked hurt, and a little shocked. "No way! Are you kidding? They'd be lost without me. Especially now that Dad's gone. Fire me?" He seemed startled at the thought.

So he still had his big paycheck. Why had Carmen left? Was it guilt? Had she had an affair with Bruno, and now couldn't face the family? Or was she feeling a more serious form of guilt? Like for murder?

"Why did Carmen leave me? I don't get it."

"Maybe she's upset," I said gently.

Graydon blew his nose noisily and continued. "When you were at the house today, I noticed that you and Carmen were talking privately. Did she tell you why she was leaving me?"

So that's why I got this special invitation to visit. Gray thought I had the answer to Carmen's behavior.

"We were talking about the party and, uh, your father." I wondered what reaction that subject would get from Gray.

"Yeah, she was mad that night. She didn't like it when Dad and I fought, but that's business, right? I mean, we're a couple of bulls and sometimes we've just got to butt heads."

"What were you and your dad fighting about that night?" I asked, quietly.

"Nothing important. No great shakes. He and I had a business disagreement about what to do with the company. He'd got it into his head that maybe he would sell. Can you believe that? But I knew deep down that he never would. That company is part of him. He can't give it up."

Graydon seemed to forget that his father was gone now.

"Carmen doesn't understand Dad. But they sure get along great."

"Really?"

"Oh, yeah. She'd go over there all the time to help out. Sometimes, when Lily was out of town, Carmen was at the house every night to make sure Dad had something to eat for dinner."

"And your father, did he . . ."

"He loved her! Of course, she's gorgeous. Dad always used to say I was a lucky S.O.B. to have Carmen."

And then he turned morose again.

"I don't get it." He shook his long face back and forth, back and forth. Even blotched by tears, his was a handsome face. His straight black hair tumbled over his forehead shading his large brown eyes.

Before one got to know him, he seemed a very attractive package: exciting job, pedigree Hollywood family, good looks. But years of being overindulged had inflated his self-esteem way beyond sense. He had this goofy, unselfconscious belief that every one of his ideas was brilliant. His every casual thought was so important, in fact, that he could hardly be expected to actually work. I guess I could figure out why Carmen got tired of it.

Gray was still suffering on the gray sofa. "She was leaving, she said. Just like that. She wanted to stay at her mother's. I said, 'What do you mean, stay at your mother's?'" He looked at me like I'd see how absurd the idea was.

"Is she close with her mother?"

"That's not the point!"

Graydon was having a bad day, all right; his father's millions gone, his lovely wife gone, his cushy job soon to be gone. He just couldn't comprehend this sudden shift in his cockeyed universe.

"Gray, I've got to go." I made a move to the door.

He didn't stand up and see me out.

"Yeah, okay. See you, Maddie."

"Oh, by the way. Did you and your brother decide what you're going to do about your father's will?"

"Bru's taking care of all that. Bru and Mom. They'll see that we get all our money. I told that to Carmen, but she didn't seem to listen."

I left, thinking I really had better stop getting involved with all these ridiculous Huntleys. Except . . . Wes was in trouble. Even if he didn't want to face it, I felt I had to.

And if trying to protect my best friend wasn't reason enough, what was it Honnett had said, as I was walking out of his office, that had bugged me so much?

"I have enough to worry about without worrying about you," he'd said, reducing me to a damsel in distress. "Don't go getting in trouble with any more of your ideas, okay?"

Yeah. The little lady has too many ideas, I fumed as I traveled down twenty-two floors. She's starting to annoy the authorities.

Dammit! Why am I the only one who's so sure I'm right?

Chapter 22

Wesley was waiting for me upstairs when I got home. As I walked up the stairs, I could hear the closing theme from the eleven o'clock news on Channel 7.

"Trying to bring back the Bo Peep look?" Wes asked, gazing up.

I kicked off the white Keds. "You'll get the full, uncensored report," I said, circling the living room sofa wearily and walking out to my bedroom. "But first, talk to me while I change."

The red print dress that had served me so well landed in a heap not too terribly far from the hamper basket. I sighed and pulled on a pair of comfortable white leggings and a long white T-shirt. I could hear only the muffled sounds of commercials coming from the living room's television set. Wes wasn't taking commands well, as usual.

When I finally came back to the living room, Wes was gone. An instant later, I heard the motor from the dumbwaiter in the dining room and I walked back in there, curious. The mechanism grew louder as it labored to rise with its load, and then after a pleasant ding, it went silent. I opened the door to the dumbwaiter, which was ingeniously disguised among other identical cabinets built into the wall of bookcases, and found a tray set out with prosciutto and melon, sliced fresh pears, a lovely ripe brie that had been baked in puff pastry dough, and a bowl of strawberries dipped in bittersweet chocolate. Alongside was a two-liter bottle of Diet Coke in an ice bucket and a couple of goblets. Wes's little welcome home gift.

Wes bounded upstairs and grabbed the tray while I took the ice bucket and we picked up our conversation as we trekked back into the living room where the comfortable seating was.

"I sure hope you aren't the murderer, Wesley. I would really miss you."

Gratefully, I started in on my late night snack and between bites, filled him in on all the grisly details of my day. The long version, as requested.

Wesley's a great audience. As always, he loves the element of gossip. And just to annoy me, he wondered what I was going to do with a cop who had the hots for me. Perhaps it might somehow be used to his advantage? I laughed and poured another glass of soda.

Wes's other comments were not made in jest. He was upset, to put it mildly, about the two guys chasing me. He kept repeating, "Madeline, this is getting too real."

But when I finally got most of the story told, he was just as baffled as I was about why anyone would shoot at me.

"What about Bru, Jr.?" Wes suggested. "If he found out you were listed in his daddy's will, perhaps he was trying to eliminate anyone diluting his inheritance."

"But I didn't get anything he would have wanted. And, besides, his biggest threat was Lily. If he was sending goons to eliminate people, why wasn't she attacked?"

It couldn't have been anyone we know. So we kept finding our way back to Hirsh.

"Hirsh could be connected to crime figures," Wes said.

"That's not what he looked like. And the name 'Hirsh'?"

"Sure," he continued. "Maybe Bruno was in trouble with the mob. Then you show up at Hirsh's house, talking about the party where maybe they had a contract out on Huntley. They get edgy, so they send some goons to shake you up."

"And that girl who played the gypsy fortune teller? Her

license plate led me to Hirsh. So how was she involved?''

Wesley thought. ''Mafia princess?''

''Way too movie-of-the-week.''

I didn't know what to think. And my mind kept puzzling over the other revelation the day had brought: the whole Carmen-Bruno deal.

''Why would Carmen have had an affair with Bruno? She may be a little bit passive and, okay, not the greatest brain in the western hemisphere, but she doesn't seem like the type to cheat on her husband. Don't you think? She just never struck me as the tough, two-timing type at all.''

''You think you are so cynical,'' Wes said, laughing. ''You think you're so jaded. And then there's lyin' and cheatin' and murder all around you, and you just can't believe anyone you know could really do anything bad, can you?''

''I just want everyone to be happy,'' I said grumpily.

''Maybe Carmen was happy with Bruno.''

''Hardly. And look at things now. Carmen is a crying mess. So is Graydon for that matter. Bruno winds up dead. If Bruno was cheating on Lily then she's in for a world of pain when it comes to light as I'm sure it will. Bru, Jr. and Gray are going nuts because their dad left them nothing in his will, not even the goddamn pots and pans.''

''Ahh. We're back to the Curse of Los Feliz.''

''Wes, I'm serious here. The family will try to prove Lily was a whore just to get at Bruno's money. That's more pain ahead. And don't forget, the cops want your head on a platter . . .''

''What kind of platter?'' Wes interrupted.

''Would you be satisfied with Limoges?''

''French. Nice.''

I ignored him and continued. ''And some violent madman with the mafia or who-knows-what behind him is after me for making a Sunday visit. Can it get much worse?''

''You can add that we have somehow lost our three biggest parties this week and cancellations are starting to roll in for Thanksgiving. Strangely, folks seem unwilling to consume food made by the caterers who were involved in a notorious celebrity poisoning.''

"Didn't you point out we did a brunch today and absolutely no one died?"

"That we know of," Wes amended. "So add financial ruin to your list of unhappiness."

"Done." I sat there munching a slice of pear. Wes and I looked at each other.

"I guess I should mention that you received a fax earlier today. I picked it up from the office downstairs when I came over this evening."

"From Lizzie?"

"Right. It's a copy of the autopsy report."

"What did it say?"

Wes picked up the flimsy fax sheets that were lying on a nearby side table and started to skim through them.

"Lots of stuff about the temperatures of various organs, which seems dumb since there were hundreds of witnesses to establish the time of death."

"What else?"

"Toxicology report on the contents of his stomach indicates Bruno tested positive for strychnine."

"No surprise, I guess."

"You know, strychnine is an odd poison for someone to use, actually." Wes seemed lost in thought.

"Why?"

"In days of old, strychnine was useful for eliminating vermin. But it's been outlawed for almost twenty years."

"How come?"

"Too fatal. Everything from pets to livestock to kids were getting themselves killed. Especially at farms where they'd mix the strychnine with oats. All sorts of tragic accidents would happen."

"So you can't buy it today? I didn't know that."

"The only way you'd find it is if someone had some old rat poison laying around the barn for years."

"Wes. The Huntleys had all that ivy on their hillside. And remember the rat we saw in the kitchen? Let's say they had some old poison around for their rat problem, maybe left over from years ago, sitting in their gardener's shed.''

"Maybe. But don't you think old Bruno would notice a couple of handfuls of oats floating around the top of his brandy?''

"Right. Well then . . .'' I shook my head. "So that's a dead-end. If the poison was really put into the brandy, like I think, it must have been in some purer form. Hey, who uses the straight form of strychnine, anyway?''

"Well . . .'' Wes stopped to think. "Strychnine is sometimes used by drug dealers to cut cocaine.''

"Now, *there's* a reason to just say no.''

"Let's say a dealer wants to make more money on a kilo of pure cocaine. All he has to do is mix it with some other cheap white powder, and he's suddenly got 1.25 kilos to sell. They use lots of things for filler. I hear that powdered baby formula is so popular with drug dealers that in some neighborhoods, the supermarkets can't keep the formula on their shelves.''

"Lovely. So why would they use something as deadly as strychnine?''

"Cutting cocaine with baby formula or powdered milk can bulk up the product, but it also dilutes the rush. And a noticeably weaker product brings down the price. On the other hand, I've read that cutting cocaine with strychnine gives the system a jolt.''

"At the very least,'' I murmured, nibbling the chocolate off a strawberry. "But isn't that just too dangerous?''

"I once heard that when kids overdose on cocaine, the emergency room doctors are always on the lookout for strychnine poisoning.''

"The things you know,'' I marveled. "Well, should we change our theory? Could it be that Bruno was a coke head? Did he accidentally overdose on strychnine-laced cocaine?''

Wes tapped the fax. "Test for cocaine negative.''

"Hmm. What about our Mr. Hirsh? Maybe he's involved in drugs. He's got that look."

"You mean unidentified white powder in his mustache?"

I had to smile. "You know what I mean. Too young, too rich, and too creepy."

"So what do you figure? Hirsh and Bruno are involved in a big drug deal. It goes south, so Hirsh gets this young woman to come to the party, dress up as a soothsayer, and pop some strychnine, which he just happens to have lying around his lab, into Bruno's drink?"

I held my tired head in my hands. "This is not working out."

Wes continued, "Bruno's the one who invited the soothsayer woman to the party. And at the very last minute. So how could this guy Hirsh know about it enough in advance to plan the murder? And how could Ms. Gypsy get the strychnine into the Armagnac?"

"She had the keys, remember?"

"True. But how could she know Bruno's odd habit of taking that special drink in the evenings?"

"Well . . ."

"Or where Bruno kept his special bottle locked up?"

"Ah . . ."

"It doesn't hold together," Wes concluded.

"You are definitely not trying hard enough to pin this on someone we don't know!"

Wes frowned. "You know, Madeline, another thought struck me. Strychnine has a bitter taste. So why didn't Bruno spit it out when he tasted his brandy?"

Just then some odds and ends fell in place. "I suspect that Bruno may have lost his sense of taste."

"Really?"

"In all the years I've known him, I can't remember him ever really enjoying food."

"So you finally agree with me? The man had no taste!"

I smiled a tired smile.

"Time for me to go," Wes said, pulling himself up from the deep armchair.

I gave him a hug and reached out for the autopsy report as he left.

Back in my bed, under my covers I could barely resist the urge to shut my eyes, but before I turned out the light, I glanced quickly through the lightly printed pages. It was all medical jargon. I wouldn't understand a thing until I went through it carefully, word by word. That would have to wait until morning, I thought. Who could follow it with a brain half-asleep? The words danced on the page, making no sense. I pulled myself back to consciousness and gave one more half-hearted try at understanding the medicalese.

The word my eyes fell on was one that I did understand. There! I could comprehend this damn report, I exulted, as I slammed it down on my dresser and turned off the light. "... vasectomy ..." I know what that medical term means. "Subject had vasectomy performed approx. fifteen years ago." That was easy enough to understand.

But, hold on. Wait a minute! Something was terribly wrong. How had a man with a fifteen-year-old vasectomy produced a four-year-old son?

Chapter 23

I had slept fitfully, tossing the quilts and pillows onto the floor, waking often to find out why it was so cold. Each time, it took longer to drift back to sleep, too many questions, swirling into nervous patterns, keeping me semi-awake.

I must have drifted off because once again I awoke with a start. This was ridiculous. I decided just to get up no matter what the time. I checked my watch. It was after nine. Apparently all that wakefulness during the night had been followed by a deep dreamless sleep.

Thoughts of Bruno and Carmen and Bruno and Lily and Bruno and "his backup"—me—kept me confused during my quick shower. I wrapped a thick terrycloth towel around myself and padded barefoot to my bedroom. The message machine was winking the number 5 from under yesterday's red flowered dress. I must have missed it last night.

I don't know about everyone else, but I get a small thrill of pleasure when I discover I've got phone messages. Maybe someone wonderful has life-shakingly good news. Phone machines bring out the optimist in me.

Pushing the buttons, I listened to the tape rewind and then click. The first message was from Arlo at 6:06 yesterday evening: "I'm completely exhausted. I hate my job. I hate this script. I hate television. I'd like to just end my life. Say, do you have any leftovers from that Huntley party? Don't call me. I may be dead. See ya."

I smiled. It was a typical Sunday night call from Arlo. He could get way too involved in the problems of writing sitcoms.

Message number two came in at 7:10. "Hello. This is Lily Huntley. Sorry to bother you, Madeline, but I didn't know who to call. I've asked Maria to box up the cookware for you. You know, the copper pots that Bruno wanted you to have. Shall I have someone bring them by?

"Oh, and something else. The older Huntley boys came over a little while ago with a court order demanding to take blood samples from Lewis and myself. Can you believe they got a judge to move on a Sunday? Anyway, I didn't see any reason to resist. After all, they seem to be implying that Lewis is not Bruno's son, and I happen to know that is absolutely absurd. So let them spend their money and prove I'm right.

"But then I got to thinking . . . Is this a mistake? I just really value your opinion. You see, Bruno usually made all the . . . Well, now I feel silly for even mentioning it. Sorry to waste your time.

"I'll have the pots delivered. Have a nice evening."

I stopped searching for my black and white gingham-checked shirt and replayed the message from Lily. Poor thing. What was she going on about? She had to know that Bruno had a vasectomy. I mean the scars from those things are visible, aren't they? So whose baby did she think Lewis was?

I thought of calling her right then, but there were still three messages left unheard from who knows whom? Could be a call from the Clintons. Chelsea's fallen in love with her psych professor at Stanford. They're thinking a lavish White House wedding. What about a champagne breakfast for twenty-five hundred to follow the ceremony? Could we possibly do the first family this personal favor and fly to Washington and take charge?

Hiding between several empty dry cleaning bags hanging in my living room closet, I found the shirt I was looking for. Coming back to the machine, I played the next message.

It was from 7:24. "This is Wes. Where are you? I gotta hear if you inherited the earth! I'm coming over."

Wes. Not exactly the hoped-for first couple requiring party tips.

I was zipping into a pair of black denim shorts. It seemed appropriate for November in L.A.

The next message was from the Whitley Heights Association. I listened to it as I looked under my bed for my low-cut black boots. They were still fighting the good fight to get better sound walls put up between my house and the Hollywood Freeway. Could I make food for the next meeting?

My thrills-per-message possibilities were dwindling. Such are the perils of high phone machine expectations.

My boots were gone, I remembered. I opened the closet in my bedroom and found a pair of sneakers that were still almost white. I tied them, folding the white athletic socks down as the fifth message played. It had been left at 9:25 this morning. I must have just missed the call when I'd stepped into the shower.

"This is Chuck Honnett. Got a few pieces to the puzzle. First, we found the bottle of brandy. That fancy Armagnac stuff was in a cut crystal decanter in the liquor cabinet like you said. We took it, and the lab is going over it today.

"Second, well, I probably shouldn't tell you this, but according to the autopsy report, which is currently under seal, the stomach contents did contain brandy. It's not official or anything. But, for my money that's one you got right. So, well . . . Thanks. If there's any more you can tell me about the shooting yesterday, call me."

That was it. I was right about the Armagnac. I knew it!

I still had to leave a witty message for Arlo and call back Lily, but I decided they could wait until after I'd gotten something together for breakfast. I walked down the stairs and almost made it to the kitchen when I heard the doorbell.

In my driveway was a blue van. Standing at the door

was Lily. Behind her, stacking up boxes and returning to the van to get more, was a man in his thirties. He looked familiar. He was dark and boyishly handsome, like an over-age jock. He wore jeans and a plaid flannel shirt.

Lily saw me staring at him and made a quick introduction. "Madeline, haven't you met Don Dana? He's a runner at Bruno's company. He's worked for us for years."

In T.V., a runner is an entry-level job. He's the slave who picks up the producer's chopped salad from La Scala Presto and makes the torturous drive to the deep Valley at rush hour to deliver a script to an actress they're trying to interest in a part, even though everyone knows she'll never do it. Because it's so tough to break into the business, these lowly runners jobs are often filled by kids hired right out of prestigious film schools. It usually takes these kids about six months of getting lunch for people less talented than they are until they either find a way to claw themselves up to the next Hollywood rung or move back to Cleveland to work at Dad's optical boutique. Don, however, looked like he'd been making a career of it.

"Donnie's being a sweetheart and helping me these days."

A "sweetheart," was he?

"Hey, cool shirt," I said, as Don came to the front steps with another box.

"It's Armani! As in Giorgio. Flannel shirt for probably two hundred bucks. Ain't that a trip?" Don asked.

In a flash I could place it. It was an exact replica of the pale shirt I'd seen little Babalu Huntley wearing the morning of the party.

Lily spoke up. "Isn't it nice? I got one for Lewis and one for Bruno, but Bruno hated the colors. Too soft, he said. Anyway, I thought Donnie might like it."

I noticed the pile of boxes.

"Why don't you come on in," I offered. "Just follow me." Don carried some boxes to the kitchen and left to get more. It would be a number of bulky trips before all the pots and pans made it into the house. While we waited, I offered Lily some fresh-squeezed orange juice.

"Did I interrupt your breakfast?" she asked.

"Join me." I rummaged in the Traulsen and found some of the salmon I'd cured for the brunch the day before.

With Lily sipping juice, and Don going back out to the van to lock up, and me toasting bagels under the broiler, I asked, "Did you know that Bruno had a vasectomy?"

"What?" She looked totally blank.

"Bruno had gotten a vasectomy. More than fifteen years ago. Didn't you know?"

"No . . ." Lily looked puzzled. "I don't think that's possible."

"Lily, I like you, but it's time to be straight. You said there's a paternity issue that may get stirred up. Only, I'm not certain you've been telling me the truth here . . ."

"But I am!"

". . . not that it's any of my business," I finished, "because it's really not."

"Look, Madeline, I am telling you the truth. I simply don't know what you're talking about. If someone gave you the impression that Bruno had a vasectomy, well they obviously made a mistake."

If she was lying, she was a damn good liar.

"Maybe," she suggested delicately, "years ago, in a romantic situation, Bruno may have told some woman that he had a vasectomy. For whatever reason." I could see that this was painful for her. She went on. "But that doesn't mean it's true. I have a son, don't I?"

"The coroner spotted it. He's a doctor Lily, and he examined Bruno's body. It's no mistake."

She looked ready to cry. When you have a baby with someone other than your husband, the jig is kind of up when people know your husband was incapable of impregnating you. Her breathing seemed to get shallow and she whispered, "If I tell you something, will you swear not to tell another soul?"

Lily continued, not waiting for my promise. "I don't see how any of this is connected. And this is very personal, of course. But I'm trying to think how everything happened when I was trying to get pregnant. See, I had trouble.

"After trying for maybe six months, my doctor thought that we should take Bruno's age into consideration and get more aggressive about getting me pregnant. She said ordinarily, a woman my age, she'd suggest we just keep trying the old-fashioned way for another year or so. But with Bruno being so much older, having a child as soon as possible was important. So he could have more time with our child."

I nodded.

"My doctor suggested we try insemination. That way she could time my cycle and at just exactly the right moment we could try for conception. I don't know how much background you have on these infertility procedures, but it's become rather clinical."

"So I've heard."

"Well, I told Bruno about it and eventually he agreed. These procedures can certainly intrude upon one's own private, intimate moments of marriage. All of a sudden you're keeping charts and taking temperatures. And your husband is giving samples into a test tube! At first, Bruno absolutely refused. But then, after a while, he suddenly seemed fine about it."

"He was?"

"Yes. No one knows about this, because I would never want to imply that somehow Bruno's sperm were not what they should be. You see, part of the procedure is to take the semen and 'wash' it somehow so that only the most vigorous sperm survive.

"When it came time for me to ovulate, I went to my doctor's office with Bruno. He had already provided her with the semen about a week earlier so it could be washed. He held my hand while the procedure was being performed. And then I had to wait there awhile so it could have the best chance to take. Three weeks later, I found out I was pregnant."

"Lily, if the report from the coroner is true and Bruno

had a vasectomy, then it can't have been Bruno's sperm. You do understand that, don't you?''

"What are you trying to tell me?" She really looked shocked. "That my husband conned me into believing that we could have a baby together? And that he went so far as to sneak somebody else's sperm to my doctor to trick me into thinking I'd had his own child? No!''

"I know it sounds bad when you put it like that. Maybe Bruno didn't want to let you down. So maybe he went a little overboard trying to give you what you wanted the most?'' Shit, I could make Jack the Ripper sound misunderstood.

"So you're saying that Lewis is not Bruno's son?" She had a steely look in her pale eyes. Like tears that are not allowed to fall, so they sort of freeze in place.

"Maybe not exactly Bruno's biological son, but . . .''

"So what's going to happen when they do those horrid blood tests? What's going to happen when they try to match my baby up to Bruno?'' She started to look frantic and I wished there was something I could do.

"It doesn't mean that you cheated on Bruno.''

"But that's what they'll say! And Lewis will be left with nothing. Nothing! Not a father to help him grow up. Not even the legacy that Bruno talked about in his will. He won't have Bruno's genes! It's all the fault of that wretched Bru, Jr. He'll never try to understand what really happened.''

Oh, brother. Lily had just discovered her husband's unthinkable trickery and manipulation, but she had already shifted the blame elsewhere. How did people like Bruno get away with these things?

Lily's voice got tighter and still higher. "Little Lewis will lose the money and the company and the land! My baby won't even have a home to live in. Bru, Jr. will see to that.'' Red patches had appeared on Lily's pale cheeks. As she worked herself up in anger, one tear escaped its prison behind her eyelids.

"You don't know that," I said. "But perhaps you should

see your attorney. Maybe that's the wisest thing. Sometimes knowing the road ahead gives you a chance to prepare.''

Lily stood up and straightened her pink dress. ''Well, thank you, Madeline. Donnie will drive me home. He's waiting in the van.'' And she was gone.

I sat down to finish my cured salmon and bagel.

Now what, I wondered, was all this with Donnie?

Chapter 24

"**S**o did you figure out who killed Bruno Huntley?" I could hear the swoosh as Holly shut the front door and the plop of her large canvas bag as it hit her desktop.

Sitting in my office next door, I sighed.

She was still talking as she appeared in my office doorway. "So, tell me, tell me!" Her voice just rang out louder as she continued on her way to the kitchen, in search of hot caffeine. "Who killed him?"

I put down the autopsy report and looked up at my computer screen. My notes on Bruno's murder seemed weak.

Cradling her steaming "Dilbert" mug two-handed at her lips, Holly returned to my doorway, slouching against the door frame and filling it with her six feet of lank, long self. She wore a purple sweater that was cropped just short enough to expose her navel, over a tiny gray skirt. Her extra-long legs were encased in opaque black stockings that came up above her knees and then just stopped, revealing a few inches of thin uncovered thigh until the top of her tight skirt took over. What else to finish off the look but a pair of black high-top combat boots?

"What keeps those stockings up?"

"I don't know. So who killed Bruno?"

"I don't know."

"Mmmm," she mumbled, pensively, as she carefully took a few tentative sips off the top of her steaming cup of coffee.

"Mmmm," I answered, equally pensive.

"You need help with anything?"

"We have recently had a few sudden party cancellations, which has cleared our catering schedule in a rather dramatic fashion. In fact, we have no parties at all this week."

"Jeez!"

"Exactly. I was just going over some of the things I'd learned in regards to Bruno's murder and I have to admit, I'm lost."

"Great! Okay! Tell me all the clues and then maybe I can, you know, just sort of see through the whole cloud of smoke and kind of pull the murderer out of the mud, so to speak."

I smiled and briefly filled in my free-spirited assistant on everything I'd discovered in the last two days. The strychnine, the brandy decanter, the cruel will, the Curse of Los Feliz, Bruno's possible affair with Carmen, his vasectomy, the Hirsh incident and subsequent chase, Graydon's marriage fizzling, who had the keys to the liquor cabinet, the missing soothsayer, and my personal opinion of all the players.

"Oh, this is too easy!" she announced when I had finished.

I laughed.

Holly laughed back, good-naturedly. "No, I mean it!"

"Okay, who did it?"

"Oh, I don't know that," Holly admitted, "but this has got to be connected in some wicked way to that scary curse of the Felizes."

"Oh, really?" Hey, cancel the cavalry. Holly had this one pegged.

"Sure, the Los Feliz curse has got to be it! My theory is you go for the weirdest part of the story and that's the one part that's got to be true."

Well, her crime-solving philosophy wasn't any more preposterous than anyone else's, and I knew how she felt. We'd all grown up on T.V. and expected a dramatic twist to every story. It was like "The Rockford Files" and

"Magnum, P.I." had crept into our existence and we felt cheated if there wasn't a surprise ending to every real life crime.

"Well if you are looking for weird . . ."

"And I am," Holly nodded.

". . . then you can't rule out the bizarre angle concerning Bruno and his sperm."

"Oh, I love that part. Tell me again."

"Okay. Lily wanted a baby. Bruno had a pesky old vasectomy that he was keeping a secret from his young wife. So one of two things must have happened. Either Lily was having an affair . . ."

"Which she vigorously denies, right? Isn't she always going on about being as pure as soap?"

"Yes. Anyway, she is either lying and has been sleeping with some other unvasectomized male, or . . . and this is truly bizarre . . . her old husband pretended some other guy's sperm was his own."

"Why not?"

"Wait! We're to believe that he brought this bogus sperm to the doctor's office and helped his wife get inseminated with some other man's semen?"

"Washed semen," Holly corrected.

"Exactly," I agreed. "Now talk about your bizarre acts."

"Love is strange. And that guy Huntley was on a major power trip. Maybe he just didn't want to admit there was anything in the world that his wife could want that he didn't have the power to give her."

"You know," I said looking at Holly with my usual appreciation, "you could be right. But where on earth could he have found some extra semen lying around?"

"A sperm bank! He probably just walked right in, browsed through their catalog and picked out some sperm that seemed to fit his physical type."

"No! People can't just walk into sperm banks and pay with Visa, can they? No!" I shook my head.

"Of course they do. Don't you know nothin' about birth-in' babies? It costs like around fifty bucks a pop. I had a friend who decided she wanted a baby but didn't like the idea of having the father hanging around and messing up the kid's head. She went to this sperm bank in Westwood and like twenty minutes later she walked out with a vial of sperm.''

"Really?''

"Uh-huh. She wanted a tall, thin child that would look like Sting, but with hair, so she picked from a list of all the donor's physical characteristics.''

"So does her baby actually look like Sting?''

"Nah. It was kind of tragic. See, she was sharing a place with two other girls at the time. Anyway, one of her roommates didn't pay the electric bill and the power was turned off. Unfortunately, the sperm was in the refrigerator at the time and I guess it kind of spoiled before she could, uh, use it.''

"Lovely story.''

"But the point is, why couldn't Bruno have just walked into some sperm bank and bought himself some sperm, like off-the-rack?''

"I'll look into it.''

"Fine. But I still think the whole murder revolves around that curse. I really do. 'The land, Katie Scarlett!' ''

"Have you just rented *Gone With The Wind*?''

"Don't knock the classics. I bet if you look further into the Feliz Curse you'll find a motive for Bruno's murder. I'm telling you.'' She wagged her finger at me.

"Okay, okay. I'll go to the library and get some more details. Will that satisfy you?''

Holly smiled, nodding, trying to keep the coffee cup at her lips from spilling in the process.

Forty minutes later I was wrapping up some note-taking and phone calls that needed returning. My last call was to the information line of the L.A. Public Library. I was put on hold. After a minute, a man's voice answered, "Reference.''

"Hi. I'm actually looking for a way to get more information about the history of Los Feliz."

"That would be held in a special file in our Los Feliz branch," he replied.

"Oh. Where is that?" I was not acquainted with every branch in the library system, but felt I was about to get an education.

"Nineteen thirty-nine and a half Hillhurst. But it's closed."

"Pardon me," I had just scribbled down 1939 ½ on the back of the nearest envelope on my desk.

"It was damaged in the earthquake."

"Ah. Is there any other branch that might have information on certain historical incidents in that area?" I felt myself slipping into libraryese, a kind of reference-speak.

"A moment," he offered, neutrally.

I waited.

"I've checked my database and there may be some information here at the Frances Howard Goldwyn Branch."

"And where's that?"

"Hollywood. Sixteen twenty-three Ivar."

I made it over to the Ivar address in about five minutes. It was just south of Hollywood Boulevard, in one of the parts of town that had been trying to upgrade itself. An artsy, iron sculpture adorned a parking lot gate across the street. The library itself had been newly rebuilt, a modern structure of the palest peach stucco with angled windows.

On the second floor of the library, I found the reference desk and asked for help in researching my curse. They acted like people come to them for help about curse research every day of the week. You can't surprise a research librarian.

I was eventually handed a copy of *On the Old West Coast* by Horace Bell. It was marked "Reference Material," not to be taken out of the library, and I was curious to see if Wesley's memory was as good as he had always claimed.

Sitting down at one of the oak tables, I started to read

about the folklore that surrounded that period of California history and that piece of land. It was certainly fascinating reading.

Good old Wes and his photographic brain. It was exactly as he'd remembered. Poor old Don Antonio Feliz had been rooked out of his land by a dishonest attorney, and the women in his family were left with very little. The more things change, the more they stay the same, as the saying goes.

It was almost an hour later when I'd finished reading. I had just been sucked into the nineteenth century and I had to shake my head to get ready to face traffic on the verge of the twenty-first. Aside from refreshing my memory about the details of the curse: blight, sick cattle, poor crops, dead oaks, wrath of heaven and vengeance of hell, I had not learned anything that could tie it to my modern-day murder.

I returned the book to the reference desk and as I turned to leave, a soft cough announced the approach of my determined librarian who had gone on to find additional materials for me.

"Take a look at these," he suggested. The label on the box of microfilm indicated it contained old photos and newspaper articles from 1850 to 1900. "They're quite a trip back in time."

Although I was ready to leave, it seemed unkind not to stop and look at the material he'd spent time digging up.

He led me to a viewer and showed me how to use the machine. You pushed a button that made the pages, which had been photographed onto microfilm, just fly by in a whir. I began to let the button go at random, then wait for the words to stop spinning and my eyes to focus. Whichever article the machine stopped at, I read. Another hour glided by as I immersed myself in unconnected historical tidbits.

There were photos and diaries kept on film that had been left to the library by historical societies. There were old photos and prints taken from oil portraits. I'd stop the whirring whenever I'd find a patch of these pictures. The dress and demeanor of the men and women appeared stiff and dark. The faces seemed very different from ones I see today, but perhaps my eyes had become too accustomed to our contemporary appearance, altered from nature as it is by cosmetics and hair mousse.

I marveled at the portrait of one settler family: seven sons standing straight-backed, their heights graduated like a staircase, seven pairs of identical pale eyes looking almost transparent in the sepia print. Whatever had become of them?

There were more articles from a newspaper dated 1862. I was getting tired, but I pushed the viewing machine button another time and it spun until it came to a large block of photos. I let go of the button and the viewer stopped on an old portrait of three people. In shock, I stared at one of the faces.

The accompanying caption read, ''Don Antonio Feliz and relatives, Los Angeles, 1862.''

It was the face that belonged to Feliz's niece, Petranilla, that had stunned me to the point that I stopped breathing. Even with bad lighting and primitive photography, even without benefit of makeup or hair gel, I recognized her. I knew that lovely face. I knew that beautiful hair.

Oh my god.

Chapter 25

I used my car phone to make a few calls and line up an address. I was swinging around the streets of Hollywood, making a fast approach onto the Highland entrance of the Hollywood Freeway when I got through to the LAPD office of Lizzie Bailey. She seemed as excited as I was and promised to meet me in ten minutes.

I felt high. I was all adrenaline and sparking synapses. I really loved this investigating thing, the rush of the hunt. I'd always been the type who liked answers. I felt a few coming and smiled.

I cut off the Hollywood Freeway to the Ventura, and exited on Coldwater Canyon. I took a left, and in the light midafternoon traffic, I was able to weave my way south into the hills of Sherman Oaks in pretty good time.

I had made a photocopy of the picture of Petranilla. At every stoplight I looked over at the copy I'd thrown on the front seat next to me. The resemblance was startling every time I looked. And every time I looked, my pulse would rev up as if it was the first time I'd seen it.

I pulled in front of a hillside home that had a large flat lot and what looked like plenty of room for a pool in the rear. The house was long and low and had enough square feet to mean big money in this upscale section of the Valley. I pushed the photocopy into my purse and walked up to the door, not really knowing what would happen from here.

Answering the bell was a tall woman with her vivid black hair swept back into a french twist. She looked to be in her midforties, but they had been very well kept years. She paused to take in my casual appearance and said, "Yes?"

"I'm Madeline Bean and I'd like to speak to your daughter."

"Come in then," she offered, cool and unperturbed.

I walked into the large living room. The ceiling was low, the carpet was the color of the earth. She waved me towards a light brown sofa, but I didn't feel like sitting. And then I saw her daughter walk into the living room from a back hallway.

"Mom, I thought I heard someone at the door."

I was looking at the face of the young Feliz niece. The one who had long ago been cheated out of inheriting the rancho of her uncle; the woman whose curse was meant to bring death and destruction to the rich and arrogant Anglo men who possessed her family's land ever since.

"Carmen?"

"Oh. Hi, Madeline. It's you."

"I had to see you. I just found this."

I held up the picture of the Feliz family from over one hundred and thirty years ago.

Carmen looked at the image of Petranilla. Both young women had perfect oval faces and large, deep-lidded eyes. Both had full mouths and high cheekbones. Carmen said in a toneless voice, "Yes. I look like her."

Not the reaction I'd expected. No protests or denials. Just Carmen's smooth, emotionless voice, as if she took for granted this striking family resemblance.

"She must be your great-great grandmother," I suggested.

"Add one more great and you are correct." Carmen's mother's voice had steel in it.

"Great," I replied with some steel of my own. "Look, I know all about the Curse of Los Feliz. Was your daughter's marriage to Gray Huntley part of some scheme to get at the land?''

''My daughter is a sweet child.''

I ignored the mother. ''What happened when you brought that glass of brandy to Bruno? Did you fight with him?''

''No. It wasn't like that.'' As she sank down into the sofa, she seemed sad. Not scared. Not defensive.

I looked at my watch and wondered what was keeping Lizzie. I felt if I was going to go on I had better set the record straight for my own protection.

''My friend, Officer Bailey, is on her way over here. I already told her about your connection to the Feliz Curse.''

Neither mother nor daughter seemed moved by the thought that the law was on to them.

''Well, something's going on,'' I continued, a little exasperated. ''Bruno died talking about the Feliz curse. And you served Bruno the brandy snifter of Armagnac that contained the strychnine that killed him.''

I could hear Carmen begin to sniffle.

The mother spoke again. ''If the drink was tainted, my Carmen knew nothing about it. The police have been here already and they believe her. Why aren't you convinced?''

I ignored her and spoke again to Carmen.

''You are involved in this thing down to the ground.'' I knew I was pushing it, but I couldn't believe how calmly they were dodging these bombshells. Well, dodge this.

''While you were married to Graydon, were you also having an affair with Bruno?''

''I was sleeping with him, yes,'' she said quietly.

''Carmen! That's enough!'' her mother ordered.

''Mama, I must confess.'' She looked up at me. ''For my soul.''

Confess? Damn, where was Lizzie?

''It's true. I was married to the son and making love to the father. I know I've sinned.'' Carmen started crying.

Yes. But just how many commandments had she cracked?

"That night at the party, maybe you told Bruno about the Feliz family's claim to his land? I can imagine his reaction. He probably laughed in your face. And in your anger, perhaps you took the legend of the curse a little too seriously."

"I know you're worried about your friend, Madeline, but I didn't kill anyone," Carmen said in her slow, sad way.

Hell, maybe she didn't. On a scale with one being passive to the point of coma and ten being hyperactive, I had Carmen notched somewhere around three. In fact, the most profoundly moving emotion I'd ever seen her express was melancholy.

What, then, did she do with her anger? Most of us women learn to deny it around that time in junior high when the cute boy throws our sweater in the mud and we just smile. After years of practice, we're on autopilot, all the time denying we ever feel rage.

But it's not like the anger goes away. It just keeps building up. And while we're busy denying how bad we feel, some of us get drunk, some of us make jokes, and some of us cut off our husbands' genitals with a carving knife. Which type was Carmen Huntley?

"That's all. My daughter did not kill the man. You've taken up enough of our time." The mother opened the door and by grabbing the material of my checked shirt, she effectively pulled me out of her house. Now this was a woman with strength. This was a woman, it dawned on me, who had the right personality and family history to commit murder. This woman was an eight!

I stopped at the doorway and turned back to Carmen. "I need to find the truth. If you didn't kill Bruno, help me find who did."

I thought I saw Carmen's face soften, but then the door slammed in my face. The mother. My heart was pumping from the confrontation, and yet I felt let down, somehow. I was having a hard time hanging onto my conviction that Carmen did Bruno Huntley in. According to the evidence she should have done it, but I was beginning to doubt that she did. Now her mom, on the other hand . . .

"Madeline."

I had just reached my car when I thought I heard a whisper. I turned my head, but couldn't see anyone nearby. I noticed for the first time that a thick cloud cover had rolled in, hanging above the Valley like a puffy gray ceiling.

"Madeline, please come here."

It was Carmen, hiding in the shade of the wood shake roof that deeply overhung her mother's wide three-car garage.

Stepping away from my car, I glanced back to check the windows of the house but couldn't see any trace of a watchful parent.

"Madeline, I have to talk to you. I didn't want you to think I could kill someone."

"You don't have to worry about what I think. I like you, Carmen, but there's an awful lot of evidence that seems to tie you to the murder."

"I know it sounds bad but I guess you're right about part of the story. I've been a horrible person. The only reason I married Graydon was that it brought me closer to the property in Los Feliz. I didn't see it so clearly at the time, but now I do. I realize what I did was awful. I shouldn't have married Graydon."

"I take it Gray never actually caught on that you were only in it for the land?"

She looked startled, as though she'd been struck. But isn't that exactly what she'd been saying?

"I just don't think you can understand what we've been through. My mother is really a wonderful woman, but she's suffered most of her life by the injustice that was done to her family.

"Her own mother was a very strong-willed woman. That was my grandmother, Sylvia. Grandma had been terribly poor when she was a child, living behind a small grocery store. The Great Depression affected many people, but to my Grandma it seemed like a personal insult. It made her feel demeaned. Growing up, eating bruised vegetables and

second-day bread, she had lived only on stories of the
wealth and prestige of our family in the old days. The injustice of her circumstances seemed so great to her that,
well, she became very bitter.''

I nodded. I had expected such a story. It was all fitting
back into my theory about the curse.

''My mother felt a very deep need to help Grandma Sylvia, to make up for Grandma's pain. When she grew up,
my mother married a very rich man and brought Grandma
here to this house. She had meant to give her mother the
one thing she had always wanted, a privileged life.''

Carmen was leaning against the yellow stucco garage,
keeping her face in the shadows. She looked at me and
smiled sadly.

''I guess by that time, my grandma was too old to get
any pleasure out of being rich. She lived here with us, but
every day she would spit out venom at the people who had
robbed her of a comfortable youth. This beautiful house
was not enough to erase her grievances. She had it in her
head that we should be living on that side of the hill.''
Carmen gestured with a graceful wave across the hills that
separated the San Fernando Valley from Hollywood. ''And
not on an acre or two, but on thousands.''

''Is your grandmother still living with you here?''

''Oh, no. She died a few years ago. But my mother has
been infected by this desire of Grandma Sylvia's to get the
land back. Mother met a woman some time ago who said
she would sell her many acres of the precious land. My
poor father! He'd given up on trying to reason with his
wife and mother-in-law long ago. But he became hopeful
that there might be an end to Grandma's weird stories and
curses.''

''What happened?''

''The old lady that owned the land died suddenly while
the young woman who was arranging the sale to my mother
was out of town. In the meantime, a relative inherited the
land and sold it privately to Bruno Huntley. My mother had

her real estate lady go to the Huntleys and try to buy it, but they wouldn't sell. It was too late.''

Carmen shook her lovely head, her shiny hair swinging. ''Just rotten luck, but my mother had another idea. She suggested I meet Bruno's son and tell him about the land. She said maybe I could appeal to his sense of chivalry.'' She shook her head again at the futility of her plight.

I understood. Trying to get sympathy out of a Huntley was like trying to get milk from a bull. Watch where you pull.

''So you married Graydon?''

''Yes. Why not? He was nice looking and I thought he had influence and authority. My mother said it made perfect sense. If I couldn't persuade my husband to get his father to sell the land, Gray would in any event inherit it one day and leave it to my children. She was not in a hurry. To her that would have been fair and just.''

''So when you found out that Graydon wasn't exactly calling the shots at Bruno's company and had little influence over his decisions, you shifted your attentions to the father.''

''Mother thought it could help things, if you must know. I had been going through a bad point in my marriage. I felt less and less interested in my life.

''I was at a family party and Bruno took me aside to show me something he'd bought, a necklace. Bruno said not to tell anyone in the family so there wouldn't be any hard feelings.''

''Was it expensive?'' I asked, knowing the answer.

''Of course. It was ridiculous, all diamonds and rubies.''

''And you started sleeping with him.''

''Mother thought if he would give me a ten-thousand-dollar necklace, perhaps the land was also negotiable.''

''But it wasn't.'' I was adding up Carmen's story, and wondering if the final revenge for all the promises and humiliation turned out to be murder.

Tears were falling from Carmen's perfect oval eyes. She shook her head. ''Bruno was so smart and strong and in charge; everything that his sons could only wish to be. I actually thought I loved Bruno then. Do you think I'm horrible?''

She looked at me for reassurance, but what could I say?

"Back then, Bruno was so wonderful to me. Some nights we would sit with our drinks and he would talk to me about his work or his plans. He was a million times the man his sons have turned out to be. He was so forceful and clever and, and generous. You liked him, too, didn't you Madeline? That's why I'm telling you all this. I know you respected Bruno.''

Had I? It had been hard not to be attracted to the man even as you were repelled by him, with his compulsive need to control you and please you and punish you.

"Did he have plans for the land in Los Feliz? Could you persuade him to give it to your family?''

"Of course not!'' It was the most force I'd ever heard Carmen expel. She was crying and growing more agitated as she spoke. "He didn't even own the land, he said. He chuckled and said, too bad Carmenita. Too bad! What did he know about how we'd suffered!''

"Wait. Back up a minute. Bruno said he didn't own the land?''

"Who knows what he said?'' She was wiping her eyes with a tissue she had pulled from the pocket of her skirt. "All I know is that I was married to a man I hated. I was in love with a man who was married already. I was no closer to helping my mother fulfill her dream. What did it matter what the details were?''

"But with Bruno dead,'' I said gently, "weren't you back in the game? Your husband might have inherited the land. You couldn't know that Bruno would cut his sons out of his will.''

"No? He was always taunting his sons about it. One day he would say they were in, and another day he'd say they were out. One night, he told me that he'd never leave a lot of money or property to his sons. He said they'd never enjoy anything they had not earned on their own.''

She smiled at that and added, "How little he knew them, don't you think? Bru, Jr. owes almost half a million dollars to some guys that aren't very patient. Do you think he cares where the money that will save his ass comes from?

"Please, I know I've been bad. I have. But you mustn't think I'd have hurt the only man I truly cared about."

Before I realized I was talking out loud I heard myself say, "I believe you."

All through her story she had been waiting for some sign from me. Some display of sympathy, or unbending of my harsh judgment of her life. Now, a flood of relief met me as she hurried on.

"All we were hoping to do was buy the land, don't you see? I'd have gained nothing if Bruno died. And as for the fact that his drink was poisoned, well it scares me. Could I have handed him that glass of death? I have no idea how that stuff got into his Armagnac. I swear I didn't put it there."

Maybe not, I thought, but what about her mother? Was that woman angry enough to fulfill her family's curse? If she had condoned her daughter's needless sacrifice to the Huntley men, perhaps she felt justified to take Bruno's life in retaliation.

Carmen must have been reading my mind, because she added, "Mother is obsessed with owning Bruno's land, it's true, but she's not a foolish woman. She has been trying to find out if Bruno was telling me the truth about the deed. If he no longer owned our land, then someone else must. She was doing research on the title to the land. She wasn't interested in Bruno. She had no reason to kill the man I was in love with."

At that moment, Carmen's mother stepped out of the side door of the garage. She'd probably been standing there for a while.

"Come inside, Carmenita," she called. "You have talked enough about these sorry things, don't you think?"

I got into my car and mulled things over.

I pulled out the crumpled photocopy of Petranilla and

her mother and uncle, smoothing out the wrinkles and staring at the women. Carmen and her mother seemed like the perfect suspects: their connection to the curse that was on Bruno's dying lips, their present-day quest for the land in Los Feliz, Carmen's messed up relations with Bruno and son, and the fact that Carmen actually served Bruno the poisoned brandy.

The thing was, I just didn't think they did it. They weren't scared, or shifty, or defensive. They weren't inventing all kinds of stories to cover up their involvement. They were neither overly clever nor playing dumb.

I was stumped. The thing was, I wanted my murderers to *act* like murderers. Stealthy, lethal, on the attack. Of course, I had to remind myself, I'd never actually met a murderer. Perhaps, this is where experience might come in real handy.

Chapter 26

I started back down the hill and had to wait at the intersection for a flurry of cars to pass. My phone rang just as I found a small opening in traffic. I wheeled right, then grabbed the phone as I straightened the car onto Ventura.

"Madeline?" It was Holly. "Madeline! I'm going fucking nuts! I don't know where you are! I'm in my car. I'm driving around looking for you, for cripe's sakes. I took your spare cell phone with me and I called everywhere I could think of. Twice!"

"What's up?" I was getting alarmed. Holly does not freak like this.

"They've arrested Wesley. He's in jail! Oh, Madeline, I knew you'd want to go see him but they won't give me any information. The only reason I even know about it is that Lizzie Bailey called for you."

"Shit!" I said, and then, noticing too late that I'd forgotten to make the necessary left turn onto Coldwater Canyon. "Shit!"

With the dozens of people in the world who really had good reasons to end Bruno's life, why were they still after Wesley?

"Geez! Arrested? Wes must be going completely mental. He didn't kill Bruno! Are the cops crazy?"

"Of course they're crazy! Why else would they take a sick job like being a cop?" Holly screamed. She was definitely not her normal cool cat self.

"Holly, you can't lose it, buddy. You hear me? I need to do some thinking and I don't want to worry about you driving into a pole," I said calmly, as I severely corrected my steering to avoid the pole coming directly at me.

"Yeah, right," she said. "I gotta pull over to the curb. I'm feeling kinda weakish."

"That's the best thing for you to do til you feel better," I advised. Meantime, I pulled over to the curb.

"The police have so little," I said. "Okay, Wes had the key to the liquor cabinet. So what? Plenty of people had their hands on that key. And, all right, Wes was mad at Bruno about that land commission. But what about the party? Don't those pinheads realize Bruno just handed us a huge fee?"

In a nonlinear, odd, Bruno Huntley way, the score was being evened out. So why didn't the cops get it?

"There's something else, Maddie. Something real bad. Something you don't know." Holly's voice sounded stressed. "They found the poison in Wes's apartment."

"What! What poison?"

"Strychnine. A shitload of it. The stuff that was used on old Bruno. They had a search warrant and went through Wes's place a few hours ago. I guess they found it in one of his canisters, you know, on his kitchen counter."

"I can't believe it! That's impossible!" Wes had a set of canisters that he'd gotten from a scientific supply house. They were impressively large glass bottles with round glass stoppers. He used them to hold sugar and baking powder and flour and . . . and . . . strychnine? Oh my god! Where could Wes have gotten the stuff?

"I have to do something," I told Holly, "but I'm not sure what."

"I know what I have to do," Holly replied, with a hint of her usual mischief.

"What?"

"It requires a toilet," Holly offered, delicately.

I turned my radio on and tuned it to the all-news station. I was hoping the story on Wesley's arrest would give me more details, like where they had taken him. As they gave the traffic report, I thought about who we could call to represent him. We had done a lot of parties for successful attorneys. Problem was, most of them specialized in entertainment law—great for a network pilot deal, not so hot for murder one.

The weather report warned that large storm clouds were gathering off the coast and could be coming inland by tomorrow. That was disturbing. Many areas around Southern California had been devastated by brushfires this past summer. After having been stripped bare by days and nights of flames, the charred earth was vulnerable. Now, these same defoliated areas were in line to be drenched by huge downpours and inundated by mud. You could tell what season it was by what disaster was most likely to strike.

I got onto the freeway and heard the announcer tease the next segment to be reported after the commercial. "Coming up," he said, "an arrest is made in the Bruno Huntley murder." But first I had to listen to an ad for a tuneup franchise. Yes, why not get a car lube while waiting for Armageddon?

"Police Chief Bernard C. Parks, today, praised the diligent and speedy work of the Los Angeles police department in the arrest this afternoon of a suspect in the killing of T.V. producer Bruno Huntley. Huntley's death on Friday night had alarmed many in the entertainment industry who had counted Huntley a friend.

"The arrest of Wesley Owen Westcott, a caterer, came after investigators found a large quantity of strychnine at Westcott's residence. Strychnine was the poison used to kill Huntley while he was hosting a Halloween party at his estate in Los Feliz.

"Police say Westcott knew the victim and had become disgruntled after a real estate deal fell through."

I had to admit, it sounded a whole lot more solid and plausible when you heard it reported on the news. I had to talk to Wesley. I had to find out about that strychnine.

My mind was reeling as all the stories I'd heard in the past few days started to shift and reshuffle themselves. The last thing I wanted to do was doubt Wes. If only he hadn't known so damn much about how they use strychnine in street drugs . . .

In my heart, I knew he'd never kill anyone, but my mind is not my heart. My mind finally had to ask the question: Did Wes kill Bruno?

Chapter 27

I put ice cubes in my glass and moved to the faucet. I had been drinking way too much Diet Coke. Feeling it was time for a health food purge, I filled the glass from the purified water spigot. It was Tuesday morning, and I had an hour until I should leave to meet the attorney over at County Jail, where they were holding Wesley.

I had called a lawyer we knew, Tom Field, the previous evening. Wes and I had done his wedding about a year ago. It's odd what you remember about clients. I remember particularly that Tom loved oysters and hated Bruno Huntley. Bruno really must have jerked him around at one time. At Tom's wedding reception, he kept returning to the oyster bar for "just one more," and he kept his guests amused by telling derogatory "Bruno" stories.

Tom Field specialized in network series packaging, but was happy to recommend a fellow with whom he'd gone to law school who was enormously respected in criminal cases.

I swallowed the water and dialed Honnett's number. I hung up. What was there to say? He'd arrested my best friend. I guessed dating him was out of the question.

Holly tiptoed into the kitchen.

"Madeline?"

"You don't have to whisper," I offered.

"There's a woman. Her name is . . ."

"I couldn't possibly." I shook my head at the thought

of someone applying for a job. I splashed the rest of my water into the sink, ice cubes clattering in protest against their ignoble end, and set the empty glass down by the drainboard.

The electronic beep-beep-beep of the timer meant my chocolate chip croissants were ready to come out of the oven. I bent to the task. Perhaps they wouldn't let me give them to Wesley. Perhaps they would. I just knew that baking had filled another hour until I could leave for the jail. The kitchen clock told me I'd been successful. It was now almost ten o'clock.

"So I should tell her to go? Or . . ." Holly was not used to me being vague, distracted.

Just as I roused myself to respond, this other woman entered the doorway to the kitchen right behind Holly. She was slender and dressed to show off her well worked-out body, in skin-tight black Lycra shorts that stopped at mid-thigh topped by a biker's black leather jacket. And hers was a face I remembered distinctly.

"Hello," she said. "I didn't want to bother you. But I simply had to see you."

Holly looked confused. She wanted to shield me from the intrusion. We both spoke at once.

"Look, I'm sorry . . ." Holly started herding the woman away from the door.

"Please come in," I said at the same time.

"Holly, don't you remember our soothsayer?"

"Holy shit!"

The out-of-costume soothsayer gracefully sidestepped Holly and entered the kitchen. She had the kind of nose and cheekbones and, for that matter, bosom that made one curious to know if such perfection was possible without a helpful surgeon. Her thick eyebrows arched beautifully over the greenest of eyes. I still found myself wondering if they were contacts.

"My name is Angelica. Angelica Sands. I'm afraid there's been a terrible mistake."

For a crazy moment I thought she was going to confess

to Bruno's murder. Police made big mistake. Arrested the wrong person. She did it. Hope is so fucking illogical.

"What mistake?" I asked, removing my oven mitts.

"You've been looking for me, right? About the party? I guess I shot out of there pretty fast. I was like devastated, you know?" She looked pretty shook up. "Devastated!" She really liked that word.

"Were you and Bruno close?" I asked, checking her out in the bright kitchen light. She seemed awfully young.

"Well, sort of. I'm going to be a big star some day. Bruno said so. And he was going to give me my first big break. He said I was a really gifted actress, like a Meryl Streep or a Lisa Kudrow. But now he's gone. Man, what a waste. Bruno was an angel, you know?"

People loved Bruno at first. The man could be very enthusiastic. Later, when they began noticing his footprints all over their dreams, they began to despise him. From her reaction, I was betting she hadn't known Bruno all that long.

"It was such a shock. A real American tragedy, like *MacBeth* or something." She looked deeply touched, and held it for a beat. "I mean he died, for God's sake, right there at the party. So I bagged it."

"Yes, I see. Well, we did want to pay you for your work that night but there was no way to contact you."

"Oh, I wasn't doing it for money. See, Bruno called me very last minute. He said I'd meet all the most powerful men in Hollywood. I did the soothsayer gig just to please him, really."

Angelica smiled at something, some memory. When she realized we had noticed, she decided to share it with us.

"Bruno had such a great sense of humor, didn't he? I wasn't supposed to tell anyone this, but I guess it's okay now . . . well, now that he's gone.

"He had this major plan. He was so naughty. He paid off some guy at the air freight company to screw up your shipment of fancy food for the Halloween party. He wanted you to send your assistant out on some wild goose chase so he could arrange for me to step in as the fortune teller.''

Bruno was behind the truffles/nightcrawlers switch? I suddenly felt off-balance.

''Well, why?''

''For fun. He gave me a list with a lot of very personal dirt on the party guests. I mean, intense. Then I predicted horrible fortunes for each one, with lots of specific details. Like I knew that actress was going to get fired off her soap because it was Bruno's show and he told me!''

She laughed at the looks on our faces as we recalled the impact of Bruno's fiendish plot. ''Really! And it went great. Everyone was completely freaking!'' She smiled. ''Wasn't he a bad boy? It was just to have a giggle.''

I nodded my head slowly. It did make a sick kind of sense. And it sounded like that old devil Bruno Huntley.

''So that guy who was nuts about his new car?'' I asked, remembering back. ''And the guy who dated his secretaries?''

''Yeah. It was hilarious. I had these big powerful men shaking! Bruno was supposed to meet me at the dinner break to get the details. He thought it was the biggest hoot.''

Holly cleared her throat. ''You predicted I would get a new boyfriend before Christmas.''

Angelica grinned. ''You weren't on Bruno's hit list, so I just made it up.''

''And what about Madeline? You said Arlo would propose.''

''Now that was Bruno.'' Angelica turned to me, smiling. ''He said I should rub in what an old maid you are.''

It figured. The joke was on me, too.

''I'm not that old,'' I mumbled, more to myself or maybe to Bruno than to anyone in that room.

''Bruno told me to think of it as an audition. So I really got into the character. Things just started coming to me. Can you believe that? I actually started getting, like, messages. I felt that something awful might happen at midnight. Isn't that wild?''

Well, Stanislovsky said that acting is believing. I could tell she'd make quite an actress some day. Maybe even a Kudrow.

In my kitchen, with the sun shining on her young pretty face, there was none of that ethereal quality I'd noted on the night of the party. If anything, there was a bit of the Valley girl.

"Nice performance," I commented.

Her dimples deepened and her shiny black ponytail bobbed.

"But wait a minute." Holly was confused. "Bruno couldn't have met you during dinner. That was when I accidentally walked in on Lily and him in their bedroom."

"Right," Angelica said, coolly. "He didn't show up. I was really pissed about it at the time." She smiled ruefully. "I thought he was going to put some moves on me during dinner."

"At his own party?" Holly asked, thrilled.

"Oh, you get to know about these directors and producers. They pretty much want what everyone wants."

"And you give it to them?" Holly was dying to know how these things worked.

"Look, why sell it on the street for a few hundred bucks when you can date these powerful men, travel first class, get great clothes and stuff, and land a career that will net you millions? Am I right?" She turned to me, like this is the way all us business women get started.

"Is she?" asked the ever-curious Holly.

"Making it in Hollywood . . ." I said, selecting my words carefully, "there are many paths. Some, such as Angelica, favor the time-honored route. Many don't. But tell us," I said, quickly steering a conversational U-turn back to the party, "did you ever see Bruno that night?"

"Never. I was stuck telling fortunes until late. Then around twelve o'clock, somebody called me on the walkie-talkie saying that Bruno is, like, dying. It just creeped me out! I mean, all night I'd been getting vibrations about midnight!"

"But you said there was a mistake . . ." I reminded her, trying to get back to what she'd said when she entered my kitchen. The comment that had given me something to hope for.

"Oh, yeah. The other night, I borrowed a car from my cousin Perry. His Bentley. See, he was out of town and I know his bodyguard pretty good. I was real careful to get his car back before he came home. But then you show up at his house! How'd you find out about him, anyway?"

"The license plate."

"Well, that was a mistake. My cousin is like paranoid. He doesn't dig strangers is the thing. He's really an okay guy, but he kind of flipped when you showed up on his doorstep. He just wasn't expecting you is all."

"I got that impression."

"So he's real sorry he got the wrong idea. He told me to make sure everything was okay. You know, with your car and all."

"Those are some dogs he's got."

"Nancy and Hillary. Yeah. But really, they're fine when they know you."

"So what does your cousin Perry do for a living?"

Angelica hesitated.

"Or shouldn't I ask?" I asked.

"Yeah. Maybe you shouldn't," she agreed, but then her tone brightened. "Oh! Perry wanted me to give you this. It's his way of saying no hard feelings." She reached into the pocket of her jacket and pulled out a white envelope.

"What's in it?"

"Money, I think. For fixing up your car. He's awfully mad at me about everything. So it would be great if you could take this money and make the whole incident disappear. Could you do that?"

I needed a minute to think that one over. "Holly, could you get Angelica's driver's license and xerox it for our files?"

Angelica looked at Holly and me and then mashed through her bag and drew out her license. Then she held out the envelope to me and said, ''Could you just forget about Perry and, well, all the shit that happened when you visited him?''

I looked at her young face. It was clearly unstruck by any slap of conscience. She had planned to accept Bruno's advances in exchange for that big break. Perhaps she had built up their future affair in her mind, had even seen herself as the next Mrs. Bruno Huntley. Was the gypsy so angry at Bruno for standing her up that she killed him?

''What were you doing with a gun at the party?''

''L.A.'' She shrugged. ''You know. It's dangerous.''

''And that white powder in your purse,'' I continued, ''what was that?''

She didn't question how I knew the contents of her shoulder bag. Still holding the envelope, she reached into her bag with the other hand. Holly, God love her, ducked.

''It's coke. You gonna bust me?'' She held up the vial.

A twenty-year-old who nonchalantly carries a gun? And drugs? Well, it wasn't the L.A. I knew personally, but I read about Angelica's L.A. in the paper all the time.

''Are you going to give me a break?'' she asked.

I took the envelope. ''This is simply to fix my windshield? Nothing else?''

''Perry just wants to know that you're his friend.''

I handed her back the envelope. It had felt thick. ''I don't think . . .''

''Oh no! You really have to take it.'' She was definitely stressed. ''He told me his dogs may have scratched your paint job. Perry takes cars very seriously. Look, he really wants you to have this. Please. Don't disappoint Perry.''

The last thing I needed right now was some sort of gang leader annoyed that I wasn't ''his friend.'' What was so wrong about letting him pay for my car's damage?

''Please,'' Angelica pleaded.

I find it incredibly hard to say no. Call me a wimp. I didn't disappoint Perry.

Angelica left, and I was startled by the time on my kitchen clock. I quickly packed the cooled croissants into a white box. I poured cafe au lait into a thermos. I grabbed Perry Hirsh's envelope and started for the door.

Holly stopped me.

"How much?"

I opened the envelope and scanned the contents.

"There are sixty five-hundred-dollar bills," I said quietly.

"Yow! How much is that? Like . . ." Holly was breathless, doing the math. "Like . . . like thirty thousand?"

"Nice paint job."

Chapter 28

*T*he attorney's name was Del Schreiner. He was extremely "business suit" in appearance, but actually seemed to have a sense of humor. That helped. When I offered him a fresh-baked croissant, I said, "I'm pretty sure this one's from the batch that wasn't poisoned."

Del accepted the pastry, bit into the delicate crust with gusto, saying, "If I get your friend off, will you marry me?"

We were scheduled to go in to see Wes in thirty minutes. I would get a mere five minutes to meet with him alone. How to tell him all that I'd found out in such a short time? That Lily may be kicked out of her home and lose the millions and the land because it was not physically possible for little Lewis to be Bruno's biological son. That through a wild scheme of semen bait-and-switch, or just old fashioned hanky-panky, unto them a child was born. And, that Carmen Huntley is really a Feliz of the "Curse of the Felizes" fame. That she and her mom were trying to buy the very same land that Wes had sold to Bruno.

I had to fill him in on the missing soothsayer and her connection to the incredibly shifty Perry Hirsh. How is he connected to Bruno's murder? I was pretty sure Wes would have a fit about me accepting the thirty grand and want to shuffle me off in the witness protection program.

What I really wanted to do was to ask Wesley about the

poison. Where the hell did it come from? Please, Wes, have a really good answer.

"So," the newly hired attorney, Del Schreiner, said after neatly finishing the chocolate-chip croissant, "where the hell did that strychnine come from?"

"Aren't you supposed to be coming up with all kinds of ways to suppress the evidence? Like illegal search or something?" I asked.

"Of course, Madeline, of course. That's what we always do when there's physical evidence so damaging that no jury in its right mind could fail to convict on it."

My mind raced, feeling trapped. "But what about the Menendez brothers? They admitted shooting their parents, and two juries were still hung trying to decide if they were guilty."

"If there is any way that we can prove that Bruno Huntley had been sexually abusing your friend Wesley for years, I think I can assure you we won't have a problem with the jury."

The thing about humor in horrible situations is this: I never really appreciate it when someone else does it.

Before I was allowed to walk into the conference room I was relieved of everything I was carrying: my purse, my box of croissants, the thermos of cafe au lait, my notebook. No one explained the rules. Perhaps they were wary of concealed weapons or drugs or chocolate chips, who knows?

Sitting on the other side of the large table in the center of the bare room was Wesley, wearing L.A. County prison blue, a one-piece jumpsuit of navy cotton. He didn't really look as bad as I'd imagined.

But as soon as I spoke to him, I could tell the difference in the man. He no longer made jaunty jokes. He was taking things seriously now. He seemed older, somehow, more sober and manly. Like maybe he grew up.

"Wesley!" I just stared at him, tears coming quickly to my eyes. Now where the hell did they come from?

I had so much to tell him, so much to ask him, and I could say nothing.

"Madeline. You know I didn't kill Bruno. You know that, right?"

"Right." Of course I knew it. Of course. How had I started doubting the one person I know best?

"The poison must have been planted in my apartment. I can't remember when the last time was when I baked a cake."

"A cake?"

"They found the strychnine powder in the large glass jar I use for storing cake flour. I was just trying to pin down when was the last time I really looked at the cake flour." He shook his head. "I just don't know."

"Wes, whoever killed Bruno had to know about your history with him, right? That would leave out most of the people involved in Bruno's company and the general Hollywood crowd."

"But why frame me?"

"You know this town. It's not so much talent as just being in the right place at the right time."

Wes smiled weakly.

An officer came over to us and said our time was up.

"Hey, Wesley. Hang tough, okay?"

He just looked at me helplessly. On second thought, maybe I shouldn't have used the word "hang."

Chapter 29

While I was out, Holly fielded calls from everyone we knew. Friends were shocked by the arrest. Clients were making sure we would send back their deposit checks as soon as possible. The tabloids were making offers. One paper was interested in purchasing the exclusive rights to the recipes we'd used for the Halloween party, including how many teaspoons of strychnine per serving. Wes's mother called. Lizzie Bailey called. Lily called. And Chuck Honnett called.

I shuffled through the message slips a few times and put the one from Honnett on the top. I stood there, in front of my desk, just staring at his name written in Holly's loopy penmanship. Then I firmly rotated it to the back of the pack.

"Madeline, I didn't write it down, but Arlo has called you every fifteen minutes. He knows Wesley's been arrested. He sounded kinda tense. Would you like me to get him on the line for you?"

"Thanks, Holly." I had meant to call Arlo last night and tell him about Wesley myself. Things were just getting away from me.

Holly called from her desk in the next room, "They're getting him."

I picked up my phone and waited. Arlo's voice came on almost immediately.

"Mad? Are you all right?"

"I'm fine. I'm angry."

"Mad Bean angry? You're never angry. Hey, I think this is a growth thing for you."

Arlo had a lot of money invested in therapy.

"I wish there was something I could do, Arlo. I wish I could take care of things so Wes could come home. But it's just beyond me, you know?"

"You always want to take care of people, Mad. That's the neat thing about you, but, hey, sometimes you have to give yourself a break. Remember we were talking about getting out of town? How about Vegas? Let's take some time to unwind."

"Unwind? No. I don't think so, Arlo. I've got to stay wound until I can figure out what was really going on at our party last Friday night. It's just a total nightmare. Not only is Wes in trouble, but my whole brilliant career is up in smoke. Our catering company has zero clients."

"Sounds like you've got a lot of grief work to do." This is what Arlo is like when he's being sympathetic. I actually prefer him when everything's a joke.

"Arlo . . ." He could hear the warning in my voice.

"Honey, why don't you and I get together for dinner?" He was trying his best to be there for me.

"Great. Where shall we meet?"

"Actually, I didn't mean tonight. See, we're still in major fucking rewrites tonight. You know how it is on Tuesdays. But how about on, well, Saturday?"

"Sure. Fine."

It's lucky we have dedicated sitcom writers hard at work in Hollywood, or, God forbid, we might not have new episodes of "Suddenly Susan" and "Woman's Work" every week.

I looked at the message now on the top of the stack and wondered what Lily was calling me about. I had become her best friend in the last few days. After dialing the number, I kept sorting through the rest of the slips and stopped, again, at Honnett's.

"Hello?" Lily's breathy voice answered after one ring.

She had called to say how shocked she was that the police had arrested Wesley.

"I guess I should be relieved that they are not seriously considering me as a suspect," Lily said, "but the idea that Wesley murdered Bruno is absurd! I called them and told them that, but they seem to believe in what they are doing."

"Thanks for your sympathy, Lily. I appreciate it."

"Ever since Bruno died, nothing has gone right. I had called to tell you that I've been asked to leave the house. In fact, the trucks are coming tonight to start packing."

"Lily! Are you serious? Why are you moving?" It was the first I'd heard that Lily didn't mean to stay in the Huntley mansion on the hill.

"It's the paternity issue. Bruno was not Lewis's father." She let out a shaky sigh, but then pulled herself together.

"That was the lab's conclusion and that's enough for the attorneys to rescind Bruno's will and award the entire estate to Graydon and Bru, Jr."

"But did you tell them what you told me?"

"Please. The attorney said that for thousands of years babies have been born by a very simple process. And no matter how technical I was trying to make it, Bruno was not Lewis's father. Since Bruno had set up his will to question my loyalty, the lawyers think he was suspicious of me all along."

Lily sounded so matter of fact. No emotion. I wondered, again, what the truth of Lewis's parentage really was.

"But what about your doctor? She'll explain that you were inseminated and Bruno provided the sperm to her office. I think you need to get a lawyer on your side, Lily."

"I never really wanted Bruno's money. Won't it seem like I'm just a greedy little . . . ?" Her voice trailed off.

"I'm sorry you have to leave the house," I said. "Do you need any help?"

"Thanks, Madeline, but the moving company will pack me up. Bru, Jr. is intent on getting me out as soon as possible, it seems."

"Lily, at least check with a lawyer. Maybe you will have

to leave the house eventually, but this moving you out in the middle of the night sounds awfully fast to me. Be careful.''

Things were not going well. I stewed over Lily's odd story for a minute. Then, remembering Holly's sperm bank theory, I pulled out the Yellow Pages.

From my open door, I could hear the phone ring and Holly picking it up. As I flipped through the phone book, looking for sperm banks, Holly peeked in at my door.

''Hi, I know you're busy returning calls, but I've got Carmen Huntley on the line. Do you want to take it?''

Did Carmen know something about Bruno's murder that she had forgotten to mention yesterday?

I thrust the Yellow Pages toward Holly.

''Would you start calling all the sperm banks to see if you can get any information on their customers. It's a long shot, but maybe we can find someone who can verify that Bruno Huntley bought himself some sperm.''

As Holly backed out of my office, her nose in the listings, I picked up the phone.

''Carmen?''

''Yes. I'm sorry to disturb you. I saw in the newspaper that your friend has been arrested. It seems the police must have made a mistake. I just don't believe that your partner was responsible for Bruno's death.''

''He isn't.''

''I called the detective and told him that it didn't make sense to arrest Mr. Westcott. Bruno liked him.''

''Well, Bruno may have liked him, but he still screwed Wes out some money. The cops figure Wes was pretty upset.''

''Oh, but Bruno was planning some big surprise. He was very excited to see your reaction.''

''What are you talking about? What surprise?''

''He wouldn't tell me the details. Just how happy you would be. You and Wesley.''

I didn't need any more mysteries. What Bruno thought

was a wonderful surprise could be downright scary to contemplate.

"Carmen, now you can see why I need to find out who really did kill Bruno. Are you sure you don't know something that would help get Wesley out of trouble?"

"Why, no. My goodness, my mother thought I told you much too much as it was. When she found out your friend was arrested, she . . ." Her voice trailed off.

"What?"

"Please don't be angry. It's only natural that she would feel relieved that the police won't bother us anymore."

How could I get angry? If the cops had arrested Carmen's mother, I know I'd have felt relieved for Wes.

"I wonder if you could tell me something," Carmen said tentatively. "Did Lily lose her inheritance?"

So this was the real reason Carmen had chosen to call. She was scouting information herself.

"Where did you hear that?"

"Gray. He called me a few hours ago and told me to come home. He's been after me ever since I left. But this time he said things had changed. He said that Lily had been cheating on Bruno and now the entire estate will go to the brothers. He's worked a deal with Bru, Jr. so that we'll get control of his father's company and all the land in Los Feliz. Bru needs cash. They worked out an agreeable arrangement."

"So you might own the land you wanted after all?"

"I don't know. I can't believe it's true. My mother said you'd tell me if Graydon is just dreaming."

"According to Lily, I'm afraid it's true."

"Oh my god." I could hear the mixture of emotions in Carmen's voice.

"So will you go back to him?" I asked.

"Mother thinks I should."

"Why am I not surprised?"

"It's just that I'm not sure I could take it anymore. Graydon was always trying to control me. Always deciding who I could see for lunch, or if I could commit to taking a dance class. He wouldn't even let me join a gym.''

"Carmen, since we're trading information, I'd like to get the chronology straight. Bruno and Lily got married about six years ago. And then, you married Gray . . . when?''

"Let's see. Graydon and I got married the next year. They had little Lewis the year after that.''

"When did you and Bruno start . . . ?'' Not exactly delicate, but she had no trouble following me.

"Three years ago.''

"So that was a year after Lewis was born. Did Bruno ever talk about what Lily and he went through to have a baby?''

"No. Of course, that was before Bruno and I got together. But I do remember there was some talk in the family. Lily couldn't get pregnant. And then there was the contest.''

"What contest?''

"Bru, Jr.'s wife Missy and I used to laugh at those men sometimes. The Huntley men. They thought they were so macho! It was kind of funny. I remember not long after I'd been married, Gray said he couldn't sleep with me for a week. This had something to do with a contest his dad had set up.''

"What kind of contest?''

"Lily was going to some fancy doctor in Beverly Hills. Bruno told his older boys that he'd had his sperm tested as part of the process to see what was wrong with Lily. Anyway, Bruno said that the doctor had never seen sperm with such high numbers. You know, for all the weird stuff they test sperm for. Bruno bragged that he had scored the highest ever on this doctor's sperm tests.''

Wait. Back up a moment. This had to be impossible. And then I got it. Of course. This was the very way Bruno used to embellish things. A man with a vasectomy claiming to have a high sperm count! Brother.

"Somehow, Bruno thought up this funny challenge and got the boys to agree. He offered a thousand dollars to the son who could top his scores on the sperm count.''

"He wanted his sons to get their sperm tested?"

"Right. He dared them to compete with their old man. Missy and I thought they were out of their minds, but it was a male bonding ritual, Huntley-style. They met one morning in the parking lot attached to the Cedars-Sinai Medical Center. The boys were to do their business into these cups, and then Bruno would take them up to the doctor to get tested."

"Wait a minute. You mean Bru, Jr. and Graydon actually drove to a parking lot, sat in their cars and . . ."

"Gave a sample, yes. Missy called it the Jerk Olympics. Get it?"

"Yes." In every sense of the word.

"See, Graydon was so competitive he insisted we couldn't sleep together for a week. In order to build up his sperm."

My head was spinning. I was beginning to believe Bruno devised this bizarre family contest for the sole purpose of gathering sperm samples. It seemed he'd dipped into his very own gene pool to inseminate his unsuspecting wife. And that meant Lewis Huntley's half-brothers were actually, biologically, his two dads. Amazing.

"Who won the contest?" I had to ask.

"Bru's sperm count was about 150 million per cc of semen and Graydon had only about 100 million."

"One hundred million sperm? Per cubic centimeter of semen?" I asked. (I made a mental note to get my diaphragm checked.)

"That doesn't tell you how lively the sperm are swimming. Now what do they call that? 'Mobility' I think," she guessed.

Upward? I smiled at my own joke.

"Motility?" I suggested.

"Something like that. Anyway, Bruno declared Bru the winner and Gray was demanding a recount." She was laughing. "Typical."

"That's one odd family you married into."

"All families are odd, aren't they? When you get to

know their secrets?'' Carmen, with her own bitter family
sorrows and strange sexual alliances, was clearly beyond
being shocked by mere macho posturing.

As I hung up, Holly entered my office and slumped in
the comfortable chair that faces my desk. She carelessly
tossed one of her legs over the rolled arm of the chair.
Today she had on black leggings and a black leather bra.
She dangled a heavy clog from the foot that was looped
over the chair.

''No luck with the sperm banks,'' she sadly offered.
''They have this confidentiality thing.''

''I figured. But the sperm question may be answered.''
I filled her in on the Jerk Olympics. Where I had been sort
of stunned at the madness of it all, she was totally amused.

''It's not such a bad idea,'' she said. ''Maybe when we
get serious with a guy we should insist he get his sperm
checked. I mean, it could be pretty important information
if you want to have children.''

''So what do you do if the guy you're in love with has
problem sperm?'' I challenged.

''Toss him,'' Holly said, unconcerned with trivial issues
like love.

''Right. Say Christian Slater asked you to marry him and
it turned out his sperm was lazy? Low motility, say. What
you gonna do?''

Holly's eyes flashed at me. She untangled herself from
my office furniture and rose to her full six feet. ''Oh, throw
Christian Slater at me, huh? Think that will win your ar-
gument?''

She walked to the door and then turned. ''Well, I'd tell
Chris and his slow-assed sperm to take a hike!''

The wind had picked up and was beginning to rattle the
glass in the multipaned windows. The sky had turned the
bruised shade of smoke, and as I fastened the doors that
led out to the patio from the living room, I saw the first fat
drops pelt the glass.

It was nearing six o'clock, and I told Holly she should
go already. Although we were critically short on bookings,

she'd had a full day of work, what with cancelling food orders for parties we would not be catering, and paying bills with money we probably didn't have. Before Holly had a chance to give me the bottom line, I shushed her and told her I'd rather hear the bad news tomorrow. She took the hint.

I decided I'd go over to Lily's and unload my sperm theories on her tonight. Why wait? Especially if her stepsons were kindly packing up her p.j.s and escorting her out of her home this very evening. I quickly changed into warmer clothes. As I stepped outside, I yanked up the hood of my camel-colored parka and wondered if I should go back for an umbrella.

I jumped into my car. Chewed-up wiper blades clicked like a metronome without much success at wiping anything. With thirty thousand dollars stashed in my underwear drawer, you'd think I'd get around to having my car fixed.

On second thought, maybe I could find an all-night service station. With a virtuous stab at my dragon of procrastination, I jumped out of my trusty Wagoneer and went back for the cash.

Chapter 30

I consider myself a pretty good driver. Except when it's dark, and the rain is pouring down in sheets and I've got less than one-quarter of a functioning wiper. I was going slow, my whole body tensed forward, trying to get closer to the windshield, as if that would clear up this mess.

By the time I arrived at the house, I was exhausted. Ahead, on the last turn of Winding Oaks Drive, stood two enormous trucks, parked on the wrong side of the street, as close as they could get to the bottom of the Huntley driveway. I saw moving men pushing dollies, walking slowly as if undisturbed by the heavy rainfall. I parked, pointing the Wagoneer uphill, headlight to headlight with the bottommost truck, saying a silent prayer to the god of parking brakes.

Mud and debris trickled down the steep road, making it impossible to avoid getting filthy, although I stepped as best I could around the worst of the puddles. As I hiked up the driveway, I noticed a number of cars had made it up the hill on this wet night and parked on the circular driveway in front of the Huntley mansion.

I thought I recognized Bru, Jr.'s Jaguar, and perhaps that BMW525 belonged to Graydon, and there were others. As I ran to the front door, damp just about everywhere my hip-length parka was not, I thought I saw a profile in one of the parked cars. Startled, I turned back to get a better look. Sitting in the front passenger seat of a Bentley was Angelica Sands. Now what possible need would anyone have for a fake soothsayer on this particular night?

I thought about going up to the car and getting her attention. But the wind was yanking at my jacket like a particularly annoying three-year-old, and I chose instead to leave my questions to a drier time and place.

The door of the house was opened by Rosalinda Luquin, the Huntleys' nanny.

"Oh, hi!" I said, stepping in and shaking myself like a retriever, droplets of water spraying the lovely Turkish carpet in the entry hall. What the hell? The Huntley boys could afford to get it cleaned. "How are you, Rosa?"

"Too bad," she told me, earnestly.

"Too bad about what?"

"It is too bad tonight, Miss Madeline. Too bad in this house. I must quit my job. Only I don't want to tell Mrs. Lily. She is having problems, you understand? Many problems in her life."

"Yes, I know."

"Now my Babalu, he is hiding from me. Ay, such a boy!"

"I'm sure Lewis will be found soon."

Rosalinda was dressed in a heavy coat and carried an umbrella. I also saw a suitcase tucked near the door.

"I guess you're leaving, then."

"I see the face. The face of a man. I see this face in the bushes by the fountain. I was looking for Babalu outside. I don't want to leave without saying goodbye to my boy, but then I see this face."

"Who was outside?"

"An old man. Skinny with long gray hair. I get scared. It is the one thing too many for me. This house it is too busy with witches." She took her umbrella and picked up her suitcase. "Mrs. Lily stay in a hotel tonight. I go now to my sister." I saw sadness in her determined face as she moved past me and out the door into the black rain.

Coming up the drive past Rosalinda as she left were two men from the moving company. They had dollied up a huge stack of large unassembled cardboard boxes. As I held the door open for them, they sloshed through the entry hall and into the living room. I followed them and found more than a few Huntley family members.

The workers set about constructing the cardboard boxes. Lily asked them politely to remove their boots as they were muddying up her floor. Before she could see me, I tiptoed back to the entry and removed my wet rubber-soled shoes.

It was then that I became aware of voices coming from the study. One was the unmistakable whine of Bru, Jr.

"See, the thing is, is everything's okay now. I've got the money, so don't worry."

"Don't worry? I don't worry when *I've* got the money, you imbecile. Get it?"

"All right! All right! Let go!"

I had to see who was threatening Bru. Just a peek. Movies can't be trusted for accuracy and I was curious to see what an "enforcer" really looked like.

He looked like Perry Hirsh.

I stepped back before either of them saw me.

"I want the money tonight, Bozo," Hirsh was saying.

"Tonight? I can't get it tonight, Perry. I mean, I just inherited it. You know? It takes a little time for the paperwork, but I'm good for it, man. You know that."

"Yeah, right."

"Hey, didn't I get your sister that audition she wanted?"

"That was my cousin, Doofuss. And you're right. I forgot to thank you. She met up with your old man and he really thought she had talent. Yeah, he wanted to put her in one of his movies. Too bad the guy winds up dead, eh? Now she won't be able to use that valuable contact, will she, shithead? You think I owe you, asshole? You think you done Perry some big favor? You've done me exactly squat!"

"Madeline? Is that you?"

I spun around to see Lily, standing in the archway of the living room.

"Hi. I hope I'm not coming at a bad time." Although I didn't see how there could be a worse one.

"No, of course not. Would you like some hot coffee? You look drenched." Ever the perfect hostess as her family and fortress crumble around her.

"No thanks. I just came over for a minute. I've found out a few things that may help you with the lawyers."

"As you can see, it's probably too late for anything like that, but I appreciate the thought."

"It's really not . . ." I let the sentence just hang there as Donnie walked through the living room into the entry hall and up to Lily. He stood about an inch closer to her than I would have thought platonic, but who can judge by an inch?

"Hi," he said to me. Then to Lily, "The guys want to know if they can start packing?"

Just then, Bru, Jr. walked out of the study and screamed, "Hey, stupid! Don't ask her! I own this house now, got it? Tell them just her personal stuff. She can take her clothes and that's . . ."

"You're pathetic, you know that?" Donnie cut him off with a look of disgust.

"You're fired, Don! You know that? You're out of here! Get out!"

"Stop it." Lily did not exactly raise her voice, but she was firmer than usual. "Donnie is here as a friend."

"Hey, man, what's your problem?" Donnie was getting riled, but it was in Lily's defense. "The movers are all over the place. Lewis is missing. Lily's got her hands full."

"I've got no problem," Bru snarled. "Just find Lewis and get the hell out!"

To this ugly scene entered Graydon and Carmen, coming from the back hallway that leads to the kitchen.

"What's all this about Lewis?" Gray wanted to know.

"Don here is real concerned about him," Bru said in a syrupy tone. "We all know that Dad wasn't Lewis's real father. So who was? Hey, Don! Want to fess up?"

I looked up to see Lily blush. Donnie was steaming now,

and he pulled back to take a swing. I'd been doing a bit of boxing training to work out, so I knew to brace myself in a more balanced stance, in case Donnie needed backup.

Before the punches could start, Carmen said, "Can't we just act like grownups? Don't you boys know how to behave when you win?"

It was an odd moment. Standing there in the entry were Bru, Jr., Graydon, Carmen, Lily, Donnie, and myself. Off to one side were the sounds of moving men making boxes. Off to another lurked Perry Hirsh, out of sight in the study. No one spoke.

Then, the doorbell rang. Who wasn't here? I wondered. The answer, as Lily moved to open the door, was Mark Baker, the attorney for Bruno Huntley's estate. I figured he was here to oversee the orderly change of possession of the property. It was about as orderly as a seventh-grade boys' locker room.

"Well. Look who we have here." He smiled as he entered, clearly not an expert in the kind of tension you could cut with a Sabatier. Lawyers.

"Hello, Mark," Lily said. "Don't worry. I was just about to leave. Only Babalu . . . that's my son Lewis, is missing. The nanny is looking for him now. Otherwise I would have been gone already."

"Good thing you're not." Mark Baker stood there, dripping onto the entry rug. I felt a little better about my own mess. "Ahem. Could we all step into the living room? There have been some developments."

"Of course." Lily took charge of the moment, and we all shuffled into the living room and just stood there.

"Sit down," Baker suggested, taking time to get comfortable in the armchair he'd used on Sunday at the reading of the will.

A few of us did, but I noticed that Bru and Gray remained standing. Bru's arms were crossed over his chest. Gray had that lost look that so often accompanied him wherever he went.

"Don't tell us that anything's changed, because it

hasn't,'' Bru asserted. ''You lawyers agreed that the estate
goes to my brother and me. That's final.''

''No, nothing has changed in that regard,'' Baker agreed.

Too bad. I had hoped that Lily's doctor had convinced
Mark Baker at the last minute, but nothing would change
if Lily wouldn't defend her own interests.

''So we get the house and the money, right?'' Bru was
gloating, looking straight at Lily, rubbing it in.

''Not exactly. That's what I've come here to advise you.
Lily notified my office that she would be vacating the house
this evening and turning the keys over to Graydon and
Bruno Huntley, Jr., and that is something I've come all the
way over here in this wretched storm to prevent.''

''What!'' That was Gray. He was just getting that something was wrong. His expression went from fuzzy to frantic.

''Calm down, Graydon,'' his brother whined. ''We'll get
it as soon as the paperwork is settled. It's all just a bullshit
waste of time, Mr. Lawyer.''

''Not quite.'' Baker pulled out a sheaf of papers from
his briefcase and then looked up at the gathered group.

''While it is true that the Huntley sons do inherit the full
share of their father's estate, I am here to inform you that
the net value of that estate at the time of Mr. Huntley's
death was one dollar.''

Oh boy.

''That's a lie!'' from Bru.

''What?'' from the ever-original Graydon.

''Boys, your father's estate does not include any assets
to speak of. No cash. No investments. No real property. No
furnishings. And no holdings in Bruno Huntley Productions
or any of the theatrical and television properties owned by
that company.'' He looked up, directly into Bru's eyes.
''Do you understand me, young man? You are to leave your
stepmother alone and vacate these premises.''

''What kind of bullshit is this? If Dad didn't own all that
stuff, who did? You gonna tell us he gave it all away to
some charity before he died?'' Bru was screaming. For
once, I guess I couldn't blame him. ''This is a ripoff! This

is some attorney's way of ripping off the family!''

God, this was familiar. Don Antonio Feliz was probably spinning in his grave.

"As you've chosen to air your ugliness in public, I am certainly entitled to sue you for slander. And I would, too, if I thought you had a penny to pay in damages. As it is, just leave at once. I don't care to see your face ever again.'' For an old man, he was cold as ice.

Bru, Jr. collapsed onto a sofa.

"Where did it all go?'' Gray asked. Not belligerent and accusing. Just . . . lost.

"That is not information that I am at liberty to divulge.'' Mark turned to Lily and offered in a kinder voice, ''Would you like me to hire a guard for you, my dear, to help you keep trespassers off the property tonight?''

Lily was looking pretty lost herself. She shook her head no, and Mark Baker stood up to leave.

I needed a phone. As Baker had a few last words with the brothers, I walked out of the living room, across the entry, and looked tentatively into the study. No sign of Hirsh. I picked up the telephone and called Rudy. I figured it was better to be on the safe side, and Lily might not realize what she was in for. Rudy said he'd be there in an hour and I told him how grateful I was.

As I hung up the phone, a side door opened, and into the study walked Perry Hirsh.

"Hi, gorgeous.'' He smiled at me.

We were friends now.

"Hello.''

"So we meet again. What is that called?'' he asked.

Bad luck?

"Fate!'' he answered his own question, like he was a brain surgeon he was so smart.

"I saw Angelica out in the car. Maybe she's cold?''

"You know, I like you better in that tight skirt you wore over to my house. Why don't you get yourself cleaned up and come on by later. We're having a party.''

"Thanks. I'm busy.''

"Some other time." He didn't seem perturbed.

"So, what gives? What was the big pow-wow in the other room?"

He'd find out soon enough, and since we were so close, I figured I'd be the first one to tell him.

"The attorney told Bru and his brother that they inherited an estate worth exactly nothing. Somehow Bruno must have spent or lost all of his money. There's nothing left."

"That a fact? So where's Bozo gonna come up with the twenty-eight large?" Perry was getting agitated, and I didn't want to see what he was like when he was really ticked off.

"Maybe we can talk later," I offered, as I left the study. Walking fast out toward the living room, I thought about this latest shift in the financial picture. In a way, it was pure Bruno to pretend he was worth millions even when he was broke, putting on that outrageous Halloween party, keeping up this enormous house and grounds. Reality had been a fairly worthless concept to that man.

The cast in the large living room had shifted. There was no trace of Bru, which was just as well. The lawyer had left, and Donnie was no longer in the room. As I approached those remaining, it was Carmen who was speaking.

". . . not if I heard that man correctly. That man said your father wasn't worth a penny!"

"Wait a minute, honey," Graydon said quickly. "Don't get hysterical. Bru will fix things. Let's go home."

Carmen stared at her husband. She just stared.

"Let's go home," Gray repeated, putting his arm around her.

Lily was watching the scene from her position, curled up on a large moss-colored velvet wing chair. The chair was so large, she seemed like a child.

"Thank God," Carmen whispered. "It's finally over."

"Honey, nothing's over. You don't know these lawyers. Listen to me, honey. I'm in business. I know all about how these things work. They're just trying to scare us, but we

Huntleys don't scare easy, do we?'' he asked her, pleading.

"I want a divorce. I want out," she said quietly.

"Carmen." His voice was getting hoarse. I could see the tears coming. "Carmen, honey, don't." He held her close to him and whispered, "You'll get the land, Carmenita. I promise. I know how much it means to you. You'll get it."

Carmen stood stock-still, making Gray's hug seem awkward. He pulled back from the rebuff, and finally let her go.

"So you're not coming home?" he asked, defeated.

"No. I'll call my mother." With that, she turned and left the room.

Gray looked up, as if for the first time noticing he'd had an audience. He didn't seem embarrassed. I was again reminded of the quaint Huntley tradition of staging their most intimate and humiliating moments in public.

"She'll come back," he suggested to no one in particular.

Well they might take these scenes in stride, but I, for one, felt miserably out of place. I tried to get Lily's attention. I needed a few private minutes to explain what I'd found out about the sperm samples and then I could leave.

"Lily," I called out.

But just then the moving men came back into the living room. They surveyed the floor. There was barely a square inch of the enormous expanse that wasn't covered by a brand-new cardboard box.

"I guess we gotta leave now," one of the men said. "I just got paged. Some lawyer just called our office and said what we're doing is illegal or something."

"Fine," Lily said. "Thank you."

"The thing is, who's gonna pay? You got 370 boxes here at two bucks a box."

"I suppose you should bill the man who hired you," Lily suggested.

"The thing is, the office told me not to leave without I get paid."

"Well, I didn't order these boxes," Lily explained.

"And it appears I have no need for them. Perhaps you should just unfold them again and take them away."

The two men laughed. "We need a check."

"Sorry." Lily spoke in her sweet breathy voice, but didn't back down. I guess it's easier to bounce back from shocking news when the news happens to be in your favor.

Donnie walked back into the room. "Hey, Madeline. There's a call for you."

"Me?"

Who knew I was here?

Chapter 31

*T*he study was empty and this time, before I picked up the phone, I checked the attached bathroom. No one lurking about. The Huntleys had three lines coming into their home and the telephone had buttons for each as well as one to place calls on hold. I saw only one light flashing and answered.

"Madeline? It's me, Lizzie. I'd just about given up trying to find you."

"This has been one wild night."

"Tell me about it! Have you been outside lately? They're calling for flooding, mudslides, the works. Hey watch yourself driving home."

"The weather is the least of my worries. Things are going nuts inside the house. The nanny quit, Lewis is missing, Bruno's property has been changing hands on an hourly basis, and now it turns out he was worth just about nothing. Movers are leaving as we speak, and on top of everything else, Wesley is still locked up in jail."

"Look, the more I think about it, the more I have to agree with you. I just can't get convinced that Wes killed Bruno."

"No kidding."

"I went out on a limb today and told my people I thought they got the wrong guy. They were not thrilled with my attitude. I figure, the only way to turn this turd into a rose is to find a suspect who looks even better to the D.A."

"You have such a delicate turn of a phrase."

"Forensics just shot us a report on the fingerprints found on the brandy decanter, which you didn't hear from me."

"Go on." I was excited. Clearly there must be evidence that doesn't point to Wesley. Perhaps I was going to get a chance to hear some.

"No prints distinguishable on the body of the decanter. It was cut crystal. But on the glass stopper and on the smooth bottom surface, they lifted four readable prints. There was one each from Bruno and Lily and their daughter-in-law Carmen, and one clear right forefinger print from an unidentified party. By the size, it's most likely female."

Or a child. "You got prints from the entire family?"

"Of course."

"What about from the boy, Lewis?"

"Be reasonable. He's maybe three years old!"

"What about Carmen's mother? Did you . . ."

"Yes. It didn't match. We even tried to match it to his ex-wives' prints, and, I might add, yours."

"And you still can't match that one print. But what does this mean for Wes?"

"That Wesley Westcott did not touch Bruno's decanter of Armagnac."

"Won't they say that he wore gloves?"

"Gloves would have smudged the other fingerprints on the stopper. And they weren't smudged."

"Thanks, Lizzie."

"*De nada.* Listen, if you get anything really incriminating over there at the Huntleys, don't do anything foolish. Just call me, okay?"

I kept thinking about the unidentified fingerprint. With all the Huntley women accounted for, I was at a loss. I left the study, and as I walked through the entry hall, a sudden flash of lightning lit up the courtyard parking area outside. The pelting rain had softened to drizzle, and looking through the leaded-glass windows, I was surprised to spot Perry Hirsh's Bentley still parked out front.

I stepped into my rubber shoes and grabbed my dripping

coat from the hook where I'd left it. Pulling up the hood, I scooted out into the night. By the time I'd covered the twenty feet to the Bentley, the rain seemed to come to a stop. I tapped with force on the window and motioned that Angelica should roll it down.

She had watched me approach, but didn't seem in a hurry to unlock her door. At the sound of my tapping, she called to me through the closed car window, "I don't want to get Perry's leather seats wet. He'd kill me."

"Come on out!" I yelled to her.

She wasn't happy about it, but she did open the door and quickly slide out. The sound of water, dripping off leaves and house, gurgling down drains, rushing down the steep driveway, stood in contrast to the sudden lull in the storm.

"I just got a call from a friend of mine," I told her. "Seems the police identified some fingerprints on Bruno's private bottle of brandy."

"So?"

"That's where the poison was, in Bruno's Armagnac."

She stared at me.

"What were your prints doing on the decanter, Angelica?"

She whipped back so fast, I thought she was fainting. But then she swung her body around and hurled her clenched fist at me. Before I could react, the garnets in her ring zoomed into closeup.

I lunged left, slipping on slick pavement, falling against the car. She tried correcting her aim as I fell, and just missed slamming her cheap jewels into my cheek. Untouched by Angelica, I still hit the ground pretty hard.

With the force of her unlanded punch, she swiped the passenger door of the Bentley. I looked up to see a double line of scratches etched into the twenty-four coats of white lacquer.

Then, she started kicking at me. Hard. From my seated position, I grabbed her flying ankle, jumped up, and twisted. She collapsed on the wet pavement as I pulled myself up.

She was wearing a party dress, and as she crashed down, the flimsy red skirt hiked up, revealing a long shapely leg in muddied and ripped hose. One high-heeled red pump had kicked off somewhere and she was scowling at her right hand. Several long acrylic nails had broken off.

I balanced lightly on my feet, waiting for her to spring up, feeling wet and sore and ready.

Angelica just sat there looking spent. "I didn't kill Bruno, if that's what you think. I just had a few drinks with him last week. I probably left my fingerprint on the decanter then. I didn't poison him."

Something caught her attention and her eyes darted up.

"Oh, shit! Shit!" she screamed, shaking her bruised hand.

The wind had picked up and I could hear the sound of rainfall again. Angelica sat there, swearing, eyes fixed to the spot where Perry's pride and joy had been scarred.

I ran the few steps to the front door of the house and looked back. Angelica's hair was collapsing in the renewed vigor of the downpour. Her dress was ruined. And by the way she was holding her right hand, there would be pain pills in her future.

I shut the massive door with a slam, twitchy in the aftermath of the fight. Then I remembered Perry Hirsh. I had just decked his cousin and she was sure to blame me for the scratches on his Bentley, but had they plotted together to kill Bruno?

Somehow, I had stepped over a line. Things had turned dangerous. I needed to call the police, but I couldn't use a phone where I might be overheard.

I raced up the grand staircase, two steps at a time, until I hit the second-floor landing. Spread out before me was a hallway so vast it was actually larger than my first apartment. Closed doors could be seen running down each side of the corridor. No wonder Holly had gotten lost the night of the party. I put a little space between the staircase and me and randomly picked a door on my left.

I shut the door quickly and turned on the light. A yellow

room. I had no idea whose. The large bed was covered by a pale yellow gingham bedspread. The plush yellow carpet seemed never to have been stepped upon. That is, until I showed up with my wet size sevens. My parka was dripping, so I grabbed the telephone and stretched its long cord all the way into the adjoining bathroom.

Holding the yellow phone to my ear with my shoulder, I shrugged the raincoat into the bathtub and stomped my feet onto a bath mat. Honnett answered on the third ring. Funny how I had memorized his direct number after staring at his message all afternoon.

"Honnett? It's Madeline Bean. I'm over at the Huntley estate. You've got to send someone over right away. There's a woman here that may have been involved in Bruno's murder, and she . . ."

"Hey. Slow down! What are you talking about? What woman?"

"The soothsayer from the party. The one we couldn't find and then she just turned up at my house yesterday. Her name is Angelica Sands. Look," I was getting impatient with all the explanations, "she took a swing at me."

"Yeah? I've felt like that," Honnett said.

"Honnett."

"Okay, okay. Just tell me something that hooks her to the murder and I'll be there myself in five minutes."

"I accused her of leaving her fingerprint on the brandy decanter and she tried to slug me."

"Are you hurt?"

"I can take care of myself. But she admitted that she had her hands on Bruno's decanter. That proves she's the unidentified fingerprint, damn it!"

"Whoa! Wait! Even if this Sands woman did leave a fingerprint, it proves very little."

"What?"

"Honey, you've got a pretty good source inside the print lab, but you gotta start flirting with the toxicology boys. Then you'd already know there was no trace of strychnine in the decanter."

If it wasn't in the decanter, then whoever poisoned Bruno must have put the strychnine into his glass.

"So even if your soothsayer had her hands all over that decanter, it proves nothing."

"Yeah, I got it, I got it."

My mind was backtracking furiously. The real killer would know there was no poison in the decanter. So why had Angelica attacked me? Because she didn't know it wasn't important. Damn!

"Now what would be real handy is finding Bruno's glass. That might tell us who poisoned him."

"It wasn't Wesley."

Honnett chuckled. "My mama used to warn me not to get involved with girls who like to fight."

"She was a smart woman."

Chapter 32

I looked into the mirror above the yellow sink. The wind and the rain had pulled my hair out of its tight chignon and it was curling this way and that. Taking a moment to wash up, I considered what I'd learned.

It hadn't exactly been easy to follow the ping-pong match of who would win Bruno's fortune, but now, even if Lily could convince the executors, there was nothing for her to inherit.

I thought about not telling her the details of her husband's sperm-gathering activities. Perhaps it was kinder to leave her some sweet illusions of Bruno, but that went against my nature. Lily was an adult. The truth means something. I had to tell her.

My hair more or less in place, my shoes wiped down, my face freshly washed, I opened the door into the silent second-floor hallway. Only the distant ticking of a clock could be heard. I padded to the landing, my feet sinking into carpet that was certainly luxurious, if a little difficult to walk on.

At the top of the staircase was a large oil portrait of Bruno. I hadn't noticed it when I was dashing up the stairs, but now I stopped and looked at the man. He must have urged the artist to play up his resemblance to Clint Eastwood.

What did you do with your glass, Bruno? Where is that brandy snifter?

And then I was seized by a memory. Bruno had invited me to share a drink with him many years ago. The two of us sat on a sofa that was placed in the atrium off the kitchen. The Armagnac was nice, but certainly not as spectacular as he seemed to think. When we finished, Bruno insisted we throw the empty brandy snifters into the fireplace.

"These are expensive," I replied, studying the Baccarat crystal, figuring them to be at least a hundred bucks.

"One hundred and seventy-five dollars per stem," Bruno informed me, smiling. "But who really gives a damn? It's fun to break something that costs a lot. You should try it."

He stood up. And with a grunt, he threw the glass into the fireplace. The droplets of Armagnac caught fire and flared as the fine crystal shattered, then tinkled against the stone hearth.

"Come on, sport. I dare you!" Bruno was amused at my resistance to wanton destruction, even on this mild upper-middle-class level. I could see it in his eyes. He knew I never would.

So I tossed my glass into the fire.

Laughing, he yelled, "Bravo! I didn't think you had the balls."

I flushed with pride and rejoiced in the freedom of my new spirit. And then he demanded that I pay him the $175.

Looking now at Bruno's portrait, I wondered if he had felt like breaking things the night of his Halloween party?

As I descended the stairs, the door to the powder room opened and Carmen Huntley, her makeup perfect, stepped out. Either this was another coincidence, or Carmen spends a whole lot of time in powder rooms, well, powdering.

"Hello," I said.

"I was just getting ready to leave. Mother should have been here by now." She sounded annoyed.

"The roads are pretty bad tonight. You know, I was just remembering the way Bruno threw his brandy glass at the fireplace one time. Was he still doing that?"

"He liked the power," she said. "When we were first

together, he'd break those expensive glasses of his all the time. Why?''

"I was thinking about the night of his murder . . .''

"Oh, Madeline. I really don't want to talk about that anymore. Okay?''

"No one can find the glass that Bruno was drinking from and I wondered . . . did he throw his glass against a wall that night?''

She looked down, her thick black lashes almost touching her cheeks. Then she looked straight at me.

"I think he did throw it. He was angry after our talk. So he gulped the liquor and tossed the glass.''

"Where was this?''

"On the path where it curves past the guest house and goes on to the tennis court. It was about halfway down that path, near the statue of the old man by the little bench.''

There was a sharp tap. Carmen opened the front door to find her mother standing on the porch. She was half-opening and closing her umbrella, as if to rid it of the rain.

Carmen zipped her leather jacket and said, "Let's go.''

"Is that all you are wearing? What's the matter with you? It's a storm outside. You'll get sick!''

"Mother. Isn't your car parked nearby?''

Just then, Graydon walked into the entrance hall. "You're leaving? Weren't you going to say goodbye?'' He seemed to be suffering and trying to spread it around.

"Who's leaving?'' Bru, Jr. walked back into the entry. "Madeline what are you still doing here? Go home!''

"My Carmen is leaving, young man. She is coming back to her family where she belongs.''

"Mother!'' Carmen spoke loudly, catching all of us by surprise.

"Yes, my little girl?''

"I'm not your little girl.'' Carmen looked at the assembled group. Bru, Jr., leaning against the newel post, haughty, mocking; Graydon, forlorn; her mother, half-opening and shutting her umbrella in nervous impatience; and me.

"Madeline, can you give me a ride?" she asked.

"Well . . ."

Both mother and husband wailed protests.

"I'm tired. Madeline will drive me. Now everybody, please leave me alone."

"Wait for me in my car." I offered her the keys. "It's the black Grand Wagoneer on the street. I won't be more than a few minutes."

Carmen swept past her mother on the front step, and walked out into the wind and rain. Without so much as a scarf, she disappeared down the driveway as I turned from the muddled group and made my way back towards the kitchen.

I just had to tell Lily about the sperm, and then I had one little idea to check out, and then, once and for all, I was out of there.

Chapter 33

"*I*'ve got to talk to you."

I was speaking to Lily's back as she sat motionless on the cushioned window seat, pressing her cheek against the cold glass. The large family room was wallpapered in an intricate green ivy pattern and filled with leather sofas and dark wood. It took Lily a while to speak.

"Can it wait, do you think?" she asked, without moving.

I turned to leave, but just then, Lily looked up at me, her head in profile against the black window. The dim light from a shaded lamp picked up the wetness of her face.

"Madeline, I know something."

"What do you know?" I asked gently.

"About the poison. About the strychnine." Her long blonde hair was in a thick and intricate braid down her back. She turned again to the window, talking more to the blank darkness outside than to me.

"I know where the poison must have come from."

It was hard to hear her, what with the clatter of the rain hitting the windows and Lily's naturally soft voice. I moved in closer and sat down next to her on the deep window seat. Her legs were drawn up under her long wool skirt, her cheek was still flush against the window. I sat the opposite way, my feet on the floor, but with my ear now close enough to pick up every word.

"Where did the strychnine come from?"

"Bruno bought it himself," she said. I was close enough

221

to watch each tear as it clung to her light lashes. "We have this miserable problem with mice and rats. We have four acres of landscaped property and another forty acres that are pretty much wild. So the rats can be horrid. We kept finding them in the house and I told Bruno I couldn't have that."

I didn't interrupt, hoping she'd continue talking.

"Bruno was planning to soak loaves of bread in a solution of strychnine and spread them over the property when we were away next week. The gardeners would have had plenty of time to sweep up the bodies."

A nasty image, but I said nothing.

"When he'd been a boy, they'd had rats at their vacation cottage in Colorado and his dad had done the same thing."

She had come to a halt, not wanting to go further. I nudged her along.

"So did Bruno buy the poison?"

"Well, yes. But of course he never got to use it. He kept it locked up," she said, virtuously.

"Locked up where?"

"In the liquor cabinet."

Oh boy. Whoever had access to the brandy also had access to the strychnine.

"Lily, the police came to the house and got the decanter of Armagnac on Sunday. They should have found the strychnine then. Why didn't they?"

"I moved it," Lily mumbled. "When the police said they were going to search the liquor cabinet, suddenly everything looked so bad. Why hadn't I told the detective about the poison right after the party? I was sure they'd arrest me!"

Fresh tears made twin streaks down her face.

"Besides, I wasn't sure who . . ." She stopped.

"Who else knew Bruno had strychnine locked up in the liquor cabinet?"

She still wouldn't look at me. Her voice was now only a whisper. "I thought to myself, how would Bruno handle this? And then I decided to move the strychnine someplace where no one would find it.''

''Where'd you put it?''

''In our bedroom safe. But when the police found a half-pound of strychnine in your friend's house, it seemed like too much of a coincidence. And when I checked my safe this morning, the bag was gone.''

Why will no one ever listen to me? Didn't I tell them Wesley was framed! And now, finally, some proof.

In as calm a voice as I could muster, I asked, ''Who has the combination to your private safe, Lily?''

''Just me.'' She thought. ''And the family.'' She paused. ''Oh, and a few people at Bruno's company, and the housekeeper.'' She stopped. ''And some former employees.''

Goodbye simple proof.

''Anyone else?''

''Actually, I don't think we had the combination changed when we married. Maybe his ex-wives?''

I stared at her.

''See we don't keep anything of real value in it.''

I rethought the situation and got hopeful again. No matter how many zillions of people had that combination, I was almost certain that Wesley was not one of them.

I reached out and touched her shoulder. Finally, she looked at me. ''Lily, you've got to talk to the police. Just tell them the truth. It'll be okay, and it could help Wes.''

She nodded and then she actually smiled at me. ''I'm glad I told you. You know, you're just like Bruno. I was feeling horrible and you told me what to do.''

Just like Bruno. Well. I'm sure she meant it as a compliment.

Donnie arrived with a tray, a teapot, and two cups.

''I'd like to check something out in the garden,'' I said.

''Not tonight! Surely it can wait for the storm to pass.''

''It's ugly,'' Donnie agreed. ''When I was in the kitchen, I heard trees coming down, the wind is so strong.''

''I better not put this off.''

As I headed for the upstairs bedroom where I'd ditched

my jacket, I saw Lily begin to pour the tea. Donnie was turning the key that started the gas jets in the fireplace.

Back downstairs, the house seemed quiet now, large and warm and snug against the howling of the wind outside. Moving through the halls, I caught a glimpse of Graydon, still here, still moping, in front of a T.V. set in a small office just off the kitchen.

Outside, the rain lashed down at a forty-five-degree angle, with gusts often whipping it sideways. I abandoned my attempts to hold the hood up over my hair and just moved as quickly as I could. I passed the same familiar cars parked in the drive: Graydon's BMW, Bru's Jaguar, and Hirsh's scratched Bentley, although any trace of the soothsayer was long gone.

Fumbling under my clothing, I retrieved the envelope that still contained sixty five-hundred-dollar bills. It was warm from being held snug in the waistband of my tan tights. With a pencil from my parka pocket, I wrote "Sorry about the scratches. Hope this covers the repair of your car. M. Bean." The door was unlocked. I left the package for Perry on the driver's seat. Ah, well. Never trust a soothsayer when she predicts you're about to come into a lot of money.

I trudged around the huge house, and soon found the large marble bust of an elderly man near the bench where Carmen and Bruno had met, she to plead for family unity and he to sip his Armagnac. So what had happened to that glass?

The path was paved with large, rough-cut stone blocks, perhaps three feet square. They would have provided a suitable surface for a nice smash, but surely the police would have noticed any shattered glass on the night of the party.

Once I stopped fighting the idea of being cold and wet, I began to feel giddy, like a child playing in puddles. My parka was holding up well, but my legs were getting soaked through their tights and the bottom hem of my cashmere tunic was soggy. Wes gave me the dress last Christmas to celebrate our first profitable year. Now the dress, as well as the business, was probably ruined. Ah, well.

Water was rolling off my head, springing my curly hair into long wet ringlets, pouring down my face like a vigorous cold shower. Giant puddles had formed where there were depressions in the uneven rock path, and I got down on my knees and put my hands into the muddy water just to make a thorough search. Twigs, rocks, nothing else.

My ears were becoming accustomed to the language of the storm; the ever-present rush of water, the drumming of rain on the bench, and the harsh clanking of metal against metal as the wind beat the nearby tennis court fencing.

What was that? I stopped splashing in the muck, startled by an unexpected sound that couldn't be explained by rain, rushing water, or wind. It sounded like gravel, like when it's kicked on a path when someone is approaching. In the dark of the storm, I twisted to see who was coming up behind me. I stared into the gloom. No one was there.

Then, again, another shuffle! Again I reeled around fast, staring into the dark. And, again, no one.

My senses were hyperalert, straining to see or hear or feel a stranger upon me. And then, once again, I heard the sound of movement. But this time, I was surprised to realize it was coming from the ivy! I stared hard at the hillside. Millions of black-green five-point leaves were dancing and jittering in the deluge of mud and rain.

In an instant, I became sickeningly certain of what had made those footsteps. Rats. Hundreds of yet-to-be-poisoned, agitated rats. Rats scurrying, excited and frightened by the storm. Rats burrowing under their blanket of wet ivy, not four feet away from where I, deeply disturbed, stood.

Chapter 34

*I*t was after some time had passed, with me staring numbly at the infested hillside, that I got the terrible idea. The idea was this: Bruno threw his brandy snifter up against the hill. The idea wouldn't go away. I hated the idea. The more I hated it, the more I believed it was true.

I stared at the ivy some more. Perhaps I could go find a rake and just poke around. Sure. And break the evidence. Who was going to get fingerprints off a shard?

I stared at the ivy some more, and just to make sure I was fully aware of all the horrible possibilities lurking just beneath the leaves, I could swear I saw a long wet tail disappear back into the greenery.

"Hell."

That being said, I walked back to where I presumed Carmen had stood with Bruno when she first brought him his drink. I sat on the soggy wooden bench where they had their chat. I stood up. I picked up a tiny stone from the path, tossed it gently at the hillside just a few feet away, and watched where it landed. I walked up to the very place and stuck my arm, elbow-deep, into the leaves and vines and, for all I knew, a hidden rat's nest.

I screamed quite a bit, too. My apprehension was almost unbearable. Would I touch a glass or a rat? Although clearly an octave higher than the prevailing winds, my screams were swallowed in its deep howl as I, now committed to this dreadful task, forced myself to feel around in the roots and vines and mud of the hill.

When I was eight, I had a friend named Imogene who lived next door to a vacant lot. We used to play in that lot, unconcerned by the tiny field mice and lizards that lived and played there as well. One day we found a baby blue jay, abandoned we thought, since it was far from any tree that might hold its nest. We scooped up the baby bird, aware that its mother would now surely reject it because of our very touch. We warmed it in a blanket made from a red cotton kerchief and built it a little pen out of chicken wire where we vowed to bring it worms and bugs on which to grow. It was the budding of our nascent maternal core.

When we returned the next morning, bugs in jar, we discovered a sickening little scene. The pen had been overturned. The baby blue jay had been attacked in the night. Its sweet head was missing and its tiny feathered body lay there half-eaten. I remember the two of us girls crying in shock and grief, losing our first child to some horrible, heartless marauder.

Rats, my father said.

I moved my hand around a few feet to the left, then a few feet to the right, then higher, then lower, my fingers cold and hurting as they scraped the tough roots and stones under the ivy. By the time my hand actually brushed against something rounded and hard, I was so traumatized with disgust and horror, that I almost passed it by. Then, fast, my fingers grabbed hold and pulled out my prize.

It was a startlingly simple moment. I had Bruno's brandy snifter. These things shouldn't work out like this. But sometimes they just do.

And then, I looked up on the hillside. Dear Lord, something was moving up there. Upset and angry, a line of rats was attempting to escape across a sprinkler pipe from the monster who was rustling and plunging into their homes.

I backed away from the hillside. Freaked but triumphant, I remembered to hold the glass at the edges, and to shield it beneath my jacket. I was actually laughing from the release of tension. And then a curious thing occurred. My ears, which had moments earlier been so sharp as to detect the rooting around of rats in the ivy, had failed to warn me that someone had walked up on the path from the house.

Nosing around other people's secrets, I can't honestly say why I hadn't been more concerned about my safety. I figured that a poisoner had to be about the least confrontational type of murderer going. In theory, as long as I didn't drink anything foolish, I'd be okay. That, of course, was in theory.

Graydon pulled his collar close. He looked at me with indecision.

"Lily told me you were looking around out here," he said, in a normal tone of voice. "Can you give me that?" he asked, gesturing to the small bundle under my jacket.

"I'd rather not."

He seemed to be thinking that over.

"Are you going to shoot me, Graydon?"

He looked startled. "I don't have a gun, Maddie."

"Then I think I better get back to the house." I tried walking past him, but he blocked me.

"Why are you out here, Maddie? It's a terrible night to be outside."

His tone was so conversational. Was he the killer? Or was he just trying to keep me from finding evidence that pointed to someone else? Someone he felt he had to protect.

"I need that glass. Then everything can go back to the way it was, okay?"

"Are you trying to protect Carmen?"

"Carmen? Why? Is someone trying to hurt her?"

He didn't get it, so that at least cleared up that question. I tried a more direct approach.

"Why did you kill your father?"

He draped his arm around me and leaned a little too heavily. With the slippery rocks underfoot, I collapsed, sitting down hard on the bench. Graydon sat down right beside me, holding me with a tight grip around my shoulders.

I was still trying to protect my treasure, hidden from the rain under my jacket.

"Everything I ever wanted, Maddie, Dad took away from me. You know? And all the stuff he ever gave me were things that meant nothing to me. I mean, he ended up paying a guy just so I could graduate from high school. So why did he make me go to college? To humiliate me, do you think?"

"No, Gray. He just didn't understand you."

"I guess. But it went too far. I told him not to sell the company. It was mine. That's what Dad said from the time I was a kid and I'd hang around the studio just to watch him work. He just shouldn't have gone back on his promise. Not this time."

"So all this was about the company?"

He spoke to me with his mouth close to my wet hair, the rain falling from his head onto mine.

"It was lots of things, I guess. Things really got bad when he got married again. He was starting a whole new life with Lily. I'd never seen him like that before. All the time, he used to tell people what to do, but it seemed the older he got, the more he was letting Lily tell *him* what to do. I didn't get it. He still wouldn't listen to a word Bru or I said. He still didn't take my advice at the office. But when Lily wanted something, she just had to snap her fingers."

"It must have been difficult when Lewis came along."

"Dad changed. Here was this important man, my father, on his hands and knees playing with his new toy. His baby. You know all the things he'd been too busy to do with my brother and me, when we were growing up? He would brag about all the great stuff he was doing with this new kid. It wasn't that I was jealous. It just didn't seem fair, you know?

"But I figured, with all the time he was out with the wife and kid, the more I could do with the business. Like I could really run things, for a change."

The rain was falling steadily. And here was old Graydon Huntley acting as if our sitting in the middle of a storm chatting about murder was not particularly bizarre. What I really needed was a rescue. But what was holding up the cavalry? Wasn't Carmen getting ticked off, waiting so long in my car? Wasn't Lily starting to worry about my whereabouts? And what the hell had happened to Rudy?

I kept Gray talking. "Did you plan this . . . thing?" I asked, not daring to use the word "murder."

"I guess I'd been pretty upset about a lot of things. I guess my dad dying seemed like a great way to solve a lot of problems. But I don't think I ever gave it any more thought than that. See, there's all sorts of problems with my wife's family. If I had this house, see, it could have made a tremendous difference to my in-laws. I think Carmen would have stayed with me, then. I really believe she would have stayed with me."

"I know about the Feliz land," I said, looking out into the darkness at the vast property that was the source of so much longing and frustration.

"Dad should have given it to Carmen! See, he just wouldn't listen about that. After he died, I was planning to do the right thing for Carmen's family. But then, with that lousy will and the lawyers and the land . . . I don't know what happened, exactly, but Dad screwed me again, didn't he? Even when he's dead, he still does a number on me. He took away the one thing I ever really wanted."

"The Feliz land?" I felt I was missing something.

"My wife. My Carmen." Graydon squeezed my arm painfully tight and spoke into my hair. "He took her away from me, Madeline. He shouldn't have done that."

Did he know about his father and Carmen?

He whispered, "Dad made her fall in love with him."

He knew. It's a lesson that Bruno never lived to acknowledge: Even the dullest blade can nick you. Graydon Huntley went after his father for seducing his wife, and that was a motive even an L.A. District Attorney would have to find compelling. But would I ever have a chance to relate this enlightening conversation to the proper authorities? I kept Graydon talking. It works on television.

"Your father was a complicated person," I offered.

"Hell. He could get any girl he wanted! Any one! You should see the actresses that came into the office, willing to do anything to get close to Bruno Huntley. So why did he have to take her?"

"I don't know."

"To show me! That's why! To show me that no matter what I did in my life or what I managed to get on my own, he could do it better and he could take it away. What makes a man get like that?"

"It's that ruthless competitive thing," I said. "It's probably the same quality that made him so successful."

"I figured one day Dad would get tired of Carmen, or tired of torturing me. I figured I could wait. I always had. But then, he started talking about selling the company in a few years. I mean, I was steamed.

"And then, at the Halloween party, the fortune teller told me that Dad had *already* negotiated the deal!"

"Graydon. Let me get this straight. You believed this gypsy fortune teller was telling you the truth?"

"Well, sure. It's the way Dad would do a big deal, keep me in the dark until it was over. And just like that, I was out of my rightful spot, in line to the throne. Oh sure, the soothsayer woman told me Dad would get me another job somewhere. But what about my legacy? What about my company?"

The irony was brutal. Bruno's great big joke, his soothsayer telling nasty, shocking, personal predictions, had actually pushed this man, his son, to kill him.

"Did you know your father had strychnine in the house?"

"He told everyone about it. It wasn't any secret."

Thinking back, I remembered something Wes had told me days ago.

"You were hanging around the kitchen after dinner. So you must have seen Carmen coming in to get your father a drink."

"Yeah! Right! She was going to Dad, again. Imagine

that. She knew I was steamed about the fortune teller, and she thought she could patch things up between Dad and me. Is that perfect? What was she going to do? Have sex with my father in the bushes so he'd reconsider selling out my future?''

Gray clutched at me harder, shoving me down against the bench until I yelped out in pain. This time he loosened his grip and I got a bit of relief. He didn't seem to enjoy hurting me, which I took to be a good sign.

"I was with Carmen when she was pouring Dad his Armagnac. She was fussing about meeting him and she wanted to, I don't know, do her makeup again, so she left for a minute. The door to the liquor cabinet was still wide open. I saw that bag of rat poison. I don't know. I think I half-figured he'd taste something wrong and pour it out. Maybe get a stomachache. I didn't really think it through, you know?''

I guess.

He stopped talking. There was really very little else to say. Lily had not come out looking for me. Carmen had not gotten bugged enough to track me down. Rudy, for all I knew, was sitting in the family room with Donnie drinking tea. Hell, I'd have settled for Perry Hirsh looking for me just to get another glance at my butt.

"We're soaking," I said. "Let's go inside and get dried off.''

"I need to see what you found. Is that the glass Dad was drinking from?''

"I think so.''

"You know, Maddie, you're really smart. I never thought about where Dad's glass could be. Lucky thing you figured it out instead of the police. But I gotta have it, now. Let me have it.''

What else could I do?

I brought it out from under my coat. Graydon grabbed it. If it didn't have his fingerprints before, it certainly did now.

"So would this have proved that I did it?" he asked.

"I don't know. Maybe it could have shown that you'd handled the glass. I'm sorry Gray. I was just trying to get Wesley out from under. You must have put that strychnine in Wesley's apartment, huh?"

"That wasn't planned. Bru told me to go into Dad's safe and take anything that was valuable. He said it was really ours, anyway. So I checked it out on Sunday. That's when I saw the sack of poison. God, I was blown away seeing it again! I mean, who the hell moved it up there?

"And then I got it. It hit me. Lily must have figured out everything that happened. She was keeping the poison locked up in the safe so she could blackmail me. If I didn't do something fast, she'd get everything: Dad's money, Carmen's property, and my company. The bag was her ace, you know? So I took it. Then, later, I guess I just went a little crazy. I'm sorry about getting your friend in trouble, but, well, it's not like he was family."

A nice warm sentiment from a man who had recently sent his father to paradise or points south.

"It's the cops' fault, really. They told us they thought Westcott killed Dad. So I just gave them a little help in catching him."

"I see."

No one was coming. I was going to have to make a move. The good news was that Gray had sort of mesmerized himself, deep in the justification of an irrational act, sitting still all this time in the soggy cold, telling his story. The bad news was my butt had sort of fallen asleep.

I jerked myself to my feet, pulling away fast down the path. Gray didn't give chase. He didn't even stand up right away.

"Hey. I still have the glass, Maddie. See?" He stood and held it up. Then with a strong, swift jerk, he smashed it on the paving stone near his feet. It was a million shards in seconds.

I took off past the tennis courts as fast as was safe on the slippery stones. Of course, he came after me.

When it comes to the winding paths through the property, I had a pretty good idea of which way they led, but soon I was at the border that separated the landscaped yards from the outer lands that were wild. I ran through a large iron gate, up an irregular dirt path seeking shelter in the tall wet weeds. Heart pounding, I ran as far as I dared on the cleared path and then darted into a tangle of tall grass and got down on my knees. I prayed I wasn't sitting in a patch of poison oak as I waited for my heartbeat to quiet down so I could listen for Graydon's footsteps.

"Maddie? Where are you? Hey, you shouldn't be out here on this kind of night. It's dangerous, you know? You could have a terrible accident."

Would he really hurt me? Kill me? After all, he'd had a lifetime of pain and abuse before he'd halfheartedly sent a poisoned drink off in his father's direction. Not exactly the methods of a determined fiend.

But he had killed once; what now? Perhaps he'd decided that he could add murder to that extremely short list of things he could do pretty well. And why hadn't I taken the time to think all this psychological bullshit through before I ventured out in this muck?

"Maddie! Come out here!" He passed quite close to where I was sitting, missing me in the dark downpour. I waited until he was a distance away, and then bolted further into the hilly country.

The overgrown chaparral abruptly ended. Last year's brushfires must have burned right to this spot, four hundred yards above the border of Bruno's backyard. Where no plants grew, there was no longer a root structure to hold the hillside up when the rains came. In a downpour like this one, it was the wrong place to be. And, then, I saw something truly awful. The earth above me was moving. Inch by inch. The hill was coming down.

I veered left, going downhill in a deep crouch, while trying to make my way clear of the mud. Around me, everything was moving: rivulets of water, debris on the ground, and the mushy soil itself. I tripped and fell hard on my hip. Black waves of mud were building on themselves and gravity was tugging it all down my way.

I pulled myself painfully up and knew I was in trouble. Moving in a crouched position was now impossible. Graydon would soon spot me. It was black night, and the rain was coming down hard again, but in my light colors, I was not exactly camouflaged.

I stood and made a run for it, trying to ignore the sharp fire in my hip. In moments, Graydon called out to me and I froze. He had been running up a section of hillside that hadn't burnt down so close to the estate. He spotted me and changed directions, crossing to the left as he charged back downhill.

I stumbled frantically, moving further left, trying to evade the horrible onslaught. The mud seemed to be shearing off, picking up momentum.

Graydon was closing in on me, cutting right to left and on an angle downward. He was moving with less caution and, therefore, much more speed. I was injured and winded and weakened from my hour in the freezing rain. I was sure I had already caught my death of cold. The rest of this nightmare was simply offering a multitude of quicker ways to cash in.

I had to get away. Gray was getting so close! And then, he went down. One moment Gray was crashing across the hillside, and the next moment I saw him fall. I tried to force myself to keep moving. Then I heard his screams. I looked back up the hill. He had stepped, unaware, directly into the path of the oncoming mudslide. The entire hillside seemed to be coming down and he was rolling down with it.

"Graydon!" I screamed into the stormy din. "Can you hear me?"

Graydon's voice floated on the wind. I couldn't be sure I heard him correctly. "Heal us!" Was that it? No. He said, "Feliz."

I started moving upwards again, checking that my feet were planted on firm ground. I hoped to pull level with where he'd fallen, the better to evaluate my options for helping him.

"Graydon?"

A flash of lightning and a clap of thunder obscured any answer he may have offered. In that brief light I could see he was tangled in some thick low bushes. He had slipped and rolled downhill in the mud until the twisting bale of branches grabbed at his clothes and pinned him down. And now, just a few yards above his head was a wall of mud, sliding closer with every drop of rain that fell.

I couldn't get in there.

"I'll go back and get help!" I yelled. I doubt that he heard me.

Staying clear to the left of the mudslide, I tried to scurry down the hill. The rain seemed to come to a stop and the wind died down. Suddenly, I could hear his voice calling me clearly.

"He's coming to get me!" he cried. "He wants me!"

I looked back. Graydon, still pinned, stopped struggling against his tight prison of black branches. He pointed up above him on the hill.

"Don't you see him?" he shouted, hysterical. "The old man on the waves? The old man with the face like a skeleton!" he yelled, gulping water, mud now up to his neck and pushing forward.

"Run, Maddie! Don't let the old devil catch you!" He turned to look up at the moving mountain of black mud that was overtaking him.

"Graydon," I shrieked. "Move! Move!"

"It's okay, Maddie. Everything's okay. I'm going to be his guest in . . ."

And that was it. Graydon vanished under tons of wet hillside.

As I scrambled down towards the estate, rescue workers appeared. They were making a human chain, passing large sandbags and warning me to stand clear. It took me a minute to realize what was going on. My cavalry hadn't finally arrived. They were there to protect the house from the slide.

Somehow, I managed to get to the house. Inside, I couldn't seem to feel its warmth. Regretting the puddles I was leaving on the beautiful old wood, I numbly walked through the entry, down the back hallway, and through the butler's pantry into the kitchen. The little liquor cabinet, sitting beneath the counter, looked so innocent.

In the kitchen I turned on the tea kettle. I only knew that if I didn't put hot liquid into my system, I might be spending the night at Cedars Emergency Room, learning everything I'd ever wanted to know about the effects of exposure.

Honnett walked into the kitchen, followed closely by Lily.

"There she is!" Lily beamed, and then got a good look at me.

"Get towels! My god, get blankets!" Honnett ordered, and Lily ran out of the room. "Get a doctor to come out here at once!"

"And you might want to get the coroner, Chuck," I suggested, my voice hoarse with fatigue. "Graydon killed his father and then, out there somewhere, he died."

One moment I was trying to remember in which cupboard I'd find a teacup and the next I was suddenly sitting sprawled on the kitchen floor. So, in an attempt to cover my graceless fall, I opened the lower cabinet that was now at eye level. As Honnett rushed over, bending down to help me stand, we both looked into the cabinet at the same time.

Little Lewis Huntley was curled up, asleep, unaware that the world around him was moving, with parts of it moving just a little too fast.

Chapter 35

*T*he police were busy on Wednesday and Thursday. Carmen Huntley confirmed that she'd left her husband alone with the open liquor cabinet on the night of the party. She also admitted to her affair with Bruno.

They identified Graydon Huntley's fingerprints on Lily's safe and on the glass beaker taken from Wesley's apartment, the one that had contained the half-pound of powdered strychnine. That poison had been their strongest evidence linking Wes to the murder.

After that, it was just a lot of details. Like digging up a hillside to find the remains of the final suspect in the murder of Bruno Huntley.

Thursday, Lily made a public statement forgiving her stepson's act. Gray's secretary turned up on "Inside Edition," confirming Gray's murderous motives. Charges against Wesley were quietly dropped.

I had spent most of the two days in bed, watching developments on the news, reading the papers, talking on the phone. Exhausted and bruised, I had thus far not developed a cold. So tell that to your mother the next time she catches you out in the rain without your galoshes.

By Friday, I'd had enough of recuperating. Wesley had been released, and we decided to meet at Pinot Bistro for lunch to celebrate his freedom. Holly and I drove there together and when we saw Wes, looking thin and handsome, none of us knew whether to joke around or thank God.

"You've lost weight," were my first words. In L.A. that's like the ultimate compliment.

"I found this terrific spa." He hugged me tight and then gave Holly a turn.

After we were seated, Wesley grabbed my hand and looked at me. "Can I say thanks?"

"You're welcome."

"You could have been killed, Madeline, you could have . . ."

"Okay, that's enough thanks. Let's look at the menu."

"Madeline . . ."

"Food!" I said, and both Holly and Wes dutifully picked up their menus.

We concentrated on what would be good with what, and what we were in the mood for and allowed the moment of too much emotion to gently wash away from our shores. The waiter took our order, puzzling over our eclectic choices, and left us.

"To freedom!" I proposed and we clinked glasses. Wes's was champagne, Holly's was iced coffee, and I was back to Diet Coke.

I waited for our first course to be served to drop my bombshell.

"I've got big news."

Wes did not interrupt his reverent plunge into a serving of green risotto with salmon flakes, sugar snap peas, and scallions, but his eyes did briefly flicker upward.

"Lily just heard from the attorneys. Guess what?"

"Bruno's *a-l-i-v-e*!" Wes did a pretty fair impersonation of Geraldo.

"Please."

Holly was stumped. "What more could they have to say? Isn't Bruno broke?"

I smiled.

Wes stopped eating.

Holly said, "Don't tell me . . ."

"He'd set up a living trust the week before he died, transferring all of his holdings into a special account. Technically, that meant he didn't own them anymore because legally, they now belonged to this trust."

"I don't get it," Holly said. "Does that mean he gave away all his money?"

"See, he turned over everything to the Bruno Huntley living trust and then he appointed himself as the trustee. That way, he had total control of the assets even though he didn't hold title to them anymore. Got it?"

"Not really. Why would he do something like that?"

"Really rich people do it all the time so their heirs won't have to pay millions in estate taxes."

"Wow," Holly muttered.

"So, this morning, Bruno's estate attorney calls Lily. He tells her that all the assets, the land, the money, everything, are residing in Bruno's living trust. Bruno had set things up so that in the event of his death, Lily would be appointed the trustee and have control of all the whole enchilada."

Wes smiled. "So you mean that everything Bruno owned is still intact and Lily gets it?"

"Right."

"Unbelievable!" Holly said with a sigh. "How much?"

"Roughly one hundred and five *million* in cash, stocks, and property."

We all thought about that number and went back to our food.

"What I want to know is, since the will is invalid, does that mean you have to give back the pots?" Holly was always the practical one.

I ignored her.

"So Bruno never meant for his sons to have a penny of the money," Wesley mused.

Our plates were cleared quickly and the main course was served. The food was exquisite, and we took a moment to savor a bite of whole lamb shank with garlic mashed potatoes here, a forkful of spicy grilled swordfish medallions there. It was our habit to taste each other's dishes, despite the disapproving looks from our neighbors at the next table.

"Seems like Lily has gotten a whole lot of weird news lately." Wes brought us back to the subject. "Nothing could be weirder than what you found out about the sperm. Nothing. It had to be like the world's first case of semen fraud."

"She actually took that news a lot better than I would have thought," I explained. Instead of being disillusioned with Bruno, in light of how miserably he'd tricked her concerning the parentage of her own child, she gave the sad event an almost romantic spin.

"Lily was delighted to find out that little Lewis contains some of Bruno's D.N.A. after all," I announced to the table.

Holly picked up the thread. "So she was glad that if Lewis couldn't be Bruno's child, at least he was like Bruno's grandchild. That it?"

"Well, yes."

We all kind of shook our heads at that one.

"I think Lily was about the only person who really got Bruno, you know?" Holly suggested. "It's like there's always somebody out there for you, no matter how weird you are."

"At least you hope there is," Wesley said.

"And here's some grim news," I said. "Lily's decided to have a double funeral. Tomorrow."

"Gross!" from Holly.

"Father and son? It'll save the family some time and trouble, I guess." Wes thought that one over. "I've never actually heard of such a thing, under this kind of circumstances. But why not? It'll be small, no doubt."

"Oh, no. Lily feels Bruno deserves more. She's expecting a thousand people."

"Really?" Wes asked. "Who's catering?"

"Wesley!"

"Hey, someone has got to be thinking about our moribund company."

We'd have to talk about the shambles that our business

had become, but now didn't seem like the right time to get depressed.

I tried to change the subject. "Oh. I've got something for the gossip-lovers in the group . . ."

Wes and Holly looked at each other in complete innocence.

"Lily says Donnie is moving into the guest house."

"Bruno's *runner*?"

"Uh-huh." I looked up for their reactions.

"Life must go on," Holly observed.

"You can always use a good runner," Wesley opined. "What do you think, Mad?"

"I just want everyone to be happy!" I wailed.

We laughed and asked for the dessert menu.

"What was Bru, Jr.'s reaction when he learned that Gray murdered their father?" Wes asked me.

"No one knows. Bru disappeared on Tuesday night and no one has heard from him. He even left his car parked up there at the house. He had to be concerned about not inheriting his daddy's fortune. If Perry Hirsh gets to him, it could be pretty serious trouble."

"He'll turn up sooner or later. On a night like that, where could he run?" Holly asked.

"He couldn't run in the hills that's for sure," I seconded. And then I had a chilling thought. Bru knew Perry was at the house. Perry's car was blocking Bru's in the driveway. If Bru was on the run and he didn't leave by car, had he tried to evade Perry by escaping into the hills? I pushed the gruesome possibility out of my mind.

"Well, what's the story on Perry Hirsh, anyway?" Wes asked. "You said you saw him again on Tuesday night at the Huntley place. Did you guys make up?"

"Yep. We're buds. In fact, I got a call from old Perry, yesterday, asking if we'd like to cater a party for forty of his closest associates."

Wes's ears perked up. "I'm spotting a trend. I see a renaissance of Madeline Bean Catering. I see us starting to pick up all the great funeral business that's in town, then moving into small catered affairs for the organized crime set. Interesting client base.''

"I told Perry no thanks." It was time to tell Wesley the worst. "I told Perry we were closing the company."

"No, Mad."

"Wes, let's not spoil this lunch, okay? We'll talk about it later."

I knew it would be hard for him to accept. Here he was, just out of jail a few hours, and instead of his nice comfortable life, look what was waiting for him. Because of the murder and our connection to it, we had gone from "in" to "out" in record time, even for this fickle community. Being unemployed was a stomach-churning thought, especially with the loans we still had to pay off, but all that could wait until after lunch.

"Oh, did I tell you?" Holly asked. "In *Variety* today, there was a little item about Angelica Sands. She just landed a big part. She's going to play the girlfriend of Billy Baldwin in the new Oliver Stone movie. Isn't that cool? Maybe we could visit her on the set."

"Quiet down. Can't you see Mad is studying the dessert menu?"

The waiter came to get our orders and, of course, we all chose different selections, the better to get a sampling.

The guilt set in as soon as the waiter left our table. "I shouldn't have ordered dessert."

"Oh, of course you should." Wes always played "good cop" in my struggle over calories. "This is a celebration. How many times does one of your closest friends get sprung from the slammer?"

"I know. But I'm going out again tonight . . ." I had this rule about how many meals I could indulge in on a given day. The "bad calorie cop" inside me was sure this one lunch had already blown my day's limit.

"So?" Wes said, helping me rationalize. "Arlo doesn't like to eat anything fun. Take him to a salad place."

"Arlo doesn't eat salad," Holly reminded him. "And anyway, Arlo's show films on Friday nights so . . ."

They both looked at me and by the transformation on their faces I could tell that they weren't such bad detectives themselves. Damn.

"So who are you going out to dinner with?"

Why prolong the heat they were about to lay on me? "Honnett," I said casually.

"The cop who arrested me?" Wes gave me that reproachful look, like Mrs. Bean really should have taught her girl better manners.

"I don't want to talk about it anymore," I said.

Both my companions smirked. I hate that.

The desserts were served and Wes remarked that he had never seen seven thousand calories displayed with such artistic flair. The chocolate mousse came scooped on a large, white plate and had a special message written in chocolate syrup around the flat, broad rim. It said, "Welcome home, Wes!"

"Oh, here's something you probably don't know about, yet," Wes said. It was a rare conversation in which Wes missed an opportunity to top us with his own gossip finds. Naturally, being detained by the County of Los Angeles, he wasn't expected to contribute at today's lunch, but Wes would not be stopped by mere bars alone.

"I got home to my apartment and there were a few messages. Friends who heard I was getting out mostly. But there was also one from Carmen Huntley's mother."

"You're kidding?"

"With all the publicity about my arrest, the story had been told a hundred times about the whole land deal I had done with Bruno. Apparently, Carmen's mom had just found out that I was the one who had made the arrangements to sell the forty acres to Bruno. Now, get this. She was making me an offer to act as go-between with Lily and help her acquire the land. She offered to pay me a ten percent finder's fee." Wes smiled at the irony.

"Oh, God! Here we go again!" I couldn't believe the circles within circles that make up our daily dance. Honestly, it's a wonder we aren't just holding our heads all the time, dizzy with life.

"Anyway, I called her back and I found out that Carmen has moved out of town."

"So soon?" I guess she didn't want to stick around for the double funeral. It kind of made sense.

"Yeah. Her mother was upset. Seems this is the first time that Carmen has been out on her own and her mom doesn't think she's strong enough to make it."

"Where'd she go?"

"To Ojai with a friend of hers from high school."

Ojai was an idyllic little grove town just inland of Ventura that attracted artists and writers.

"Ojai. Yeah. It's a jungle out there." We all enjoyed the thought of Carmen being on her own. Maybe the best outcome for her was simply going it alone for a while.

Bringing Wesley up to date had taken us the better part of a two-hour lunch. We sent a note back to Octavio in the kitchen, thanking him for the brilliance of his cooking as well as his generosity. The chef had insisted on treating us and would not accept payment for our bill.

In our two separate cars, we headed back to the office. We had to plan the closing down of the company and get serious about finding ourselves employment. In one week, we had gone from Hollywood's culinary rising stars to something exactly like yesterday's news. The catering business, when played out on such a high profile, trend-setting stage, is like a souffle. One lousy client gets murdered and poof!

As we walked in the door, none of us really wanted to face it. Holly, as always, led the way.

"So, do I call the lawyers and tell them to start up bankruptcy proceedings or what?"

"What's on the floor?" I asked, avoiding the inevitable answer she was waiting for.

"On the floor? Oh! It's a fax." The long white roll of fax paper had been keeping itself pretty busy while we'd been out.

"What is it?"

Holly bent down and rolled it all up, trying to get to the beginning. "It's from Six Star Pictures," she said.

Wes looked at me. "We've never done any parties for them, have we?"

I shook my head. Six Star was the result of a merger between two of the oldest and most venerated broke movie studios in Hollywood. Two years ago a Japanese car company spent billions and bought them out.

"What's it about?" I asked Holly, who was still reading.

"Oh my god!" she exclaimed. "Read this."

I looked at the letterhead, which was from the head of legal affairs at the studio. Puzzled, I read on.

Dear Ms. Bean and Mr. Westcott:

As per the terms of an agreement dated October 31, 1997, between SIX STAR STUDIOS and BRUNO HUNTLEY PRODUCTIONS for the purchase by SIX STAR of that company, Mr. Huntley specified that certain monies be paid, certain stock rights be transferred, and guarantees of consulting contracts be offered.

In addition to the above arrangements, and as a condition of sale, Bruno Huntley required that SIX STAR tender a purchase offer for the company known as MADELINE BEAN CATERING for the purchase price of $3 million.

In the event that the owners of MADELINE BEAN CATERING choose not to accept the offer by SIX STAR, the monies offered will revert to Mr. Bruno Huntley and be added to the purchase price agreed upon for acquiring BRUNO HUNTLEY PRODUCTIONS.

Please call me at your earliest convenience to let us know if you will be selling your company to SIX STAR.

That was as far as I read. Wesley, who had been reading over my shoulder, was silent.

"Bruno arranged all this. He was selling his company to Six Star for big bucks, and as a little twist of the knife, he forced them to buy some insignificant catering company as part of his deal," I said in wonder.

"Why would he do that?" Wes asked, stunned.

"To piss them off, I expect. Just for fun." I started to reread the fax.

"Does that mean we get three million dollars?" Wes was just catching on.

"If we want to let go of this treasure."

"But then what will we all do?" Holly wondered.

"We've always wanted to move up into major event planning full time. How about Mad Bean Events?" Wes suggested.

"And why must all of our ventures feature my name?" I asked, full of curiosity.

"Because you're so lucky!" he said, with the exhilaration of discovering all of his bills were about to be paid off.

"But I'm still mystified," Holly said. "Why did Bruno arrange for Six Star to give all that money to *us*?"

"Maybe he just got a kick out of making the Japanese buy something they couldn't possibly want. The power angle. Or maybe he felt it would pay Wesley back on that old Los Feliz score and, this way, it wasn't even coming out of his pocket."

"You should hear yourself," Wes said. "You still have a soft spot for that monster. You think of him as a prankster, a naughty kid bugging the big corporate grownups, a guy just out to pay off an old debt!" Wes shook his head. "More likely, he was after you, Maddie. He was planning to offer you one of his legendary bribes."

Bruno had dealt in a sick kind of barter; celebrity contacts, the glamor of his lifestyle, the money, the parties, Hollywood's largest dreams . . . anything you wanted.

Wes was warning me. Accept the bribes, and Bruno

grabbed your soul. And it appeared that death hadn't slowed him down much.

Holly said, "I'll go get you a Diet Coke."

Wes was thinking of something else, now, because he was staring at me with a silly grin on his face. "Remember the soothsayer?"

"Angelica."

"Well, yes. But, no. Think of her as the soothsayer on Halloween. She predicted you'd meet a dark man. That's Honnett. And she said you'd come into a lot of money."

"I thought that was the thirty thousand, but of course I gave that back."

Wes said, "Think bigger. Like a hundred times that. Then didn't she say something about a change of career?"

"We're selling the old catering business and starting a new one. Yikes. And didn't she tell you, Wes, that your life was soon to be in jeopardy?"

"Right. And I laughed. Was there anything else she said? 'Cause I'm getting frightened here."

"She said Arlo was going to propose, but of course, Bruno put her up to that one. Angelica told us that he was trying to scare everyone, and that is a pretty scary idea."

Wes eyed me to see if I was serious. I avoided his look.

"And let's see," I went on, shifting quickly. "Didn't she warn me to wear sunblock?"

"What?"

" 'Beware of the sun.' That's what she said."

"The sun? Oh, my god. She was warning you about the *son*! About Graydon."

I looked at him. I mean, what could I say?

Holly walked in, breathless. "Madeline. It's the phone. Arlo's calling. He said he's drunk and he's quitting his job and he wants to marry you and move to Montana. He's so funny."